D0445188

THE MONSTER WHO WASN'T

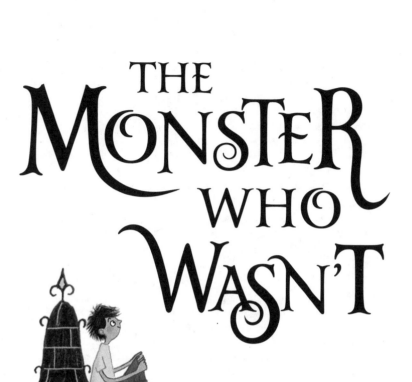

THE MONSTER WHO WASN'T

T. C. SHELLEY

BLOOMSBURY
CHILDREN'S BOOKS
NEW YORK LONDON OXFORD NEW DELHI SYDNEY

BLOOMSBURY CHILDREN'S BOOKS
Bloomsbury Publishing Inc., part of Bloomsbury Publishing Plc
1385 Broadway, New York, NY 10018

BLOOMSBURY, BLOOMSBURY CHILDREN'S BOOKS, and the Diana logo
are trademarks of Bloomsbury Publishing Plc

First published in Great Britain in August 2019 by Bloomsbury Publishing Plc
First published in the United States of America in September 2020
by Bloomsbury Children's Books

Bloomsbury books may be purchased for business or promotional use.
For information on bulk purchases please contact Macmillan Corporate and
Premium Sales Department at specialmarkets@macmillan.com

Library of Congress Cataloging-in-Publication Data
Names: Shelley, T. C., author.
Title: The monster who wasn't / by T.C. Shelley.
Other titles: Monster who was not
Description: New York : Bloomsbury Children's Books, 2020.
Summary: Imp, hatched in the underground monsters lair looking like a human boy,
does not know where he fits, but Thunderguts, king of the ogres, has a dangerous
destiny in mind for him.
Identifiers: LCCN 2020016585 (print) • LCCN 2020016586 (e-book)
ISBN 978-1-5476-0456-2 (hardcover) • ISBN 978-1-5476-0518-7 (e-book)
Subjects: CYAC: Monsters—Fiction. | Gargoyles—Fiction. | Belonging (Social psychology)—
Fiction. | Kings, queens, rulers, etc.—Fiction. | Fate and fatalism—Fiction. | Fantasy.
Classification: LCC PZ7.1.S5128 Mon 2020 (print) | LCC PZ7.1.S5128 (e-book) |
DDC [Fic]—dc23
LC record available at https://lccn.loc.gov/2020016585

Typeset by RefineCatch Limited, Bungay, Suffolk
Printed and bound in the U.S.A. by Berryville Graphics Inc., Berryville, Virginia
1 3 5 7 9 10 8 6 4 2

All papers used by Bloomsbury Publishing Plc are natural, recyclable products made
from wood grown in well-managed forests. The manufacturing processes conform to the
environmental regulations of the country of origin.

To find out more about our authors and books visit www.bloomsbury.com
and sign up for our newsletters.

To Richard, for all the love, support, and encouragement;
and to Tess, for being my muse

I t is a well-known fact that fairies are born from a baby's first laugh. What is not as well documented is how monsters come into being.

Monsterkind is divided into three categories. The Great Monsters—identifiable by their huge size—include trolls, ogres, goblins, dragons, abominables, and other such monstrosities. The subgenus, Imps, covers all stunted and smaller species— pixies, brownies, leprechauns, sprites, gargoyles, bogeymen, and so on. And, lastly, of course, there are the Monster Witches: banshees, Baba Yagas, snitches, hags, wyrd sisters (hatched in triplets), and the wet witches like sirens and Jenny Greenteeth.

All species of Monsterkind are born from a human's last sigh, and the vileness of the monster is in direct proportion to the depth of the sigher's regret. Unfulfilled dreams, disappointment, and bitterness settle into the human soul like sediment at the bottom of a bottle of vinegar. Once freed, the last sigh grows, turning in the air, solidifying into a dark, resentful shape: as tough as loneliness, hard enough to cut a diamond in two, but as supple as a lie.

After absorbing every bit of misery and loss in a room, a released sigh makes its way to The Hole, the native country of monsters, hidden in dark caverns of filth. Upon its arrival, the ogre king breathes on it to begin the hatching process. When great evil has been done by the sigher, the sigh will be incarnated into a powerful and hideous beast. Whereas a life lived happily and full of goodwill generates very little regret, enough to produce nothing more annoying than the smallest of Imps. The Great Monsters are often disgusted by how darling the littlest ones appear.

The breath of the ogre king also grants the new monster some knowledge of the world. Ogre kings do not allow their underlings too much insight, as they see knowledge as power and transfer only a few useful bits and pieces into the heads of new monsters: some basic language skills, remedial literacy and numeracy, and a thorough understanding of how to grovel before superiors.

From The Monster Hunters' Journal

CHAPTER 1

Old Samuel Kavanagh studied his granddaughter's face. His son and grandson had brought her for the evening. It took him a lot of work to keep smiling so his boys wouldn't know his thoughts. They worried about him enough. He peered at the sepia photo of his wife on the dusty sideboard. Despite his smile, she'd have seen through him and right into his thoughts. She'd have shared them.

He missed her.

The ten-week-old baby girl lay on his lap. She smiled at him, exposing bare gums. She'd been born with a full head of ebony hair, as they all had. His grandson reclined at his side, perching on the chair's arm. Only two years into his teens, he watched his grandfather with Kavanagh black eyes, the young man he'd become hiding politely beneath the surface.

Then Samuel turned to look at his son—graying at the temples, hovering over his daughter with lines of concern carved into his forehead. What wouldn't the old man give to lift that load from him?

He sucked his tongue, feeling the air move from that bottomless place in his stomach. He held it back, but the sigh won, hissing out into the room. Regret and misery, pain and weariness blended and solidified.

The baby laughed, and her music burbled into the polluted air. She watched her laughter turn into a bead of light and circle the old man's head, dancing and casting sparks over his thin hair. The baby reached for it, and the sparkle ducked between her fingers, teasing her. It shot upward joyously and got caught in the toxic fog of the sigh. It hit against the sigh's insides and gleamed through the dark surface.

The blend coughed and spluttered and struggled, but the laugh and sigh stuck together. The mixture sagged, its serpentine tail curling in as the baby giggled again.

Samuel's grandson grinned. "I've never heard Beatrice laugh before."

"Ah, Nicholas, it's a wonderful sound, isn't it?" The old man ran a finger over the baby's face.

Unnoticed by the older humans, the muddle turned in the air, tightening into a tiny black lump. The laugh held it in the room for a moment, sparking as it soaked in the loving atmosphere. When it grew tired of fighting itself, it flitted toward the old man's bathroom and slithered down the rusted drain in the sink.

4

The visitors didn't stay long. The baby's giggles settled to whimpers, and she began to fuss.

The old man stood to see them off.

"Sorry to leave you, Dad," his son said. "Your show's on next. We'll let you watch it in peace."

His grandson kissed him on the forehead.

Familiar music wisped from the television as Samuel waved them out. He saw the glow of their car's taillights heading south.

He leaned over and picked up his wife's portrait, setting it on his lap and stroking the picture frame.

"I don't know why, but I think they'll be fine, Annie, my darling," he said. "And I'm not worried anymore; maybe my prayers have been answered."

He settled to watch his show, but he would never move again. He drifted away remembering his granddaughter's giggle.

At the window, a pair of pretty green eyes looked in on Samuel Kavanagh. They had witnessed everything. They'd seen with some surprise the sigh rise smoke-like and congeal into a small and scaly cloud, and they had creased into a smile as the old man breathed his last. Then their owner turned away and slipped into the darkness.

The tiny black gem fought with itself as it traveled the pipes, turning a normally quick journey into a struggle lasting days. The laugh itself wanted to burst free, find fresh air, see the sky, and head for a bright star singing a singular, irresistible note. But the sigh was heavy; it needed to sink and merge with dark water running through rusted pipes into murky sewers.

It looked odd too. It was not pure regret—not merely loss and wasted opportunity. The laugh had brightened it, and though the nugget was black, like all last sighs, it gleamed. It had held back long enough in its absorbent state to nab the humor, the kindness, and the love of a family. It had soaked up a lot of humanity.

It took five days for it to arrive in The Hole.

It zipped over the heads of the monsters gathering in the center of The Hole's Great Cavern, the huge hub of the monsters' lair, deep under the Earth's surface. One end stretched three soccer fields from the other. The cavern walls rose high and dingy, so high not even a monster's nocturnal eye could see the roof.

Near the middle, a thunder of ogres played soccer with a gargoyle's head. The little sigh flew over them and joined the hundreds of other sighs flitting around, gnatlike, into the faces of red-coated leprechauns and pixies wearing newspaper hats and burlap undies. The trolls batted at them. Bogeymen climbed headfirst down impossible walls to watch sighs fall into a heap inside a circle of rocks. They were overshadowed by a rough-wrought throne on a raised stone platform.

It was Hatching Day. A day of celebration, a day to listen to cracking and crunching of hard dark shells as the latest crop of sighs spat out grubs and pups of the various monster breeds. The monsters had gathered from every corner of The Hole to see if there were any new members to their packs. Some even came down from the world above, abandoning attics, cellars, bridges, tunnels, and other human-built residences to have a look at the new additions. The stronger the beast, the closer to the throne and the circle of dark eggs they shoved themselves, which annoyed the weaker imps, as they couldn't see much at all.

At the front of the crowd, trolls shoved leprechauns, which in turn bit their toes. One ogre with a head like a damaged pumpkin grinned down at a clutch of shivering pixies and sucked his fleshy lips. Toward the back, a batch of brave brownies waited for their moment. After the goblins and ogres pushed forward and settled, they squeezed between comfortable butts to fill gaps. Being breakable, the gargoyles hung at the rear of the mob, away from ogres' feet, and listened to the few snatches of news that were passed back to them. They readied themselves to rush forward and grab any new-made gargoyles before ogres crushed in the hatchling heads.

Ogres on guard circled the mob, making sure no one ate anyone else before the new-mades hatched. It was exciting. A festival of sorts. Even the soccer players stopped their game and pressed close, elbowing banshees and goblins out of the way.

When the ogre king entered, an avenue formed as the crowd parted so he could ascend his throne upon the flat stone. The king was the largest of all the monsters. He had two fangs like elephant tusks poking from his top lip, and though his left hand consisted of the same compact muscle and meat as any ogre's, his right curled into a solid stone fist. It weighed on the end of his wrist.

The creatures bowed low, muttering "Your Majesty" and "King Thunderguts" under their collective smelly breaths as he passed. A pixie squeaked as a bogeyman trod on it, desperate to get out of his way.

King Thunderguts blinked at his scraping underlings and took one large step to ascend the platform. As he did, the sighs hiccupped and bumped each other in front of him, rolling, some already cracking in a hurry to become little monsters.

The ogre king's attention was caught by the sight of a sparkle. He studied all the beads and spotted one that was shining. Even among hundreds of dark jewels it stood out, with its unnatural and (Thunderguts's mouth felt sour as he thought it) *pretty* glow. He shifted from one hip to the other; he knew he should waddle down there and pick it out. It was lovely, and nothing so lovely could produce a half-decent monster. It would be best for all if the thing was destroyed. No point telling one of the underlings to do it. They'd be holding up every bead and button until teatime before they got the right one.

He stepped forward, ready to descend into the pit of sighs to collect the shiny little reject, but before he could, a panting, puffing crone in bedraggled, venom-green rags shoved through the crowd.

"Majesty, Majesty." The frail creature pushed past a bear-eared ogre. It flinched and stepped aside for her. "Majesty?" She stood wheezing beside the platform.

The king nodded, and a troll with a nose like a cow pie lifted her onto the dais.

Thunderguts leered at the crone, studying her twisted face, and stepped to his throne. He wiggled his huge behind between his long-suffering arms and sat down. His red eyes widened, but even the strongest of the cavern's yellow lights could not make them glow.

"What's got you so excited, Crone?" He spoke low, although the crowd's attention had turned back to the black beads in the pit, watching them pop and jump like fleas in a pot.

"It's happened. And the bead, it's a little different. I think this one will take."

"Well, which one will it be, then?"

The hag looked out over the myriad black stones. She shook her head; there were so many. Then she smiled and pointed at the glowing gem among the dull black nuts.

The ogre king chuckled. "You're sure it will work?"

The crone sighed and opened a small metal box. It was full of sparkling powder. She took a pinch and snorted it, clicking the box closed again. "It has to, I won't last much longer."

"Well, get down there and grab it before some oaf forgets himself and steps on it." The king lifted his stone fist onto the arm of the throne and issued an exhausted grunt. "It's time to hatch these beads!" From the comfort of his seat, he tutted his tongue to the top of his mouth and bellowed his heavy breath all over the new nuggets. Then he watched with the rest.

A goblin helped the crone off the edge of the dais, and she hobbled through the mob. The monsters shuffled aside for her, jostling and pushing and peering back at their ogre king. Thunderguts felt their curious glances on him. His people knew he didn't normally wait to watch the new ones emerge once he had set the hatching in motion.

Crowds of monstrosities and imps huddled closer and raised eyebrows as the first of the black gems snapped and erupted. A dark boulder began hatching before all the rest, expanding as the ogres cheered. Its surface cracked and a claw burst through the top. Two ogres helped the young ogre climb out, and they leaned forward to hear its first word.

"Meat?" the confused creature said. Its new pack shouted encouragement, and the little ogre tried to grab a yellow-jacketed pixie.

Next a batch of brownies burst out of their kernels like popping corn. *Pop! Crack! Knisper!* Adult brownies gathered them in arms before the trolls could shove them into their mouths. At a safe distance they stopped, pushed together, and laughed as the hatchlings struggled to speak.

"Slackle," one said. The brownies giggled. It tried again. "Spackle." The tiny creature looked around to eager faces. "Sparkle." The brownies hoorahed, and the whelp repeated the new and exciting word.

Leprechaun arrivals received approval for their cries of "gold," "profit," "coin," and "commerce." One excited cub yelled "business" over and over until it vomited. The leprechauns shook its tiny hand.

"Shall we call it Kean?" an old leprechaun laughed.

The fledgling yelled out its name—"Kean, Kean, Kean"—until it vomited again.

Thunderguts's gaze narrowed. He ignored all the hubbub and excitement, focusing on the sparkling nut. It was one of the last to hatch, and the crone almost had it, but as she bent down, a newly hatched pixie grabbed it away. The bead cracked in the little imp's hand. The pixie yelped in pain and dropped it, staring at its fingers.

The crone held back.

At first, the hatchling grew like many of the other larvae, its shape bubbling and popping. Legs snaked out, arms appeared like worms. It spread out limbs as usual, although Thunderguts flinched to see the odd budding of straight, slim arms.

Nearby ogres and trolls squinted at each other. Goblins shifted. Nobody knew what to expect: a puck, perhaps?

Thunderguts raised an eyebrow and smirked as the shiny nugget grew. A head formed: one ear on each side, two eyes facing forward, the nose too short (even for a puck), and a mouth filled with small, even teeth with no sign of a fang. Hair sprouted like dirty wheat from the top of its head, but not its chin. Hands burst from the stumps of arms, small and dainty.

A troll grunted its distaste.

The soft, pale thing opened its eyes, and the monsters nearest him inched back, muttering. Even the new-mades shuffled away.

"Good grief. It looks human," something hissed.

"Let's not start imagining we can hatch our own humans, shall we?" a green-vested leprechaun said, waving calming hands in the air.

"Yummy," said a small ogre.

Thunderguts grinned, drool collecting on his bottom teeth as the new creature sat up and sneezed.

The crone pushed the other new-mades aside. When she reached the creature, she leaned down and kissed it on the mouth, making several brownies yuck and gag as she did so. Kissing was not normal monster behavior.

They all heard the hiss as a long sliver of fresh air filled the new-made's lungs. Then the crone stared at it, as if she was waiting for something.

Thunderguts's voice carried across the space. "Is it . . . is it . . . all right?" he asked.

The crone grinned, her eyes disappearing into the crimping folds of her face. "It's perfect," she cried back.

The ogre king laughed. As enormous as the cavern was, his bilious chortle filled it. The noise startled the remaining new-mades and many cried.

"Got nothing to do wivvus. S'not one of ours. S'get outa here," a goblin said. It bombed past the crone, pushing her out of the way as it snatched up a tiny goblin.

"Let her work!" Thunderguts bellowed, and jumped from his throne. Monsters nearest him backed away, desperate to escape the king's flailing fist. A sprite hustled forward, seized three fresh pixies, and fled with them. Other waiting packs, wanting to collect terrified hatchlings, forced themselves in, grabbing at grubs.

In the midst of all the mayhem, a brownie scuttled between the crone's legs. It tripped her as it snatched a pair of soft-haired mewlers. Sprites and bogeymen scooped up more pups.

"Oi! Oi!" yelled Thunderguts in growing frustration, and jumped down into the pit. "Get out of her way. Stop!" He threw his stone fist around and hit an oversized leprechaun in the face. The imp flew backward into the throne, clanging on to the chair, sending shudders through the ground.

The crone dragged herself up and reached for the strange new-made imp once more. Everyone else was trying not to touch the deformed creature, but the growing pandemonium threw it up and over piddles of pixies and a glut of shivering tommy-knockers. The crone crawled toward the new-made imp, but it bumped farther away. A gaggle of bogeymen tripped in front of her, dragging at hairy cubs. The crone sat back on her bony bottom and screamed frustration into the cavern roof.

Thunderguts's bellows reached the crone across the chaos. "Hurry up and get that…" Thunderguts could not find a word for the new imp. "Bring it to me. It's mine."

CHAPTER 2

The new imp stared at the buffering, battering monsters around him. Things came to him in flashes and flits, skimming the edge of actual ideas. He tried to form words with his . . . he put a hand to his lips. What was this thing?

"Mouth," he said. He smiled at his cleverness, but no one praised him for his first word. The other monsters were busy with grabbing and groping and getting their own new-mades to safety. A pixie gave him attention in the form of a sneer.

Out of the chaos, a huge monster loomed over him and gazed at him with interest. More words sprang up inside the imp's head—a dozen sound pictures all at once. He chose two that needled him.

"Ogre," he said. "King."

The imp assessed Thunderguts's gleeful leer, drool sliding off

14

his bottom lip as he approached. Another creature was hurrying up behind the ogre. A crone. The one who had . . . kissed him? She was wearing a grin that reached to her poisonous green eyes. He didn't like either look—their faces had something in common that told him to back away. None of his new words quite fitted the expressions on the monsters' faces, but he grabbed at the closest.

"Hunger," the new imp said.

It was a dangerous word, one he didn't fully understand. Other words threw themselves up, vying for use—"greed," "desire," "yearning"—but "hunger" seemed the best.

His limbs reacted before he'd processed the meaning. He scuttled backward, trembling as the crone's grasping claws came for him. The next word popped into his head.

"Run," he told himself. His legs knew a little of the word and shook as they rose under him.

"Don't be afraid, kitty, kitty," the crone said.

"Run," he told himself again. Then he yelled it. "Run!"

The word startled the monsters as he dashed by them. They obeyed its command. Brownies gathered up brownies and hurried away. Leprechauns grabbed bearded calves wrapped in swaddling clothes and dashed off.

Thunderguts roared at the sudden stampede. The crowd fled together, their faces twisting at the king's rumbling yells. The imp found himself carried with them, bumping along between frantic bodies.

The imp's feet cycled to make contact with the dirt, and he grabbed his chest, patting at the pumping sound inside. As his toes touched the earth, the rhythm told him to keep running. He shuddered at the king's continuing bawl. He risked peeking behind, and saw the crone's stringy arm still stretched for him, but her creaking hips and worn knees slowed her. So did the brigades of bogeymen at her feet, and a scuffle of sprites squealed as the crone stepped on their fingers. When they nipped at her ankles, the shock of their teeth made her shriek, and she tripped backward, clawing the air. She fell hard onto her bony backside again, her ragged dress tumbling around her, and wailed.

He'd managed to slip her grip, so he darted for the wall with the other escaping imps, increasing the distance between himself and the crone.

"Is that a boy?" a brownie asked as the imp followed a pus-eyed bogeyman into the dark edge of the cavern. The imp didn't stop to wonder what a "boy" was. A snatch of bogeymen rushed into the gloom with him, and he found himself surrounded by shaking fur. He peered out to the lit center of the cavern to see the crone hobble back to the king and hunch next to him. The king's incoherent bellows shook more dirt down on them both.

A new-made bogeyman tucked under its pack leader's hairy armpit sneered at the imp and licked his elbow. "Tasty," it said.

"Don't do that." The larger bogeyman cuffed its head. "He's Thunderguts's dinner. Can't you see? We gotta get as far from him as we can." They scuttled away along the dark rim of the cavern.

The imp boy scanned the mob for anyone who knew how to get away from the awful noise of the king. Most of the creatures were changing direction and hunkering where shadows clung darkest. A creature made of stone stomped past, brushing his shoulder, followed by two more. They gathered in front of him and stopped. Even in the dark the imp boy could see moss growing in patches on their gray stone backs.

The first had four legs and a broad face. It looked about with a grimace. "We all good?" It patted its partner, a creature with a beak and two legs.

"An' all in one piece too," said the third. This one was also four-legged. Pointy ears stuck through a mass of hair that encircled its big head.

Gargoyles, the imp boy thought.

"Let's get out of here then," the broad-faced one said.

"Time to make our exit," pointy ears said.

The gargoyles did not see the imp boy, nor hear him. Their heavy feet drummed louder than the thumping inside him, covering the sound even in his own ears. He trailed them as they ran, using their cacophony for cover.

As the ogre king's rage faded with distance, the imp boy began to relax, but even as the bumping inside his body softened, his small mitts wouldn't stop shaking. He shoved them under the crooks of his arms. The imp followed the stone pack out of the titanic cavern, hoping they headed for a nice, quiet exit.

He studied his surroundings as he trotted. Above him, a vast expanse faded into starved darkness, and holes littered the walls. Nasties of every kind crawled up and down like congregating flies. White, bloated faces peered out of shadows. He copied the gargoyles, who leaned into the dark as the big monsters passed. Great trolls and ogres strode the dimly lit paths, laughing and spitting at flights of pixies skittering along.

The imp boy gasped as an ogre grabbed the gargoyle nearest him, the two-legged one, by the head. It made a disgusted raspberry and threw it across the path. The stone creature clunked onto a walkway fifteen feet away, howling as its foot broke off. The imp boy stopped in shock as the broken creature stood up and put its snapped-off foot against the edge of the severed leg. The pieces sizzled and reattached, and the gargoyle hobbled back toward his pack, and they all ran on.

The imp boy trailed them, keeping within reach of the feathered tail of the limping pack member. As they passed a herd of imps, the dirt-dressed brownies and pixies in sickly yellow hurled abuse at them. The pointy-eared gargoyle snarled. The pixies giggled.

They ran on again, the imp boy puffing and panting. He started to lag at their breathless pace and almost lost sight of them when they turned into a tunnel. He used the last of his effort to keep up, rushing to where he'd seen them disappear into the dark. It was just a gouge in the wall, but after a breath, he stepped inside. The noise of the Great Cavern cut out with a sharp click, and he saw the gargoyles blending into a single shape ahead of him. Their voices were muffled in the tight space.

"Good grief, that was a bit much," one loud voice said. The imp boy tiptoed closer and saw the hairy gargoyle with pointy ears speaking. "Hatching Day shouldn't be such a to-do. Thought the ogres might go on a smash 'n' grab. How's your leg, Spigot?"

The two-legged gargoyle, the one the ogre had thrown and broken, gave a gabbled caw the imp boy didn't follow, but the wide-faced gargoyle nodded as if it understood what it had said. "Yes, too right. An' Bladder an' me is proud of how quick you did that."

"Sizzled your leg right back on, you did. You know how to move," said the pointy-eared gargoyle. Bladder, the imp boy guessed. Its circle of stone hair tumbled around its face. "What was Thunderguts's problem today?"

"Hush, mustn't talk like that," the wide-faced gargoyle replied.

"Oh, like His Dirtship's gonna hear us in here. Wheedle, you are soft in the head sometimes."

Spigot squawked something. It could have been agreement.

The imp went over the names he had learned, happy to be adding to his little store of knowledge. The two-legged feathery one's name was Spigot, and Wheedle had the wide face. Bladder was hairy and pointy-eared and grumpy, although nowhere near as grumpy as the ogre king.

The imp boy's sense of achievement calmed him a little.

"Weren't anyone watching the hatching before all the chaos started?" Wheedle stared at Bladder. "I thought it was your turn to keep an eye on the beads."

"Who can see from the back? Them modern cathedral packs, they're the ones get all the new gargoyles."

"So you weren't watching?" Wheedle asked.

Spigot squawked at Bladder.

"I was not scarfing toffees," Bladder replied.

"You're always scarfing toffees," Wheedle said.

"Almost choked on one when Thunderguts started making that noise," Bladder replied. "I suspect he spilled his hot mud again. Throwing another tantrum. That's why I hate coming down here. Can't we give Hatching Day a miss?"

Wheedle scowled. "You know what would happen to the new ones if we didn't come down. We need to be here to look out for them."

"Oh, yeah, pushed to the front, you were so eager. It weren't you two I saw breaking your necks to get to the nearest exit then?" Bladder said.

Spigot harrumphed.

The imp boy's legs felt numb as he listened to the gargoyles' bickering. He slid to the ground, his new limbs trembling. Being away from the noise and the hungry face of the ogre king felt good, but all the other emotions, the wetness and shakiness he'd been pushing down, began to bleed out of him. His eyes oozed water. His mouth leaked moany, groany sobs. Confusing sensations seeped out of his body, and he let them.

The gargoyle pack swung around. Spigot screamed.

Wheedle yelled, "What the . . . ?" and the trio shuffled back.

The imp boy did not get up from the ground. He watched them, expecting them to race away and leave him shaking in the dirt. They didn't: they shuffled forward, stepping closer, toe by toe.

They gathered around him, sniffing, growling, mooing.

"Where'd it come from?" Wheedle asked. "It's shaking."

"More importantly," said Bladder, "what in the world is it?"

CHAPTER 3

Wheedle sniffed him. "Smells like an imp. Not a pixie or brownie though. Could be a gargoyle. We come in all shapes, right?" Despite the gargoyle's stoniness, there was kindness in Wheedle's face, and the imp boy found himself leaning forward to meet its gaze.

Spigot screeched.

"No, it's not a gargoyle hatchling—can't be," Bladder said. "It's not hard enough. And what's it doing in our tunnel? No one knows it's here but us three. Don't like that."

Wheedle sniffed the imp boy again. "Are you sure it's not a gargoyle? It found our exit, and it smells new. Plus it's making a noise inside, thump-thump, thump-thump, like it's got a . . ."

"Shut up! Not here."

"Come on, little one." Wheedle turned to the imp boy. "Up you get." The gargoyle nudged the imp under the arm.

The imp boy studied the gargoyle's face more closely. A ring ran through its wide nose and it had flat teeth. Two horns grew sideways out of its forehead.

"Wheedle? What are you doing?" Bladder asked.

"What we always do with the new ones," Wheedle replied. "Or shall we leave him behind? If he's a gargoyle, he'll get smashed."

"He ain't a gargoyle. More like a good meal for a troll."

"He don't look like much, but he smells nice. An' he's enough like a gargoyle anyway. I think he is inside. Let's take him upstairs."

"Don't go sappy on me, Wheedle. It ain't the inside that counts. Look at that skin, soft as a puck, he is."

The imp boy put a finger on Wheedle's ear. Its skin was certainly stone, but it dipped where the boy's finger touched it.

Wheedle stared at him. The gargoyle brightened as he understood what the imp boy meant by poking him. "We're made of living stone, we are. Right now it'll give, but there's times we're as hard as rock. An' we break like it too. Did you see what happened to Spigot's leg?"

The imp nodded.

Wheedle carried on. "It's being made of living stone what protects us from the sun, too. Gargoyles is the only monsters can live in the sun. Leprechauns, brownies, and a few others can cope with dusk and dawn, but not noon. All of them, they all turn to ash. That's what Bladder's worried about for you."

"Ain't worried for him." Bladder said and sniffed, before turning back to the imp boy. "But if you come up with us and you see the sun, you'll turn to ash. Only gargoyles can cope with sunshine."

Spigot cawed in agreement.

Wheedle ignored them. "Sun's not a bother to gargoyles at all. We can stare at the sun without blinking. Not even humans can do that."

"But you know this, don't you? Thunderguts breathed it in you?" Bladder asked.

The imp boy nodded. Somehow he did know these things.

"Well, he's definitely a gargoyle then," Wheedle said, ""cause, he knows his monster knowledge, 'n' he don't look like no brownie or pixie or puck, nor nothin'. And we gargoyles is the only imps that you got no idea what shape we'll turn out to be—animal, vegetable, or mineral. He found his way here. And he's got a—*you know*." Wheedle gestured to his chest.

"He can have all that, but he ain't *stone*." Bladder glared at Wheedle. "It's better for him to stay put. All right? You sit! Sit!" Bladder waggled a claw at him.

The imp boy looked down at his haunches. His bottom was already in the dirt.

"Good boy. Now, stay."

Wheedle stroked the imp's head and sighed.

The trio moved off.

The imp boy peered back to where they had come in, the dark wall behind which thousands of monsters and a demanding ogre king hunted him. He couldn't go back there, and he didn't want to sit in this dark hole forever. So he scrambled after the gargoyles and began trotting behind Spigot once more. Spigot screeched.

"He's following us, Bladder," Wheedle said. "Can't we keep him? Go on, let us."

Bladder sighed. "You'll be ash before morning's done. Do you want that?"

Turning to ash sounded less painful than having Thunderguts's teeth in him. The imp boy nodded.

Wheedle cheered softly and winked at the boy.

"On your own head be it," Bladder said. "It's gonna end with Wheedle in tears, I tell you."

They wandered up into the dark tunnel, the slope rising higher and higher. The imp boy stared around, marveling at the neat brown walls curving up and over the group. He put a hand on the brick. It was so different from the rough sides of The Hole. Like someone meant it.

He looked at Wheedle. How did he ask about this place?

Wheedle looked from the imp boy's face to his hand, and frowned. "Are you wanting to know where we are?"

The imp boy nodded.

"This is a sewer. It's the midpoint between our world and theirs. Underground, but made by one of *them*," Wheedle said.

The imp boy screwed up his mouth.

"Wheedle means humans. Wet, soft, pink, and stupid. They look like you actually." Bladder poked him with a claw. "A waste of space."

"Ignore him," Wheedle said. "Bladder is cat by shape and catty by nature."

"I'm a lion," Bladder said.

The imp boy studied Bladder's face again. He liked the big head and the jaw full of sharp teeth, and the imp boy wanted to touch the mass of stone around his head, which swayed when the gargoyle moved.

The imp boy reached up to feel his own head. Tufts came out of the top but—he touched his cheeks—nothing grew out of the sides.

Wheedle laughed. "I think he likes your mane, Bladder."

"What's not to like?" Bladder asked. "I expect you want one too, Wheedle."

"I'm fine with being a bull." Wheedle turned and poked his head at the imp boy. "See? Horns. It's gonna be great to be a pack of four again."

"What! If he don't turn to ash you can keep him. You even get to clean up his muck. But don't start thinking he's pack." Bladder considered the imp boy and grunted. "Stupid beggars, the lot of you."

The imp boy followed the gargoyles as they trotted single file along a sidewalk by a stench-riddled sewer. He recited the new words in his head: lion, bull, mane, sewer . . . *human*.

They'd said he looked human. His hands certainly didn't look like Bladder's claws, nor Spigot's talons, nor the four-toed feet at the bottom of Wheedle's legs.

After a short walk, they arrived under a dark circle. Its outline glowed with white light. Bladder scurried up the wall. Spigot crawled up beside him and did a turn, catching his tail feathers in his beak. The pair hung upside down from the sewer ceiling like bats.

Wheedle nudged the imp boy. "One hand on the bricks.

It'll stick. Easy." The stone bull's nose ring rattled as he climbed up a few steps. When the imp boy copied this, his slender legs slipped, and he slid knee-deep into the sewerage. It felt cold, nasty, and thick.

Bladder snorted. "It won't look pretty for long. Shall we give it a dunking?"

"No time. Got to get back before dawn," Wheedle said. "'Sides, it does look human. If we keep it looking nice, we can send it for chocolate."

"Pipe dream," Bladder muttered.

Wheedle turned to the imp boy. "Go on, have another go."

The imp boy put his hand on the bricking again. This time his skin shucked as it fastened to the surface. He put his other hand higher and pulled himself upward holding fast to the wall. His legs flailed and dangled until the balls of his feet hit and stuck to the surface. He looked down.

"He climbs like a gargoyle," Wheedle said beneath him.

Bladder grunted.

The bull-faced gargoyle stared up at the imp boy and pulled its mouth open so the sides lifted into a pleasant curve. The imp boy liked the way it looked and mimicked it. It felt good to do that with his face.

"Ooh, that looks painful." Wheedle laughed. "It's called smiling. Keep going."

The imp boy clambered toward the opening. He enjoyed the way his arms and legs stretched, and he had no desire to rush, taking time to feel each movement instead of a blur of sensations.

He put his head through the opening and peered out.

Outside it was dark like the Great Cavern, but it was a darkness alive with color. He knew the word "sky," and "sky" meant the expanse in the background. It started so purple at the top it was almost black, but he marveled at the other colors, not bitter and cloying, but gentle gray streaked with a wash of reds and pinks near the bottom. In front of this, one clean light shone from a streetlight and cast a glow onto the path of a huge, dark building.

Yes, those were the words: "sky," "lamp," "building."

A movement whipped past him and made him shiver. He didn't like it.

Wheedle laughed at his grimace. "It's called 'wind.' Also, you'll know 'building' already, but this one specifically's a *cathedral.*"

"What are you doing?" Bladder asked Wheedle.

"Don't you remember how few words you knew when you was hatched? I remember my first cathedral, my first morning. It won't learn if we don't teach it."

Bladder grunted. "Go on then, teach it its last words."

The imp boy straggled behind as the gargoyles slouched toward the building. Bladder tapped his front paw on the sidewalk in front of the cathedral.

The imp boy put his hand on the wall. The building seemed black against the sky, but up close, it was stone gray, the same color as the gargoyles.

"We're going up there," Wheedle said.

Spigot flicked out his wings to balance himself.

The imp boy opened his mouth, and then closed it again. He had to think of the right words to fill his question. When he'd picked the best ones, he said to Spigot, "Do you wing?" His voice sang as it bounced off the walls.

The gargoyles stopped.

"Oh, it's found its tongue, has it?"

"Hush, Bladder." Wheedle turned to the imp boy. "Do you mean 'fly'?"

"Yes." He nodded, and he felt warm at being understood. "Fly."

"Spigot might have wings, but he's a stone eagle. He's too heavy to fly."

Spigot stretched out his impressive expanse of granite wings.

"Gargoyles don't fly," Bladder said. "Only wholesome little whatsits like butterflies and fairies do that, and don't get no idea you can neither, or you'll fall down and break that scrawny neck of yours."

Wheedle patted the imp boy's back. "It's good to know you can talk."

"Enough now. If we're gonna do this, up you get," Bladder said.

The pack climbed the walls of the cathedral. The imp boy felt the stones again, bigger bricks than the sewer, but solid and safe. He followed the gargoyles to their perch high on the top of the building.

"This here's a pinnacle," Wheedle said. "You can see everything from one of these. The spire's even higher." The imp boy followed the direction of Wheedle's hoof-toe as he gestured at a tall roof.

The building's sharp peak pointed into the sky above as if

wanting him to see the wonderful colors. The imp boy looked back down into the street below, distant shapes in the darkness blurred, squared, and pushed up against each other. A regular series of lamp posts lit up the space between the blocks, shedding twinkling white light. He couldn't find a word to express it, but it made him feel a bit like he had when Wheedle smiled.

"So, what does it know?" Bladder asked. "Do you know who's in charge?"

The imp boy frowned, and the warm feeling fled. "Thunderguts." He shook to say the name. "The ogre king."

"An' you know where we gargoyles belong in the pecking order?" Bladder asked.

The imp pondered this, gathering words to himself, working to put them in the right order. "Big monsters at the top, then witches. Imps lower down, and gargoyles at the bottom. Gargoyles are . . . odd."

Bladder grunted. "Yeah, Thunderguts *would* breathe that tidbit in. What else you know?"

"Ogres, goblins, and trolls only come out at night. They can't stand the . . ." The imp boy frowned. He couldn't find the word.

". . . The sun. Remember? We told you this," Wheedle said. "Ogres don't think real monsters should like the sun, let alone be able to live in it. Makes us almost human to them. The more you like it, the more they think you're pond scum."

"Imps like pixies, brownies, and leprechauns can come up when the sky is . . . is soft?" the imp boy said.

"Dusk, dawn. Bad weather," Wheedle suggested. "Not sunny though—even they can't do sunshine."

Yes, that was also part of the imp boy's knowledge. "There was a time when it was always dark, even during the day?"

"Oh yes. The Dark Ages, they called it," Wheedle said. "Dark minds and dark days. Ogres loved it back then."

"When the sun comes, I might turn to ash?" The imp boy nodded and looked down at his body paling in the new sky.

"Too late to run now," Bladder said.

Wheedle harrumphed.

Bladder's voice softened. "S'pose you might be a gargoyle. Got up the church wall all right, and it's only gargoyles can climb as good as that. Now we just need to wait and see if you can survive the next few minutes. It's almost dawn."

Bladder and Spigot turned to the horizon. Traces of gold poked over the edge.

"Here we go," Bladder said.

The imp boy leaned into Wheedle, who gently pushed him away. "If you do turn, I don't want soot all over me. Hard to get it off. Good luck though, ay?"

They sat on a ledge of the pinnacle and watched the golden glow spread above the horizon. The warm colors settled on the dark blocks, and the imp boy could see they were buildings too, little light ones.

A low instinct told the imp boy to run, to get into the deepest, darkest place he could, but stronger still was the desire to feel the sun on his skin, and it held him there. Anyway, he thought, if the sun did turn him to ash, he could float away and never worry about being hunted or having to go back to The Hole.

The sudden radiance hit the cathedral, spilling over them all, and the gargoyles glowed in soft gray.

The imp boy waited to burn, to break apart. He wondered how long it took and if it was painful. The gargoyles stared at him, three pairs of eyes wide and waiting. His skin glowed gold and precious.

The imp boy turned his paws over and over. They hadn't changed at all. He guessed that was good.

After a short time, Wheedle smiled again. "He's still soft and pink. There you go, he copes with sun. Must be a gargoyle."

Bladder rolled his eyes.

Wheedle grinned. "I bet he's got our ears and nose too."

The imp boy touched the soft nub in the middle of his face.

Bladder snorted. "He means, can you hear and smell as good as us? Necessary when all monsters wanna stomp you."

"Why do they stomp you?" the imp boy asked.

"We like it up here," Bladder said. "Once we come up, gargoyles only go back to The Hole for Hatching Day. Makes 'em all mad."

"An' 'cause we got . . ."

"Don't tell it that, Wheedle. We still don't know what it is. You really can't keep a secret."

Wheedle stopped talking and looked at the gold spreading toward them. He grinned. "Right, can you hear that squirrel?" Wheedle pointed down at the square of green boxed between the cathedral and stone walls.

The imp boy saw a leafy structure, a tree. In the branches, a flash of gray movement and, inside that, a whirring sound. He listened and breathed, taking his time to understand the noise until he could make out a pitter-patter. He touched where his own body thudded.

"A . . ." He tapped at his chest.

Wheedle stared at the imp boy's chest. He turned to Bladder. "See?"

Bladder glared at him. "He's not a gargoyle. Keep your mouth shut."

Wheedle coughed. "Still, not bad hearing. Especially at this distance."

"Well, he's survived sunup and he's not totally useless. Your pet can stay." Bladder grimaced at Wheedle's big grin. ". . . For now. Alrigh', no more playtime. Get to work." Bladder turned to move down the pinnacle.

"Work?" the imp boy asked. "What's work?"

"We guard this building from anything that'll harm it. Some places there's vampires and werewolves every second night." Bladder sighed. "Not a lot of activity here though, so we just annoy humans during the day."

"They don't pay much attention," Wheedle said.

CHAPTER 4

The imp boy surveyed his new world. The cathedral guarded a gated ground. Hanging seats chained to a frame swung in a playful wind. Beyond it, he saw a town stretched out in soft gray buildings. Vibrant color reflected from trees and grass into windows, and litters of thin-boned bicycles leaned against brick walls.

He watched a creature take hold of a bicycle and jump on, before moving off at a great speed. He wondered if the creature was human. It had yellow hair and a pink face. The rest of it was white and gray and it looked like it might be as tall as a witch, but with a similar body and paws to him.

No, not paws, *hands*. The imp boy clapped his own at understanding. A white wave—*fabric*, he thought—spread out behind the human as it cycled by, and the imp boy applauded. The beating thing inside him startled awake at the sight.

The imp boy climbed the spire. It was higher than everything around, and he could see the broken tiles on the houses below. In one direction there was a stretch of lively green, and in the other, a blue expanse. Then he turned his attention toward the golden face of the sun and blinked as bright gold poured from it.

"It's . . ." he started, speaking out at everything curving off toward the horizon. He knew lots of names for things but few words to describe how they made him feel. He wanted to describe the bright vision before him, to tell this new upstairs world that it made him feel different than the way he had when the ogre king was yelling or when the crone chased him. In fact, if anything, he felt totally the opposite.

He stood on the ledge, spreading his arms out to embrace the skin-gilding rays. "It's . . . not . . . It's really not . . . AWFUL!" he yelled.

He knew he wanted to say more, but stood there hoping the sun-covered earth would be satisfied with his effort.

"Ahhh," said a voice close by. "It's wonderful. Tell yourself how wonderful it is. Tell yourself it makes you glad to be here."

"Wonderful?" The word sweetened his mouth, and the imp boy turned to see a figure standing next to him. It had arrived without sound. At first he thought the word "human," but it was much taller than the one he'd just seen, maybe eight feet tall, as big as a small ogre, and it balanced itself by stretching out wide, white wings. They were feathery, not stone or concrete. It glowed softer than the sun, golden-red hair floating over its shoulders. The imp boy put a hand up to his own matted head. His hair was more like this creature's than Bladder's.

The figure was terrifying. He wanted to hug it, or run and hide. He couldn't decide and gulped instead.

"Wonderful?" he asked again. The creature might know lots more words. It had already taught him one; maybe it could teach him more. "Are you . . . human?" he asked.

The winged creature stared at him, frowned, looked over its shoulder, and looked back at the imp boy. "Can you see me?" it asked.

The imp boy scratched his ear. "Yes," he said. "You're very big."

Its feathers ruffled. "Well, goodness me! Are you feeling all right? You're not up here doing something . . . dangerous?"

"I don't think so," the imp boy said. He stared at the being. "What's 'wonderful'?"

"Oh, you know, it makes your insides lift, makes you happy to be alive? You are happy to be alive, aren't you?"

"I think so." The imp boy held his stomach.

"Well, what an odd little creature you must be. Standing naked on top of a church is not an everyday activity." The creature chuckled to itself. "So, you don't know 'wonderful'? Someone has been quite remiss with your education."

The imp boy slumped. "I know other words. I learned some new ones today."

"Like?"

"Cathedral, house, windows, squirrel." He listed them, but didn't want the being to think he was stupid so he mentioned the essentials too: "I also know blood, meat, and maim. Pus, grime, dirt."

"Oh dear."

The imp boy cocked his head. "Bulldozer, gun, building, car, bicycle, police. I learned lion and bull earlier."

"Your childhood hasn't been pleasant, has it? Do you know what a dog is? Every child should know at least one good dog."

"It's a biting animal that guards humans." The imp boy clapped his hands at his own knowledge.

The figure frowned. "Not the best definition. What about 'bird'?"

"No. What's that?"

The figure gestured to a swirling, living cloud celebrating morning over the city. "Those types of birds are called starlings."

"I know Spigot's an eagle."

"Spigot? You mean the gargoyle?"

Before the imp boy could answer, someone coughed. Loudly. He looked down to see Bladder and Wheedle's faces below, staring up at them from a pinnacle.

"Isn't it a bit early for you to be annoying us?" Bladder yelled up at the figure.

"You know this lot?" the winged being asked, pointing at the gargoyles.

The imp boy nodded.

"How do they know you?" The figure seemed to be asking the sky. It turned to the imp boy. "Shall we go down and talk to them?" it asked, and fluttered down, while the imp boy scrambled after.

When he arrived on the pinnacle, the winged figure sat

stretched out with one wing around Wheedle and the other squashed and tucked up trying to avoid touching Bladder.

"It's an imp," Bladder was saying.

"A gargoyle," Wheedle added.

"No! Really? Made from misery?" The figure leaned forward, pulled the imp boy closer, and sniffed his hair. "Unbelievable! You *smell* human. Well, not quite. There's a touch of baby laugh, and... other smells, but the mix is perfect. You could pass for human. You certainly fooled me."

"Are humans made of last sighs?" the imp boy asked.

"Humans are born," the being said.

"What's that?"

The gargoyles sat up at this question and stared at the winged figure intently. The figure opened his mouth, closed it, held up a finger, then put it down again. It pulled a face, then blushed. "Maybe another time."

The gargoyles groaned. "He's never gonna tell us what that means," Wheedle complained.

The imp boy sat down. His tummy rumbled.

"Are you hungry?" the winged figure asked.

"Hungry?" The imp boy thought of Thunderguts. Was this grumbly-tummy sensation what he had seen on the ogre's face? He shuddered.

"If it steals some chocolate we can *all* eat," Wheedle said. "Chocolate's lovely."

"You're stone and you eat chocolate for pleasure. It's more than likely he needs real food," the winged figure said.

Bladder glared at Wheedle. "If it was a proper gargoyle it wouldn't need food."

"What's food?" asked the imp boy.

"It sustains body and mind," the winged figure said.

"Do *you* need food?"

"Of sorts. Not the same as you. Though a good raspberry tart is nice." His golden-red hair caught the light. "But angels live on faith, hope, and love."

"Angels?" the imp boy asked. It was a pretty word.

"Yeah, Angels feed off humans like leeches," Bladder said. "Sucking 'em dry."

The imp boy stepped back.

"No, Bladder," the angel replied. "It's like mother's milk. It's not painful. It makes both parties happy."

"An'..." Bladder crawled to the imp boy and purred into his face. "...When angels want to breed, they lay eggs in human guts which grow until they burst through their chests, and the baby angel claws its way out."

"That's aliens," Wheedle said.

"You sure?"

"It's in your favorite movie."

"Angels. Aliens. Easy mistake," Bladder said.

The angel turned to the imp boy. "Were you cold this morning?"

He didn't know the word "cold."

"It was all shivery and shaky. That's cold, right?" Wheedle said.

"Gargoyles don't get cold." Bladder stroked his stone exterior with a hard paw and sneered. The imp boy couldn't decide which made him more uncomfortable, Bladder's scorn or the cold itself.

The angel took the imp boy's arm and ran a finger over his wrist. It tickled. "This is called skin. Humans are covered with it, and it's very nice." The angel turned to Bladder. "And do you have a bed organized?"

Bladder gagged. "A bed? Oh, come on!"

The angel sighed. "If he gets hungry and cold, you'll find he gets tired too." He turned to look at the sky, and his eyebrows glowed with the same copper light as his hair. The imp boy touched both hands to his face, found his own eyebrows, and smiled.

"It's not a boy; it's a monster!" Bladder stamped his foot, dislodging dust.

"He's a boy."

"No boy gets made from a sigh."

The angel laced his fingers together. "He may not be human, but he's definitely a boy."

Wheedle stared at the imp boy. "I thought it picked that up in the sewer."

"Human males and females have different . . . er . . . anatomy . . . er . . ." The angel peered at the imp boy and went red again. "You're a bit young for this conversation. Anyway, he also has a belly button."

"So?" Wheedle said. "Goblins are boys and girls, and one troll I know's got a belly button. Gargoyles come in all shapes and weirdnesses. It's part of our charm. Don't you worry; you're just the same as the rest of us."

"Yes, but the combination of all those things—the belly button, the hair, the eyes, no fangs, everything—it's perfect. There's something going on here." The angel tapped his bottom lip and fell to thinking. "Hmmm, who might know how this creature came into being?" His head bobbed up. "What's his name?"

The gargoyles glanced at each other.

"We ain't given it one yet." Wheedle sidled up to the imp boy and nuzzled under his arm. "What about Gutter? We can call him Gutter."

Spigot squawked.

"Yeah, that's a good one," Wheedle said. "Tile-Mold."

"Slimeball?" Bladder offered.

They all peered at the imp boy.

The angel winced. "Do any of these feel right to you?" he asked the boy.

The imp boy repeated each a few times to himself, but Wheedle answered for him. "No, none of them. It don't suit a gargoyle name. Let's call it 'Imp' until we can come up with something special."

"Do *you* have a name?" the imp boy asked the angel.

"Oops, sorry," said Wheedle. "I neglected the introductions. Imp, this is Daniel, Caretaker of the something-something blah blah, Overseer of the third whatsit."

Bladder sang, "Dani-elle, Ari-elle, Rapha-elle. You angels have such samey names. Why'd they all sound so girly?"

Daniel studied the imp boy. "El is one of the Boss's names. He names those He calls into being after Himself." He bowed his head, looked up again, and grinned. "Back in a minute."

Then he spread his wings, caught a breeze, and wheeled off into the wind, soaring upward on an air current. His silhouette turned into a great black bird.

The imp boy watched him leave. "Does Daniel often visit?"

Bladder snorted. "Every day. Part of his caretaking. He says we'll break bits off the cathedral if he's not watching. One little buttress it was, and now we're constantly being performance managed."

Wheedle said, "If he gave us a day off, we'd go to the playground, scare some kids. I've never been on a slide."

"Why bother? There's always some flapping busybody around no matter where you plunk yourself," Bladder said, then they all turned. "School time. Here they come! Spigot? Where are ya?"

The gargoyles fled down the pinnacle, leaving the imp boy living alone in the sunlight. He watched the human movement in the streets below, fascinated by the color of their hair and their various fabric covers; then he climbed back to the top of the spire to study the larger city, hearing the gargoyles teasing and blowing raspberries at passing children.

He watched the slow climb of the sun, until it no longer sat on the lower edge of the world but rose so it was eye level with him. His stomach rumbled like a small ogre and threatened to get louder.

"Hello again," Daniel said, touching down on the tiles and handing the imp boy a thick-strapped, green bag. "A few things you could use."

The imp boy turned the pack over in his hands until Daniel flipped the buckles. A beige object sat on top. "That's pie."

"Pie?" The imp boy held the pleasant weight. Daniel ripped the plastic and mimicked biting. The imp boy nibbled.

His eyes widened at the sensation. It made his mouth feel better, sweeter.

"You're starving," Daniel said.

The food disappeared in rapid bites. "It's wonderful."

"'Wonderful' is better for people. People can be wonderful." Daniel gestured toward the green and soft gray city, human voices rising from the streets. "How about 'tasty'? Pie is tasty."

"Tasty." Then the imp boy pointed at the golden disk in the sky. "You said the sun was wonderful."

"Well, it is. It's also 'magnificent.'"

"Magnificent. Mag-ni-fi-cent." The imp boy closed his eyes. "I like that sound."

Daniel laughed and pulled clothes from the pack. He handed them to the imp boy. "That's it, shorts on, T-shirt over the head. Most boys are a bit nervous about running around naked; you don't want to stand out. Pants and sweater in the bag for when it gets cold."

The imp boy struggled to put on the clothes. His skin tingled under the fabric. He'd seen the other humans below wearing clothes, and he smiled, knowing he looked more like them.

The angel tugged out another bundle. "This is a sleeping bag. You roll it out and crawl inside." The angel laughed. "Not head first. Feet first."

The imp boy opened and closed his mouth. He didn't have a word to say to the angel.

"You say 'Thank you,'" Daniel said.

"Thank you?"

"It means you're grateful; you think well of the effort."

"Oh?" the imp boy said. "Thank you."

"And if you need to ask for something, you say 'Please.'" Daniel patted his shoulder. "Is there anything you would like?"

"Please," said the imp boy, "can you give me a name?"

CHAPTER 5

Daniel did not answer right away. He stared about the spire and the town, then shook his head. "Sorry, angels aren't allowed to name outside our species. It can't be me that names you. You might not be human or gargoyle, but you're also not an angel. And, admittedly, you do look like you might do well with a human name."

"Am I one?"

"You have a heart, and a heart is a good start, but you need a soul as well as a heart to be human."

"What are those things?"

"Well, your heart is a little machine that pushes the blood around. Souls are something humans are born with—it's what makes them human. An inner entity, a powerful, unstoppable force."

"It sounds awful, like an ogre."

Daniel stroked an eyebrow with a forefinger. "Actually, a soul is an amazing thing, and you'd think humans would always want to convey how amazing their souls are. So much power and light in such tiny vessels. They don't always show it. Sometimes they are barely nice; sometimes they are awful. Occasionally, they are magnificent."

The imp boy sighed. He patted his face. What was leaking out? "What's wrong with me?"

"You're sad. Some creatures cry to show that. Gargoyles, humans, animals. There's a rather interesting species of German fairy that spends half its life in tears. Sensitive little creature."

"I'm sad?"

"Seems like it."

"Why am I sad?"

"You'll have to tell me," Daniel said. "What are you thinking right now?"

The imp boy studied his hands. They were full of the hot wet stuff trickling from his eyes. "I wonder if I belong anywhere. I mean, really?"

Daniel flicked out one gorgeous wing and spread it around the imp boy, blanketing him in a sweet, stomach-aching smell. "You don't want to stay with the gargoyles?"

"I don't think Bladder wants me around."

"That won't stop him from taking care of you. He's a better creature than he first appears." Daniel squeezed his shoulder again. The imp boy felt the warmth of the angel's hand, and something new: a growing sense that maybe this first day could get better. It built under the angel's touch.

Daniel took his hand away, and the warmth on the imp boy's shoulder faded. "Maybe you don't belong here. We do have to ask a few questions of the right person . . ."

The angel glided off.

The day moved fast, and soon shadows cast dappled light over different sections of ground. The imp boy watched humans until Bladder shrieked, "Imp!"

He slumped over to the edge of the spire and peered down at his gargoyle guardians. "Yes?"

"Get down here," Bladder said.

He climbed down head first and sat on a thin ridge in front of Bladder.

Wheedle sidled over. "We want you to steal us some chocolate. You think you could?"

Bladder pointed down the street. "There are shops down there. I'm sure you can put a box of choccies under that T-shirt the flying freak gave you. What do you see?"

"Big windows," the imp boy replied.

Wheedle put his head forward. "Can you read?" He pointed out a sign on the street.

The imp boy sounded it out. "Sss-L-Oh-Wer. No, slow."

"Good work, Imp," Wheedle said. "You're looking for words like 'sweets', 'chocolate', and 'confectionery'. You'll find them written on storefronts. Go inside and take some."

The imp boy winced. The street was crowded with humans of all heights and widths. Not as big as ogres, but there were a lot of them, and they gathered together into tight packs.

"Off you go," Bladder said, and poked him in the back.

"We'll be here when you return," Wheedle said.

He clambered down toward ground level and watched a couple pass along the sidewalk. If they saw him, would they be able to tell he wasn't their kind of people? Neither one looked in his direction, and he put his bare foot onto the horizontal cement and stood up straight, on two legs, like all the humans were doing.

The gray church sat in the afternoon flush, its black windows strengthened by bars, the main door hanging open. It looked darker inside, but a thin stream of blue light poured onto a spot just inside the door. He hadn't seen light that color before. The imp boy glanced up. The gargoyles weren't watching, so he darted into the church.

The inside blazed with colored glass. A picture of a serene-faced man with a mane of blue had been captured in a window. The sunlight through his hair was creating the stain on the floor. The place sat in hush, a gentle calm filling the empty space.

The imp boy could hear the gargoyles chortling outside on the roof, far above him. He could make out every word they said about chocolate and their preference for substantial drama over horror movies. Human voices, far lovelier, sang in from the streets, humming with community. He heard a tiny creature digging a hole in the dirt outside the building. He filtered them out and stood in the cocooned quiet of the high-ceilinged room.

The imp boy looked around at the warm wood paneling and white marble floors. At the front, behind a long table, two statues stood. They had sober, white faces; one was a man holding a staff and the other a woman with a baby.

"Poor thing."

"He does look sad, doesn't he?"

"You want to wrap them in your arms when they're like that."

The imp boy gazed at the statues and walked toward them. The voices stopped.

"Hello?" the boy said. He glanced from one to the other. Up close he saw their fine straight noses and high foreheads. He watched the woman but sensed movement at the edge of his vision. He turned, and the first statue, the slim man in a marble crown, stared at him with wide, stony eyes. It wasn't the same position the boy had seen him in when he'd arrived.

"You moved," the imp boy said.

"He got you, Benjamin," said the lady with the baby.

Benjamin sighed. "Hello, young man. What's your name?"

"I don't have one."

"That's a shame," the lady said. The baby burbled.

"What are your names?"

"Well, you've met Benjamin; I'm Beth. And this is Henry." The baby burbled again and waved its hand.

"They are lovely names. Where did you get them?"

"From our maker, the sculptor who made us. He named us after the models he used," Benjamin explained.

The statues went quiet while he looked around. "Do you like it here?" he asked.

"It's lovely," Beth said, "but we've been here for . . ."

Baby Henry began counting on his fingers. "An awfully long time," he said, his rumbly deep voice echoing around the cathedral.

"The world's changed since we arrived," Beth said. "I wish we could go outside, but anyone could see us."

Ben added, "Sometimes the people in here—not often, mind— but sometimes they light up enough for us to not miss the sun. And we do get *some* entertainment. The services are occasionally interesting, and someone left their iPad behind once. We watched films until the battery died. Our angel, Daniel, visits."

"Ah, Daniel," Beth sighed.

"Groupie." Ben pursed his lips.

"It's good to have someone come and tell us what's going on outside," Beth said. "So what are you doing today?"

"I have to steal chocolates for the gargoyles."

"The gargoyles?" Ben gestured at the roof. "But you're not a gargoyle."

"I was made like an imp."

"Still, nobody's ever proud to say they're a thief," Ben said.

"Maybe you could *ask* for chocolates instead," Beth said.

"Humans aren't generous," Henry said. "You could sing for your supper."

"What's singing?" the imp boy asked.

"Oh dear," Beth said. "You don't know much. How old are you?"

"Half a day."

Beth patted his head. "You know, you're a cute little fellow, in a rumpled, dirty kind of way. Try asking."

"It may only work once on the same person; but you can always move on to a different target the next time," Ben said.

Beth pouted. "Great, you say don't be dishonest but encourage him to panhandle people. Excellent work, St. Joseph."

"Don't call me that, you know I hate it when you call me that." Ben looked at the imp boy. "Eh, she's right. Come back and tell us how it goes. Tell us absolutely everything."

The group stopped talking as they had all heard footsteps resounding behind them. The statues resumed their stony positions. Beth risked a wink before the imp boy ran out into the sunshine, dashing past the black-robed man in the doorway, who turned to watch him go.

He stood in the street looking down the row of stores next to the church.

"Ask," he said, and gulped.

Dresses filled the windows of the closest stores; he stared at the bright colors shining through the glass. Strange, twisted foods jam-packed one window. Long meats hung between yellow and red circles. Rich and somber smells came through the doors; some so salty he could taste the shadow of flavor on the back of his tongue.

One dark window, backed by a black cloth and filled with pretty metal shapes and sparkling stones, echoed the movement of people behind him. The letters on the window spelled "Jewelry Store" between the reflections of bright red buses rushing alongside many-colored cars.

The window also mirrored a white oval studded with two dark eyes. He gasped to see the face staring at him, then realized it was his own. He touched his head; his other self touched its head too. His hair was matted and dark, not golden like Daniel's, but it framed the shocked pale circle that was his face. He patted his nose. Straight, very human-looking, also like Daniel's. Except for the scruffiness he looked like everyone else on the sidewalk, although a few people cast glances at his bare feet.

Then he caught the scent of something beautiful. It didn't matter in the moment what Wheedle and Bladder wanted, he needed to follow the scent. He hurried from store to store, the aroma growing sweeter and more intense until he stood outside a window decorated by a name in curling white letters. Inside, beautiful boxes and long flat parcels lay next to trays of tiny gifts wrapped in shiny sky-colored paper, a twist at each end. He caught the ghostly likeness of himself again in the glass, The smell sweet, like new words opening his mouth, the scent filling his nose. He stared at the curling letters, but he couldn't understand them—La Chambre du Chocolat. The last word was close enough to "chocolate," so he guessed he was where Wheedle and Bladder wanted him to be.

He stood at the door waiting, bewitched, until an older man with sparkling blue eyes walked out to a tinkle of silver bells.

He smiled down at the imp boy and said, "You know, whenever a bell rings, an angel gets its wings."

"Oh," said the imp boy. "I thought angels already had wings."

"Well, I may have got my facts wrong." The man wandered down the street, his warm laugh fading.

The door began to close, and the imp boy darted in before it shut.

A young woman stood behind a glass counter with her back to him. She glowed a little but did not turn, and it gave him time to study the room. Lines and lines of white, brown, and black circles of gargoyle-delight-covered shelves on every wall. The air smelled sweet and rich. The imp boy's stomach rumbled. *Hungry.* That word again, the one that reminded him of Thunderguts. He didn't like it. He did not want to associate this lovely room with the ogre king.

"It's a different kind of hunger," he reassured himself. "It's not the same type."

"Oh," said the woman, and turned. "I didn't realize someone'd come in." She peered at him, looking from his messy hair to his bare feet. "No pockets?"

The imp boy shrank back. He wondered what pockets were.

The woman smiled, and her gentle glow brightened. The imp boy thought it wonderful, like sunlight.

"So, no money," she continued. She looked at his feet again. "Your parents in the street?" She laughed and showed even, white teeth. "Someone to pay for your treat?"

"No one, sorry." He added, "Ma'am."

"Well, you look nice enough. And polite for your age. Some boys are snatching and sneering by the time they're— what are you? Twelve?"

The imp boy tried to think of something to say to this. "Do they? Sorry."

"Aren't you a dear?" Her smile lit her face all the way to her eyes. "Would you like a hot chocolate? I'm making myself one."

The smell of the room assailed him. "Yes," he said, then remembered. "Thank you." He wondered if the chocolate would be too hot to eat right away.

A machine in the corner grunted and gnashed in an ogrish manner, and then the woman gave him a red mug with frothy liquid in it; three white pillow-like things floated on the surface. He poked in the end of his tongue to test the heat, took a delighted gulp, then set the cup down to push the pillows with his fingertip. They bobbed in froth.

"Do you live near here?" she asked.

"Up the street."

"Ah, so you know your way home then." She peered at him over the top of her cup, studying the top of his head. Then she peered at his feet. He curled in his toes. None of the humans outside had had bare feet, and he wondered if it was important. "Your family nice?" she asked.

The imp boy pondered this. He hadn't heard the word "family" before, but he sensed that it was close to "pack." "My family? They're gargoyles so they can't help being grumpy. Wheedle's nice." Then he remembered Beth's words. *Ask*, he thought. "They've sent me out to get chocolates. They told me to steal them, but the man in the church said I shouldn't."

"Well, he would, wouldn't he?"

"So, do you think you could *give* me some chocolates? Please. They don't have to be your best ones."

She laughed a tinkling bell of a laugh. "You aren't going to scarf them yourself, are you?"

"Oh no, I won't get any."

She paused and looked at him. "You're serious? Won't they leave you any? That's awful. No wonder you call them gargoyles. If I give you some, will it make your day a bit easier?"

The woman didn't wait for an answer; she disappeared out the back door and returned with a box of chocolates.

"It's full but got left out in the sun, and they've melted a bit. We can't sell them, so my manager won't mind. Now you put a couple in your pockets first."

The imp boy tucked the box under his arm and turned to the door. He still didn't know what pockets were and wondered why she had told him to put chocolates in something she'd noticed he didn't have.

"Thank you. I do really think well of your effort."

"Oh, you are an absolute darling. You finish your drink. The afternoon crowd's not in for ages." She patted a stool at the counter, and the imp boy sat down. "My name's May. What's yours?"

"I don't have one."

May laughed. "You don't have one, or do I need to guess it? Is it Rumpelstiltskin?"

The door tinkled again. May looked up, and the imp boy turned around. A woman shuffled in. She wore a beige dress and carried a leather bag. She was distracted by the wall farthest from the counter, peering at boxes prewrapped in red foil.

May slid her cup under the counter and winked at the imp boy. "Sit nice and quiet."

The woman hurried over to May, digging in her bag. She handed the imp boy a set of keys without looking up.

"Hold these, Nick," she said.

The imp boy took the keys as she pulled papers and half-wrapped food out of her bag. She put a pacifier and a packet of baby-wipes on the counter.

She didn't have much success with her search.

"Nick, sweetheart," she said to the imp boy, "I need you to run back to the car and get my purse. I promised Dad I would—"

The door to the shop tinkled again. "Sorry, Mom, I got caught up at the skate shop," a voice called from the door.

The imp boy turned to see the person coming in. He was taller than the imp boy by a head, his hair brushed smooth, but the pale face and the large dark eyes were like the imp boy's own. He could have been another reflection.

"Oh ho, gargoyles indeed. To think I almost believed you," May said to the imp boy. She turned to the woman. "Your son doesn't half tell a good story."

The imp boy turned to see the woman staring at him. Hunger again, though not quite like Thunderguts or the crone's. Her eyes glowed like May's, and yet the rest of her hung in gray, as if she had enough color in her to fill only her starving brown eyes. "My son? Oh, no, no, he's not . . . I'm so sorry, I took you for . . ." She looked to the boy at the door and back to the imp boy, studying his face with greed.

The imp boy was afraid she would grab at him, and he edged back. He returned her keys and she took them, her hand hanging midair. He felt the moment around him stop and go silent, regardless of the thundering starting inside him. Then his legs and hands, instinctive and quick, moved again. He grabbed the box of chocolates May had given him, swung off the stool, and raced past the boy at the door.

"Hey!" Nick called. The imp boy glanced at the boy's face, his dark eyes, his black hair. The doorbell rang frantically as he lunged through.

And he ran.

He heard them in the shop, his ears keen to hear their voices no matter how far he fled.

"He's really not yours?" May said. "I'm sorry, I just assumed you were related . . . he's the spitting image of *you*."

The imp boy worked hard to keep the conversation clear, as his body thumped inside and out trying to drown outside sounds.

He clambered up the side of the cathedral.

"Maybe he's . . ." Nick's voice began, but then his voice cut out.

"He got a boxful! He got a boxful!" Wheedle cheered. "I told you he was gonna be brilliant."

The imp boy jumped up next to him. His breathing came hard, hurting his lungs.

"Bring it here," Bladder said.

The imp boy shoved the box at the gargoyles and barreled past Bladder to lean over the street side of the roof. He wanted to see if he'd been hunted, to see if the two from the chocolate shop were near. He scoured the humans passing alongside the church and saw the two of them coming up the sidewalk.

"Unwrap the green one for me?" Wheedle begged, passing a chocolate to the imp boy. The imp boy didn't take his gaze off the street as he unwrapped the first sweet for the bull-faced gargoyle.

"Wheedle," the imp boy asked, the hammer in his chest pounding at his ribs, "do humans often look alike?"

He saw the woman on the sidewalk frown, the boy scanning the street, searching for something. Neither of them looked up.

"All of 'em look the same to me," Bladder said.

He shrank back as the woman and the boy called Nick walked beside the church.

"Is there anyone else from the family visiting?" the imp boy heard Nick ask.

The gargoyles moved to the edge of the building to see what the imp boy was watching so intently. He pointed at Nick.

The gargoyles peered down. "I see what you mean," Bladder said.

"... Not supposed to arrive until tomorrow," the woman was saying. "Maybe ... but have you seen anyone in the family that much ..." She trailed off. The hungry look on her face had gone. The imp boy wondered why she'd frightened him. She was nothing like Thunderguts.

"Do humans eat humans?"

"Not often that they tell you about," Bladder said, "although they really are nasty brutes."

"You think one of them wants to eat you?" Wheedle chortled. This grew to huge guffaws. "You have so much to learn, kid."

"Nope, he's got 'em figured out," Bladder said. "Can't trust a human."

Nick and the woman walked by. "That boy does look a bit like you," Wheedle said. "But it's just a coincidence; I wouldn't let it bother you."

"What's a coincidence?" the imp boy asked.

"You know," said Wheedle, putting his hoofish toes together and apart as he spoke. "When a series of happenings happen and you don't expect them to. But they do, and they're odd."

The imp boy had no idea what that meant.

"He really does look like you," Bladder said. "Not that I'm a good judge of human appearance. It's all skin and hair and eyelashes as far as I'm concerned."

A gust of wind announced the arrival of an angel, and Daniel alighted next to the pack. The imp boy didn't turn to greet him. He continued watching the woman and Nick as they turned the corner.

"Daniel, can you tell him what a coincidence is?" Wheedle asked.

"An uncredited miracle," the angel replied.

Bladder grunted. "Oh, yes, very helpful."

"What coincidence do you mean?" Daniel asked him, but the imp boy's head was already over the side of the building and he climbed head first down the wall, hoping to see where the woman and the boy called Nick had gone. A small girl with a yellow cap stared at him as he descended, her blue eyes as wide as her mouth. No one else noticed.

He found their scent riding on the warm breeze. He wanted to see Nick again. Their smell came to him, the woman's scent floral on the surface but creamy underneath. Nick smelled stronger, earthier, like he'd been running.

"Your heart is racing," Daniel said. He'd fluttered down to the sidewalk.

"Heart?"

The angel pointed at the top of his body.

"Oh?" The imp boy put his hand on his chest. The beating thing within him. That was his heart? It was important, he knew, but he had no time to think about it. First he had to understand why Nick looked like him.

He turned from the angel and followed the human smells down the street. He couldn't hear their voices any more; they had stopped talking. He wished they would speak again.

"There was a boy. He looked like me." The imp boy gestured at his face and stalked to the corner.

"Humans often look alike. Dark hair and dark eyes aren't uncommon."

The imp boy wondered why they'd been shocked to see him, then. And May, she had said so too. He hadn't been the only one to see the similarity.

He scuttled on toward where a gap opened between two parked cars. The air felt warm. Even in the few minutes he'd been in the street, he'd learned that cars gave off heat. This one had just left, traveling south, its chemical smell hanging in the air, dragging with it the woman's flowers and the odor of the boy called Nick. But cars moved fast, too fast for him to run after them.

The imp boy looked at his feet. Round, hot water bubbled in his eyes. He couldn't hear their voices any longer, even when he strained. They could be anywhere.

Daniel put his hand on the imp boy's shoulder. He felt a bit better.

"I don't know where they went. I want to see them again."

Daniel frowned. "Some strangers?"

"Please."

CHAPTER 6

The imp boy stood under Daniel's chin. The angel put his hands around the imp boy's waist, then spread his wings and took to the sky.

"Hold on steady now." Daniel soared faster.

The world became enormous as the sunny town and the countryside spread out around them. Gray and red buildings glowed in the sunlight, and the fields tessellated in yellow, green, and brown. In the near distance, the mystical blue sparkled.

"The sea," Daniel explained. "Now, which way did they go?"

The imp boy sniffed the air, gestured to the road west, and Daniel turned toward the water.

The imp boy extended his hand into freezing air. The iciness on his fingertips invigorated him.

He shuffled in Daniel's arms and watched the world unfurl. The edge of the Earth bent in a wide curve.

"Magnificent?" the imp boy asked.

"Exactly."

A small red car bustled under them; the imp boy could smell the aromas of Nick and the woman breezing up from inside.

"That's them!" he called out over the wind.

"Remind me to take note of the strength of your olfactory system," Daniel said.

"Do humans have good...olfactory systems?" the imp boy asked.

"Your ability to smell far surpasses any human's. Although monster hunters can be trained to heighten their senses, none are as good as yours."

Then Daniel flicked out his wings, followed the little car, and glided westward toward a band of white separating the town from the water. As they got closer, the imp boy saw the creamy edge of the sea frothing onto a beach. Pale houses stood over it on a raised road.

Daniel descended to a street, landing on the sidewalk in front of a house with blank, staring windows.

"Not here, Daniel. They're around the corner, up that way, I can smell them."

"Yes, you're right," Daniel said. "But the houses here are empty. Humans can't see me, angels are invisible to their eyes, but they'll see you, and no one should spot a boy dropping out of the sky."

They walked to the top of the street; the sidewalk sloped up, past a few cars parked along the edge of the pavement. Weeds poked out around the lamp posts, eager to greet the warm day and sway as the imp boy and his angel trotted past. The sea breeze pushed by, racing them to the top.

At the intersection, the sea to their left caught the sunlight, and another gust greeted them. The salty wind lifted the hair on the imp boy's neck and ran its cool hand across his skin.

On the opposite corner, a little cottage sat away from the homes on the crammed terrace. Older, more lived-in, its windows and doors hunchbacked under heavy, dirty brick and brown tiles.

They stared at the house.

"Come on, let's go and have a look." Daniel pushed him forward.

They crossed the overgrown front garden, and Daniel shoved through bushes, pulling the imp boy behind him. A blind blocked out the dark window. Daniel touched a long finger to the glass, and the blind opened, the slats tilting so they could see inside.

"It's a living room," Daniel said. "This room feels important."

The woman was there with Nick. She'd pulled her hair into a dark, practical ponytail. Through the window, the imp boy could hear her sniffles and the creaking sounds of the floorboards under her feet.

Nick breathed in. "It smells of his tobacco and leather polish. What do we do with the furniture?"

"I'm not sure; we should get rid of the chair, but the rest just needs steaming. Maybe we can ask Aunt Colleen what she wants. We'll show the photos at the wake."

"I can make a slideshow."

"That's an idea. When you're done, we'll put the real pics along this wall." The woman held up a photo and closed her eyes.

"Hey, that's one of all of us when I was little."

"Look at my hair."

"I know, Mom, what were you thinking?"

"Nicholas Seamus Kavanagh!"

Nick laughed.

The imp boy spied the picture over the woman's shoulder. It was her, but younger, standing with a small boy he guessed was Nick. He watched as the woman ran her finger over the outline of her younger self's full belly, tiny Nick leaned into her knees. She picked up another. The Nick in it was only slightly younger than the real one inside, his forehead wide and nose already strengthening. The imp boy touched his own face, tracing the line of his forehead and nose. The picture could have been of him.

"Very similar," Daniel said. "Not identical. Nick is heavier set than you, his face squarer, but the confusion is understandable."

The woman gazed dreamily toward the window, as if she were looking for something. She realized Nick was watching her. She said, "Get me a box; we'll collect them up."

"He really threw you, didn't he? That boy?"

"I forgot Aunt Colleen's chocolates." The woman's eyes glittered, and she touched the heels of her hands to each one.

The young man glanced at her over his shoulder as he left the room. The woman came to the window and pushed it open, letting in a warm breeze. The imp boy pulled back, but the woman's gaze rested on the windowsill and the blinds.

"Nick," she called.

"Yes, Mom."

"Can you find a dusting cloth too?" She rubbed her palm over her eye. "Poor old Pop, he let everything get so filthy."

"Is she crying?" whispered the imp boy.

"Hmmm." Daniel put his hand on the window. "So much love here. Loss too. Maybe this is not a good time to visit."

He pulled the imp boy close and took to the sky. "Let's go back."

"He's called Nick? Nicholas Seamus Kavanagh?" the imp boy asked as they flew. "And she's Mom?"

"No, Mom is short for Mother; she's his female parent." Daniel smiled at his confusion. "He's her child, so he can call her that. It means they belong to each other."

The imp boy focused less on the green patchwork of the meadows and more on the houses they flew over. Inside, people interacted with each other, belonged to each other, called each other by their names or affectionate versions of them.

"Are there lots of mothers and children?"

"And fathers, and grandparents, and aunts and uncles. They're called families."

The imp boy remembered May using the word. "Do they like being in families?"

"Mostly they take it for granted," Daniel said, and cradled the imp boy's head.

"Where have you been?" Bladder demanded as soon as Daniel set down.

"Worried, were you?" the angel asked.

"Course not! It's just rude to fly off without telling anyone. You've never flown off with one of us before."

"You weigh half a ton."

Wheedle shoved his head into the conversation. "There was a bit of a kerfuffle while you were away. It got overcast, and a pixie showed up an' asked if we'd seen a human look-alike. I wanted to sit on it till the sun came back. That woulda been fun."

"It would turn to ash if you did that," the imp boy said.

"Exactly!" agreed Bladder. "One gray moment in an otherwise beautiful day and those nasties are up annoying us. I'd like to teach 'em a lesson."

Wheedle exhaled. "It said the ogres would make it worth our while if we see him. Said he's valuable. When he didn't come back we thought the pixie'd already nicked him."

"So you *were* worried?" Daniel chuckled. "What did you tell the pixie?"

"Ain't a snitch, didn't say nothin'. Besides he didn't ask many questions or stay long. It couldn't've been that interested."

"The ogre king tried to grab me on Hatching Day," the imp boy said.

Daniel raised his brow. "Really?"

"So you're what all the fuss was about at the Hatching? You coulda tol' us this earlier." Bladder glared at Wheedle. "Thass troublin', that is."

"Doesn't have to be," Wheedle said. "Thunderguts is probably just curious about what you are. It's an inconvenience him bothering us to look for you, that's all." Wheedle studied the street below. "I'm sure we got nothing to worry about. Just got to wait it out."

Bladder snarled, then said, "Dint even know he was on Thunderguts's radar."

Wheedle coughed. "Which reminds me. Snack time! Peel us some more chocs."

Daniel sat silently. They all did. The imp boy tried to meet the eyes of each one, but they pondered hands, hoofs, or claws and no one looked at him.

The imp boy sat wondering how long the silence would last, when Daniel touched his head and said, "You gargoyles will watch out for him?"

"Course we will. Won't none of us survive if we don't watch each other," Wheedle said.

"Well, just take care."

Bladder snorted. "Don't you have something to do that don't involve pointing out the obvious?"

"Are you all right?" Daniel ruffled the imp boy's hair.

The imp boy felt his chest. The thing inside him that Daniel had called his heart, it felt off. The rhythm raced instead of rapped. "I don't know. You have to go now, don't you?" he asked.

Daniel nodded. "My apologies. That side trip cut into my break time. Back later. It's not common practice, but maybe my assistant, Yonah, can bring my scrolls and we can do some office work from here this evening."

"Oh lovely—you're going to spend even more time with us." Bladder glared at them both and stamped down the pinnacle. Wheedle followed.

"It's unlikely that the pixie will be back today," Daniel told the imp boy. "But stay concealed if you hear anything odd. Like Bladder said, it'll blow over."

The imp boy watched the angel fade into the clouds and looked around. He grabbed the chocolate box and climbed up the pinnacle, watching for any movement of the drains and manhole covers on the roads. Bright sunlight played on the chocolate box lid, and the imp boy pulled out the leftover wrappers to see their colors, letting each one escape and fly on the wind.

The tone of the sky transformed as the sun moved, and he felt sleepy. Since his arrival, he had discovered so many things, seen real humans close-up. It tired him so much. His eyes struggled to watch the sunlight; as they fluttered open and closed he wondered what was wrong with them. He sighed and thought of the boy he looked like: Nick.

CHAPTER 7

He woke and thought he must have turned around. The sun was on the opposite side of him. He clambered up the ornate spire, high above the town, where the air smelled clean and sweet, and inhaled to his belly. Daniel was balanced on the very tip-top of the spire and waved. The imp boy closed his eyes as more sunlight hit his face.

"Did you enjoy your nap? You must have slept for hours. We came back, and you were out, all curled up into a little ball."

"Nap?"

"Human bodies need to sleep. It's likely yours needs a lot. You are basically a newborn."

The imp boy frowned. He thought through his basic knowledge, but could find nothing about naps.

A gentle flap of wings disturbed the silence, and a small white bird landed on Daniel's head. It chirped quietly in the angel's ear.

"Yes," said the angel. "They're all fine."

The bird flittered across, landed on the imp boy's shoulder, put a keen eye close to his, and stared.

"He's fine too," Daniel said. "My friend, this is Yonah, my assistant. She's a peace dove." The dove pushed out her chest so the imp could see a small badge decorated with a single bright leaf on a green twig. "She's taken it upon herself to get some information on you and may check on you at regular intervals today."

Yonah rubbed her small, soft head against his cheek. The imp boy's heart slowed. The sky looked calmer, more still.

"And here." Daniel handed him another plastic-wrapped square. "It's a sandwich. Your stomach has been rumbling since we got here, even in your sleep."

The imp boy threw out a thank-you and ripped the plastic. He took a bite as his stomach snarled. The sweet softness outside reminded him of pie pastry. The green leaves inside sent fresh coolness into his mouth. The other part tasted salty and smooth.

"Remind Yonah or me to give you something to pack for a late snack. The gargoyles aren't intending to go back into The Hole, are they? We can't go down there to watch over you."

"Why not?"

Daniel shook his head. "We die in a place with no hope. Humans can't stand that awful place either. Those few who stumble their way down there rarely return. Unless they get back out quickly, they die."

Bladder and Wheedle appeared. Wheedle took a spot close to the imp boy, shoving his bottom into the tiles. The tip of his stone wing touched the imp boy's shoulder.

"Not that that's what we're planning," Bladder said to Daniel, "but if we ever do decide to take him back downstairs he'll be just fine, because he ain't human. He was made just the same way we monsters all was, and if nothing takes it in its head to kick him, he will survive that place well enough. Stop filling his head with your stupid ideas that he's not a monster."

Wheedle reached out a claw and felt the imp boy's head, twisting it before giving it a hard rap with his stone knuckles. "His head's solid as concrete. His bones are troll weight. He could fall from this cathedral and get up without a scratch."

"I wouldn't fall," said the imp boy. "I can climb walls."

"Not exactly a human trait, is it?" Bladder chortled.

"He needs to eat," Daniel said.

"Like an ogre."

"He sleeps."

"Like a troll."

"He's a 'he.'"

"Like leprechauns and pixies and quite a few others."

"No, they only appear male or female," Wheedle said. "You know they're not either."

Bladder glared at Wheedle.

"He has a heart," Daniel said. "He really feels. You've seen him cry."

"Are you saying we don't feel? I . . ." Bladder started. "Wheedle feels. He's a total sap."

"Hey!" Wheedle said.

"Wheedle's only a century or two old," Daniel said. "And isn't it just sentiment in the end? You feel anger, envy, and resentment sure enough. But what good things do you feel?"

"Gargoyle feelings don't just go away," Wheedle muttered. "It's . . ."

"Yes?" Daniel leaned forward.

Bladder growled. "None of your business."

Wheedle shuffled back down the spire and rejoined Spigot on the pinnacle.

"Go off and annoy your other victims." Bladder stormed after Wheedle. Below, all three gargoyles set to making faces at humans. A small schoolboy ran by squealing.

Daniel smiled after the gargoyles; then Yonah peeped at him. "Sorry, we have a lot of work and can't stay here too long," Daniel said. "There was so much to do for you this morning, my other chores have gone undone. Thank goodness it's a long day."

"Your other chores?"

"A caretaker cares for lot of things. There are other statues, anthroparians, and golems that need assistance. The homunculi wanted lots of attention this morning and didn't receive it."

"But you'll be back?"

Daniel smiled. "Yonah will split duties with me today and help me catch up. We'll return early evening. Don't worry, there are many hours of light ahead and we have some office work to do. It's as easy to do it on a church roof as a desk. Be safe, my friend."

The angel flew into the warm, blue sky. Yonah trailed after.

The afternoon passed with little event. When the sun slid lower in the sky, hanging over the houses at the edge of the town, Yonah appeared carrying a plastic box twice as big as she. She dropped it onto the imp boy's shoulder and rubbed his face with her tiny head, making his skin tickle, then she nested on his backpack, her eyes drifted closed, and she cooed as she napped. The sound was a distant choir, and hinted at words the imp boy would never understand. It took him a while to realize he had to open the box. Inside he found another sandwich, some small red baubles with green leafy tops that burst sweetly in his mouth, and yellow-white salty squares.

When he finished, Yonah woke, took the box, and flew away.

Wheedle came up for him and prodded at the trash on the roof. "You know, I'm not so fond of strawberries, but I do like a bit of cheese. I could smell it, but I don't fancy that dove telling his wingship I took your food."

The gargoyle looked wounded, and the imp boy wished he had saved some "cheese" for Wheedle. He liked the word and said it a few times.

Wheedle sat on his haunches, pushing into the stone of the roof to get comfortable. "Gargoyles do feel, you know. We've got . . ." His hoof hovered over his chest for a moment. "Oh, it don't matter. Forget about feelings. I'm trying to. If the ogres ever found out, they'd probably hate gargoyles even more than they do now."

The imp boy didn't understand anything Wheedle said.

"Oi!" Bladder called from below. "Down here, you two."

The imp boy and Wheedle descended.

"Time for another chocolate run," Bladder said.

"Do I have to go back to the same shop? I don't know if May will like to see me after today. Is there another candy store around here?"

"That's your job to find out." Bladder turned his back, and the imp boy skulked down the side of the church. He walked the length of the road looking for another chocolate shop. He found a deli and smelled the sweets inside, but the woman behind the counter yelled at him and he ran back into the street.

He found himself outside May's store, peering both ways to see if anyone was watching him, before risking the tinkling of the door. He wondered if Nick and his mother had been back. He'd have heard, wouldn't he? Maybe not while he was asleep.

"Rumpel! You're back." May smiled as he entered. Her gentle glow brightened so much, he wondered why he'd been worried. "Wasn't that an odd coincidence? I'm so sorry for that. Your face, you poor thing."

Coincidence. She used the same word as Wheedle. He decided to start a book that listed words and their meanings.

"It's cool enough now for choc milk, don't you think?"

She gave him a chocolate drink with ice in it, and he found he liked ice as much as marshmallows. Only one man came in, picked up a pink box, paid, and rushed back to the sidewalk.

May gave the imp boy something she called an apple and asked him numerous questions he could not answer. She didn't understand where he lived and inquired if he was "homeless" and did he have somewhere to sleep that night. She asked several times if he was okay.

"I'm a little concerned about the ogres, but I think I'll be all right."

She peered at his face and scrutinized him before saying, "I have about five of these damaged boxes. I'll get you another. You can get one tomorrow, and the day after, if you like. Maybe I'll bring some soup to work. What do you think?"

"Thank you," he said.

When the imp boy returned to the church, Bladder let him have a chocolate. He sat sucking it at the top of the spire. Yonah sat there, watching him with small dark eyes. He waved; she bowed.

"He don't come himself but he's now sending that pigeon." Bladder's voice traveled up to him from a pinnacle below. "That's about the fifth time I seen her today. I look up and there's a disgusting blot of white on our nice gray building. Unwrap me a peppermint cream."

Wheedle was still chewing on a toffee-centered chocolate. "Thee's jutht washing outh for him," he said.

"What she think we're gonna do to him?"

"Maybe thee's contherned with wath we're all contherned about."

"What have you got us into, Wheedle? Ogres are lookin' for him. Great way to keep us all safe."

The imp boy heard Wheedle swallow his toffee. "You think we should hand him over?"

"Thass not what I'm suggesting, but what if they come back tonight? What's to stop Thunderguts sendin' up some real nasties to hunt him out once it's dark? That pigeon knows it 'n' all."

"We keep him bundled up here and nobody's gonna see him," Wheedle reassured him. "We convince them we've never seen no human-looking imp. Besides, ogres aren't so eager to go hunting. If Thunderguts just wants a homemade meal, it's only the one, he'll forget soon enough."

Spigot shrieked.

"My question too, Spigot. What if he don'?" Bladder asked. "We never seen anything like him before. I know we told the imp it'll all blow over, but in truth, if Thunderguts wants him so he can figure out a way to make his own dinners, he might hunt him forever."

The gargoyles fell quiet. Above them, the imp boy shivered.

It was early evening by the time Daniel reappeared. The sky had softened to silver, but the disk of the sun still glowed. Yonah cooed a greeting that carried over to the imp boy, and he scrambled up the spire only to watch Daniel flutter to the roof of the main building below. He scurried down again, hearing Yonah's cooing chuckle as he descended.

"Daniel!"

"My friend. Hello."

The angel had folders under one arm. He set them down on the roof and they slipped apart.

"There is much work to do, but you are welcome to keep us company while we work."

75

"What do you do?" the imp boy asked.

"Part of my job as curator is to look after legendary swords. Yonah helps me. We make sure they are accounted for, and when they are moved or change hands, our job is to make sure everything goes smoothly."

The imp boy found that he knew the word "sword," and with it came others. Slash, slice, war. Power.

"If a legendary sword falls into the wrong hands, it can have catastrophic consequences. The Arthurian swords are keeping us particularly busy at the moment."

Yonah tapped a beak on the top folder. It read "Excalibur, Caliburn, Clarent."

"Is there anything I can do?" the imp boy asked.

"Not really," Daniel said. He flicked through the folders and put a few down behind him. Then his face softened. "Why don't you rest some more—keep your strength up." Then he turned back to look at the page Yonah was pecking.

The imp boy sighed. He'd waited for Daniel to return, and now the angel was being as dismissive as the gargoyles. Together they'd taught him so much in his first day of life, but he couldn't help feeling there were more things not being said. Thunderguts's face came into his mind.

He slumped on the roof and blew air from cheek to cheek. When he realized the pair weren't going to be distracted, he went to the spire top and looked out at the world again. The view satisfied his heart somehow, filling it the way a sandwich filled his belly. He went back down wanting to tell them about it, but Yonah was still cooing, and although he could see the beautiful photographs of swords over the bird's head, he couldn't read the words. He'd love to learn the words that explained swords.

He sat down again and looked at a stack of folders Daniel had pushed to one side. Daniel didn't seem interested in them. He reached out to feel the texture of the top folder's cover. The surface moved with suppleness under his fingers, and it had words on it. He liked words. He decided you could get hungry for words as well as food. Hunger was an interesting thing.

"Can I look at these?" the imp boy asked.

Daniel didn't turn. "Whatever keeps you busy," he replied, and carried on talking to Yonah.

But he couldn't read the word on the top cover, which was ذ. الفقار. Maybe he'd try another.

The next folders weren't any more promising. The second one was titled चन्द्रहास, and the third was меч-кладенец.

He blinked and wondered if his eyes were working. Or maybe he couldn't read anything other than street things. He sighed; if that were true it would be very disappointing.

He picked up the next folder, entitled Hrunting and Nægling. The letters seemed familiar, but when he flipped the pages inside he didn't recognize the words. The folder held some beautiful pictures of swords, but even the labels didn't make any sense to him. He went to put it down, but his eye was caught by the final folder. The Vorpal Sword, it read.

One more try. He opened the cover and lifted out the first loose sheet. It was illustrated, and the letters, crushed together in a beautiful hand, glowed green and gold. Sad faces created a border. Some poked their tongues at him. The paper was thick and yellow and covered with words written in the same long, elegant hand as the cover, and he found them easy to read.

It started mid-sentence.

. . . and thus we endured this Dark Age; full many years of blighted crops and failing children. Murd'ring monsters walked among us with their endless appetites, and no soul traveled abroad at night, or under o'ercast skies. They were a plague on those of us left living.

No one knoweth who commissioned the forging of the blade. Mages and sorcerers were summon'd to protect us from the vile beasts. One magician, knowing the strongest fabric ist the human soul, did bid the rest to build these into a metal. He stole a hundred thousand souls from a hundred thousand bodies, his conjuring draining them out and pulling them into the design.

It honoureth me not to admit I, a freeman, halted not this most Vorpal of all magicks. We have sacrificed the eternity of the few for the lives of the many.

I sleep no more, for conscience is as persistent as Furies.

The imp boy leaned in. He found reading more exciting than he expected, and it was becoming easier, and here was a history of his kind. He wanted to know more. The next page was printed, although the letters were blurred and smudged. It too was entitled The Vorpal Sword.

Before the sword was wielded, everywhere humans lived in a world populated by beasts and brutes. Humans themselves were no less brutish than the ogres and goblins they feared.

The King of Ogres, the Great Jabberwock, centuries old and bloated with arrogance, believed himself unkillable, for no blade wrought of earthly metal could pierce him.

Howev'r, Sword of Souls, this very Vorpal blade, is made of human souls, and the soul is the strongest matter in all the universe.

A young knight, innocent of heart and pure of intent, carried the sword. The boy went out to face the ogre alone and with the blade he bested the Jabberwock. After killing the beast, he took its head, then did report he saw a blaze of lights issue from the blade and about him all dark creatures turned to ash.

Afterwards, the killing ceas'd. Since then, in darkest night, and most overcast of days, the people hath walk'd fearless.

The next page was thin and white, and scrawled in an untidy hand were bold, red words:

SWORD STATUS: THE HOLE.

There was nothing else on the page but a red wax mark stamped at the bottom.

The imp boy reread the pages and then looked at artists' representations of the sword. Some were of huge two-handed swords; others rough and brutal. He fell to studying a picture of a delicate rapier blade before he heard Bladder's voice. "What are you readin'?" Some of Feather Brain's diaries? Can't imagine there's anything interesting in those: '*Said mealy-mouthed things to a bunch of humans. Told gargoyles to stop having fun.*'"

The imp boy detected the movement of white to the side and saw that Daniel had stopped talking and had turned his focus on Bladder and himself. The angel waved his hand, and Yonah soared off into the blue sky. She disappeared into a creamy cloud.

"So." Daniel peered at the imp boy with the folder open in his hands. "You're reading that. It's a sad thing."

"Well, that's something we agree upon," Bladder said.

Daniel lifted one golden eyebrow. "What exactly is your problem with the sword? It can't affect you; you're not a human-eater."

"Because that blasted thing stops the ogres and trolls eating their num-nums, they take their frustration out on the rest of us. Do you really think it would be so much fun for them to play 'Crack the Gargoyle' if their tummies were nicely full of policeman or a nurse?"

"No. But you don't hate humans so much you would prefer the ogres eat them all."

Bladder muttered. Even the imp boy didn't catch what the gargoyle said.

"Excuse me?" the angel asked.

"The lot of them, selfish and self-absorbed," Bladder replied.

"You're probably right. For me, the greatest problem is the souls that are trapped in the sword. Stuck down in that vile place. So sad for them."

"But if they were free, they couldn't control the monsters

you hate so much. You can't have it both ways, Turkey Dinner."

Daniel's wings wilted. "It is a dilemma, certainly."

"If it stops them doing what they want, why don't the ogres just throw it away?" the imp boy asked.

"Can't touch it; turns 'em to ash. Can't kidnap a human; turns 'em to ash. Can't eat someone; turns 'em to ash."

The imp boy thought hard. He hadn't been given that knowledge. He said so.

"Nah, imps don't. We're not meat-eaters so not necessary," Bladder explained. "Although, I heard a rumor that Thunderguts got a leprechaun to steal a girl. So, it might be it makes new-mades useful to him as well."

Daniel frowned. "Why would he do that? He couldn't eat her."

Bladder shook his stony mane. "I didn't ask questions, did I? I heard it while running from a bear-fisted troll. Wasn't gonna stop an' have tea, was I?" Bladder glared at the angel.

The imp boy thought about what Wheedle had said about Thunderguts hunting him forever. If the ogre king couldn't eat humans, it would make him desperate to find the one human-like creature he could eat. "So, ogres don't eat humans anymore, at all?"

"Oh, there are pockets," Bladder replied. "Ogres who'll give up their home in The Hole so they can hunt humans, but they can never go back again. The moment they hit the Great Cavern, poof! Ash pile!"

"And even up here in small groups they die out. People fight back for a start, and monsters only hatch in the Great

Cavern. In the end, misery loves company, so most won't trade that even for the delight of hunting," Daniel said.

"An' Thunderguts would probably kill them if he caught 'em."

The imp boy pondered all this. "Then they're probably desperate for a human they could get away with eating, I suppose?"

Bladder narrowed his eyes and he studied the imp boy.

"Which is why the sword has been useful." Daniel exhaled. "Some good came from it, but it is a great evil to enslave a soul. A soul is the essence of a person—all the things that make a person who they are. The part that goes on, that loves."

"What's 'loves'?"

"Yeah, tell him about 'loves,' why don't you," Bladder said.

The angel's face shone so bright at this, his troubles forgotten, and he reached out a long arm and put his hand on the imp boy's shoulder. His hand did feel warm on the imp boy's skin. He realized the angel hadn't commented on Bladder's odd desire for him to keep talking, nor noticed the gargoyle clambering away. "That's the best question you have asked so far. Love is the greatest of all things; it is the source of all courage and creativity. It's wanting people to be the best possible versions of themselves and doing everything one can to make that happen."

"It sounds . . . ?"

"This is a time when 'magnificent' applies."

Yonah returned with a red fruit in each claw. She dropped both in the imp boy's lap and landed on the angel's shoulder.

"That's a plum, by the way," Daniel said.

The imp boy struggled to say thank you but his mouth was full of sweet, dark fruit.

Yonah waggled a leg at Daniel's nose. "What's this?" the angel asked. A soft orange piece of paper wrapped her ankle. "Is this paper from the Boss's desk?" Daniel said. "Well done, Yonah." Yonah rubbed her head against his face. "Yonah has taken it upon herself to find out what she could about Nick and his family."

Daniel unscrolled it and they all leaned in to read.

It said *The Kavanagh Family*.

Daniel read the words underneath aloud. "Samuel Kavanagh survived his wife by ten years. He, in turn, is survived by four sons, and a sister. His youngest son, Richard Peter (married to Michelle), visited the day Samuel died, taking with him his son, fourteen, Nicholas Seamus, and a daughter, two and a half months old, Beatrice."

"Nicholas Seamus Kavanagh?" the imp boy asked.

Daniel nodded. "Yes, Nick." A flash of blue caught the imp boy's eye. "There's something on the back."

Daniel turned it over. Written on the other side in a beautiful cursive hand were the words *Samuel Kavanagh = last sigh. Beatrice (infant) = first laugh.*

"Beatrice?" The imp boy liked the sound of her name.

Daniel sniffed him. "A sigh. And a laugh. That's what you're made of."

"Okay."

"And the only one on record we have."

"Is this about me then?" The imp boy blinked. "The family we visited, I come from them?" His insides fell quiet, as if all the noise had been sucked from him.

The imp boy settled down to sleep that night in the dirt on the roof of the cathedral. The sun bobbed on the horizon, not even below it. He smiled at all the things he had learned that day, crawling into the sleeping bag Daniel had given him. He could hear thunderous noises traveling up from the streets. They could have been cars or ogres in the distance roaring and yelling. He knew he should be afraid, but he was too tired. His eyes would not stay open, and he curled up, a hand under his head.

CHAPTER 8

He woke in the dark with his head hurting. Wheedle held a hard hoof over his mouth.

Below, from the cathedral roof, he heard Bladder say, "Well, I don't know, do I?"

"I fink you know more than you're saying," a rumbly, grumbly voice replied.

"Nah," another dark voice replied. "What does a gargoyle know?"

The imp boy expected a rude reply from Bladder, but none came.

"We'll be back to talk to you. Don't go anywhere, if you know what's good for you."

Heavy feet like falling boulders traveled away from the

cathedral and then zipped away, disappearing into the nearest manhole, the imp boy guessed.

Thump! The three gargoyles were on him.

"Put the sleeping bag around him," Bladder said. "Hurry."

They pulled at his sleepy limbs. Wheedle tugged the bag off and wrapped it around his shoulders.

"Now the backpack. That's it. He's got to look completely different. Not just a lumpy head."

Spigot nipped the cloth through the imp boy's arm straps. Bladder shoved a length of fabric on the top of the backpack near his head.

"Go and watch for us, Spigot," Wheedle said.

"What's happening?" the imp boy asked.

"Thunderguts is still looking for you," Bladder said. "A couple of trolls came sniffing around asking. Get a bit nervous climbing human buildings, bits come off too easily, so they didn't come up here, but you need to go away."

"If Thunderguts just wanted you for a snack, this would have blown over already," Wheedle said. "He's sent some of the big ones on a hunt to find the 'look-alike.' They're so loud. How'd you sleep through it?"

"I was tired. Where's the sun?"

Bladder shook his head. "Been gone ages. It's early. In the a.m." He poked the imp boy's backpack into an uncomfortable position. "They've threatened to come back a second time, which means the cathedral's a bit too interesting for my tastes. Any sign of 'em?" This was directed at Spigot, who squatted on a pinnacle, blinking into the darkness. Reflected lamplight glowed eerily into his ruff and the underside of his beak.

"We saw a goblin earlier an' all. There's never goblins about here. We're going before there's too much chance of getting noticed. Head down, all fours. Don't look at anyone with them pretty eyes of yours. All right?"

The pack scurried toward the wall. The imp boy heard the motor of a single car growling from the streets below.

Bladder peeked over the ledge, studying the sidewalk, before signaling them on. A few humans wandered the sidewalks, but no one looked up.

They began climbing down, pressing against the wall. The imp boy spotted a swarm of bogeymen scurrying onto the sidewalk from a sewer grate, giggling and running, and head up the street in the direction of May's chocolate shop. He wondered what other kinds of monsters walked these streets at night.

"Let's head for the school first. They won't look for you there. I'll check the street is clear before we run for it," Bladder said.

Wheedle whimpered. "I ain't never seen it so busy."

Bladder growled. "You causing us such a bother, Imp." He climbed headfirst down the cathedral wall, and the imp boy hurried behind him, putting his foot onto the cold ground cover. He couldn't help being fascinated by it. He put his hand to it and let his palm brush the pliant green fingers.

"It's grass," Wheedle said.

"Not now, you two. We got more important things to worry about. I knew I shouldn't a' let you bring the runt home. Now we got goblins and trolls up and down our road."

A group of pixies walked past them, dancing toward the swings. One looked at the imp boy, stopped, and peered harder, but then another called its name and it ran over to clamber onto the hard wooden seat.

Bladder's sigh echoed against the gray brickwork. "The disguise works at least. We may all get through this in one piece. Come on."

The imp boy trotted to keep up with the jogging gargoyles. His backpack and the deformed sleeping bag jiggled and flapped around him.

"Where do we go?"

"We stow him away and then get ourselves back here," Bladder said. "It's for your own safety, Imp. You're on your own now."

Wheedle nosed the imp boy in the back. "Just for the night. You find a place to hide, and we'll tell Daniel in the morning. He'll come and get you. You'll be okay."

They stood in the street, looking up and down. There were no cars, most of the streetlights were working, and the only other visible lights were red dots over the doorways of the stores farther up. The imp boy's skin dampened beneath the pack and the sleeping bag's layers, heat and fear sweating from him, his untrained heart punching at his chest. They sidled along the cathedral wall, making little sound; just the clipping of stone feet on concrete. Bladder waved them to the sidewalk. Wheedle, the imp boy and Spigot stepped out under the street-light in front of the church.

Something scraped, just the sound of hard skin against stone, somewhere back near the cathedral door. Bladder turned first, his shadow spreading out along the street in the sharp lamplight.

A figure moved out from the base of the cathedral. They halted, staring, as a mass taller than the door itself stepped away from the wall. Its tread caused the road to shudder. Wheedle eeped. Each of the ogre's hands was bigger than the imp boy, its huge claws reflecting lamplight. Deep-set, dull eyes peered out of its pumpkin-shaped, boulder-sized head. Bladder moved quietly in front of the imp boy, sheltering him from full view.

"I'm searching for an imp. Looks human," the rumbling-truck voice called from the doorway. "You haven't seen anything like that? They said you might be the pack we was looking for."

Wheedle whimpered. "Who said? Thunderguts?"

But the ogre didn't answer him. He was staring carefully at the swaddled imp boy. "There he is."

Bladder lurched forward. He stood as a barrier between the ogre and the imp child. "He's not . . ."

"Do I look stupid? Give me the imp and no one gets broken."

Bladder opened his mouth, but he couldn't form words. He managed something that sounded like wind whistling through drains.

"You think I look stupid?" the ogre repeated. "Is that what you're saying?"

"No, no." Bladder cowered as the ogre approached, its eyes fixed on shivering stone.

The imp boy put his fingers in his mouth, forcing down a scream. He looked to the horizon, the first traces of pink arriving.

The ogre took two earthshaking steps forward, reached down, and grabbed Bladder. "I won't stand for insubordination."

"I'm sorry, I'm sorry," Bladder said. The ogre lifted the gargoyle to his face. Bladder pressed his eyes closed and whined. When the ogre lifted him over his head, the gargoyle wailed and wriggled.

"Come on!" Wheedle hissed at the imp boy, and he and Spigot darted into the church's shadow.

The imp boy turned to see Bladder flailing his paws and scratching at air. He was sobbing like a kitten.

The ogre grinned, then looked over his shoulder to make sure the imp boy watched. "Just stone, little prince," he said. "You don't want to have to be stuck with something as pathetic as this, do ya?" And he dropped his arm to the ground.

Bladder's front legs snapped off onto the road. His scream echoed, repeating his anguish. The ogre laughed.

The imp boy stepped forward. "We'll put him back together."

"Not now. Not now." Wheedle dragged him. "Get away! Climb!"

Spigot shrieked.

"I know ogres can climb!" Wheedle wailed. "Where's safe? He'll smash us all."

The ogre lifted Bladder again. The gargoyle yelped and squealed as the monster threw him down.

This time Bladder's cry cut off as he hit concrete, his neck breaking and his head rolling, once, twice, three times before stopping in front of the pack, staring at them with dead gray eyes. Spigot let out a pained squawk.

The massive ogre clapped his hands together, dusting concrete powder from his palms and striding toward the imp boy. "Enough stalling. Let's talk, little imp."

A bang rang out as the church door crashed open and a white figure lunged forward. "In here," it called.

"Ben!" The imp boy grabbed at Wheedle and pulled him inside, looking back to see Bladder's lifeless cat face distorted by pain. Spigot rushed after him as the ogre's earthquake feet stomped toward the building and shook the ground.

Ben slammed the door and locked it. The doorknob jiggled and creaked as a heavy hand outside turned it.

The imp boy sat and shivered between two stone families. Beth was standing just inside the door, holding Henry. Spigot and Wheedle had wrapped themselves together, Spigot's wings stretched around them like a shield.

The doorknob creaked again, and the wood groaned as something heavy hit it. The eagle shrieked.

"It will hold," Beth replied, but her voice quivered. "It's an old oak door, meant to take battering rams."

The noise stopped.

"Has he given up?" Ben asked.

A roar shook the windows and walls. Dust flew off high beams and sills to rain down on them. Saints huddled in stained-glass windows, holding hands to the roof as their faces fractured. The bellow came again, and the pews quaked.

Henry screamed. The imp boy shuddered as the church door boomed at the tremendous weight ramming it. He put his hands over his head, trying to block the noise of the beast's battering grunts. Sharp talons scraped the door. Henry bawled as Beth comforted him. As the door shook and shuddered, their gray-shot marble eyes bulged. Ben hugged his stone robe around himself for protection.

An animal howl bent the panels inward. The door bowed and the black lock rattled and chewed on wood. Its metal grip loosened as woodchips spat from the door onto the church floor.

"Please," Beth said. She looked to the ceiling.

The imp boy could see the lock giving way. Only its iron held the doors together. If it fell off, the monster would be inside in seconds and no one could hide. Spigot and Wheedle made a solid lump in their terrified hug. The imp boy jumped up, darting forward as the screws shook again, and pushed trembling hands onto metal heads to hold them in place.

The door strained, and he knew its weight could crush him. Oak chips soared, and a claw smashed through a panel, grabbing his arm and yanking him to the door, pulling as much of him through the hole as it could. He cried out in agony as the joint in his shoulder stretched and cracked. The deep voice purred like a huge cat, and a wet tongue licked his hand, tasting him.

"You belong to us, imp. Come with us, we'll give you nice things," the ogre rumbled.

The imp boy cried out as the monster twisted his arm.

Beth screamed.

The ogre pushed at the door again, and the imp boy's legs slipped away, jarring his arm. He shrieked.

"Oh come on, little prince. I ain't got much time! You don't want to be here no more."

Just as the imp boy felt he could hold on no longer, the claw let go of his arm. The brute outside swore, and its yell rumbled like a fleet of cars. He thought he could hear the clinking and chinking of stones rolling, then feet thudding away like fading cannon fire.

The group looked around, dazed, and sagged to the floor. They sat there groaning.

"What was that?" Ben asked.

The imp boy looked at his mangled and twisted arm and sat against Wheedle, wondering if he'd ever use it again.

Beth rocked Henry.

"I'm all right, I'm all right," Henry said between sobs. "I forget myself sometimes. I am three hundred years old. I am three hundred years old." The baby controlled his hitching breath.

With a soft gentle prod, a touch of gold shone under the door.

"Sunrise!" Wheedle said, and jumped up, letting the imp boy collapse on the marble. Ben opened the door and stepped outside, the gargoyle right behind, yelling, "Bladder, Bladder!"

Beth helped the imp boy stand, and he staggered after Wheedle and Spigot. His heart raced as he held his shattered arm, and the quick pain in his shoulder seeped into the rest of his body, stretching to his neck and his back.

The sun crawled over the eastern sky. The street was empty. No broken pieces of gargoyle lay on the road.

"That brute took Bladder," Wheedle said forlornly. "Collected him up in bits and took him. Why? What good is he to him? He broke him so good I doubt he could ever be put back together. We'll never see him again."

They all looked at the sad bull face, and no one answered.

Spigot put a wing over Wheedle's back.

Beth copied the action with the imp boy. "You'll be all right. He can't hurt you now," she said. "What happened?"

Spigot ruffled his stone feathers, folded in his wings, and warbled.

"He knew where we were." Wheedle rocked side to side. "Poor Bladder. His broken face staring at us."

"He killed Bladder to find me." The imp boy felt cold. "I'm so sorry."

Wheedle wheezed and said, "Bladder broke brave. Gargoyles are loyal to their own. It's not your fault, Imp, but we all gotta get somewhere else."

Beth peeled hair off the imp boy's sweating face. "Not now you can't! Look at him. He's the color of dying grass. And it's daytime and sunny. None of those monsters will come looking for you now. Give yourself time to make a plan."

The imp boy was glad of a reason to rest. The scream in his shoulder built. He lay down on the cold marble and let the voices of the others fade.

"Wait until Daniel gets here at least," Ben said.

Spigot sobbed and squawked. Muddy water smelling like drains dripped from his gray eyes.

The imp boy tried to stand, but made it two paces before falling flat onto his backpack. He howled. Beth plumped the sleeping bag under his head in the shadow of the church, while the imp boy shivered and groaned.

The imp boy had no idea how long they waited for Daniel to arrive. It felt like hours, but the sun's glow through the stained glass suggested it hadn't been long at all. Beth and Ben watched up and down the street for human movement, rushing back in when they saw anyone and pointing at flowers and birds. Despite the drama, they were outside.

"What's going on?" he asked as Daniel lifted his head, and Yonah peered from the angel's shoulder.

"You tell me." Daniel reached to take the imp boy by his deformed shoulder and elbow, putting shining hands on the pain. The imp boy prepared to scream, but instead the agony drained and disappeared. He twisted his arm and wrist and marveled at how strong they felt, how straight they were again.

Wheedle related everything that happened.

"So sorry about Bladder, but there's no time for delay. We need to get you away from here, my friend," Daniel told the imp boy. "Have you got all your things?"

"Where you taking him?" Wheedle asked. "No, don't answer. Best we don't know."

Spigot peeped a small chick sound.

Wheedle nodded. "We won't forget you, Imp, we're long livers. Who knows when we'll see you again. It may be ten or twenty years, but we'll know you. By your smell at least."

"Ten or twenty years?" the imp boy asked. He was a day old, and yesterday had been a long day. Where was he going without Wheedle and Spigot? And poor, poor Bladder.

The imp boy looked at the stone faces, Ben, Beth, and Henry too. Everyone looked so solemn, waiting.

"There are many hours of light. It gives me time to find a safe place for you two later," Daniel said to the gargoyles. "But this boy has to go. Stay here for now. The cathedral offers some protection. If it gets overcast again, the pixies may come, but you should be able to handle them. Yonah, stay here as lookout."

The imp boy's backpack was still twisted around his body, the sleeping bag humped on top. He took off the bag and shoved everything inside it before straightening his clothes. The ogre had mangled the arm of the T-shirt.

The angel grabbed the imp boy around the waist and flew. Far below them the gargoyles, the statues, and the cathedral grew smaller. He waved at them, and they waved back, until the imp boy could no longer see anything familiar.

CHAPTER 9

Daniel landed far in the garden, next to a bush flowering in purple buds. The yard filled with noise, and person after person wandered in through the back door, carrying plates and flowers.

The imp boy retreated, hiding in the flowers and watching the crowd of people. Some ferried babies. Women wore black dresses, while men sported white shirts with black armbands. He recognized Nick, his face reddening as he pulled at his collar.

"I didn't think they'd be so many people here," the imp boy said.

"Me neither," Daniel agreed. "Maybe it's . . . Oh."

"What?"

"It's the old man's wake. That's why everyone's here."

"The old man?"

"Samuel Kavanagh. The one on the paper. Your sigher."

The other end of the yard heaved with children: they played ball, poked sticks into a pond, drank from colorful cups, and sat in the shade of a willow tree dominating the flower beds.

"We don't have time to find a different place. And the gargoyles need to be moved since the cathedral is the last place Thunderguts's messenger saw you. The statues too." Daniel shook his head. "Perhaps this could work to our advantage. Just stay back here in the bushes and, if you do get found, there are dozens of Kavanaghs here and you look like all of them." Daniel surveyed the children playing. "This crowd of humans will offer you some protection. There's lots of light here, enjoy it. Yonah will research a better place, and we'll figure it out once everyone's far from ogres. Right now, the gargoyles are more of a concern. Where can you put gargoyles where they're safe and can't cause too much damage?"

Daniel left without looking back down at him.

The imp boy stood in the yard staring.

A little girl with soft blond hair came over. She stood a head shorter than the imp boy. "What did you do to your hair?" she asked. "Look at your clothes."

The imp boy blushed at the state of his T-shirt; it was ripped and stained. "I don't have anything else to wear."

"You can clean your face in the laundry room. You better change too. I just did; I'm not allowed to play ball any more. My mommy does baking at these things."

"These things?"

"You know, family fusses. That's what my dad calls them. Who did you come with?"

"I came with Daniel."

"Who's that?" A ball hit the back of her head, and she turned on the throwers. "Stop it, will ya!"

While she was distracted, the imp boy wiggled farther behind the bush, but she turned, grabbed his hand, and led him to the kitchen. Adults stalked around gathering plates and talking about "taking it in the living room."

"My name's Henri," the girl said.

"I have a friend called Henry." He hoped they were safe. He wondered if Daniel was already back at the cathedral, and what Spigot and Wheedle were doing.

"It's short for Henrietta. After Auntie Henrietta. You know, she always wears lots of mascara?"

He had no idea what mascara was.

"You all right, Seamus?" a woman with great arms and a fleshy neck asked a young man who was staring at the tiles, before turning to the imp boy and Henri. "Come on, you two, hurry up and into the living room. Oh my goodness, you need a cleanup first, my lad."

The woman grabbed the imp boy's once-injured wrist, dragged him into the laundry, and ran a washcloth under the tap. She scrubbed at his face until he felt his skin burn. Henrietta watched with a terrified grin.

"You got proper clothes in that pack?" the woman demanded.

"No, sorry."

"Forgot them, did you? I hope you don't do this all the time? Henrietta, grab James's spares. He'll need socks at the very least."

99

"Yes, Mommy." Henrietta scarpered and came back with a flushed face and the clothes.

The woman yanked at his backpack, then had the imp boy's T-shirt off to scrub at his neck.

"You Moira's boy?" Before he could answer, she started on another question. "Is there any part of you that's clean?"

When she seemed satisfied that the imp boy looked pink enough, she loaded him into a starched white shirt. She handed him a pair of gray trousers and shoved him into a small room with a large bowl set into the floor.

The imp boy swapped his shorts for the trousers, fiddling with the metal zipper at the front. He shook his hips to see if they would come apart again. He put the lid on the bowl down and tried to sit. It was big enough for a chair, but he hit a button of sorts and the loud noise of water gushing echoed from inside the bowl. It made him jump, and he backed out of the room, staring at the bellowing porcelain.

"There you are. Thank goodness, Henrietta's managed to stay clean this time. No chocolate cake, all right, Henri?"

"Yes, Mommy." The girl stared at her feet.

The fleshy-chinned woman assessed him once more. "So, who's your mother? You look like Seamus. Except his hair is neater than yours, and he'd never let himself get as grubby as you. Oh, look at the time! Come on, best behavior now."

Henri led the imp boy out of the door as other children came in from the garden.

"You're all in the same clothes."

"Course we are," Henrietta said. "It's a wake. We're supposed to wear this; that's what Mommy says. I bet Granny will drink too much and wanna kiss us."

From Henri's tone, this was not a desirable thing.

The imp boy studied people's faces as Henri dragged him along. Some had gold hair, some had blue or gray eyes, but most looked like him: dark-haired, dark-eyed, and all in dark clothes.

The group pressed him along with them and squashed into the living room until the walls strained with people. Pictures plastered the wallpaper, and the side table had been covered in a hundred or more photos. An object hung next to the window with a black cloth over it. A clock on the mantelpiece stood with a solemn face, its hands stuck pointing up. All the furniture had been pushed out except a long, low table everyone stood back from, and the chair, the one thing the imp boy remembered the mother saying she would move. An old lady sat in it. She was wearing a voluminous, time-faded black dress, large sweat stains soaking into the armpits. Her head rested on her cane.

She didn't look up but spoke to the floor. "Shall we bring him in, then?"

Four men left the room as another man's voice rose above the conversation. His voice crooned warm and ponderous as he told a story about someone called Paddy Reilly. The imp boy liked the sound of it, liked the way his body moved to it. Although when he looked at the faces around him, he found their smiles and tears coming together made no sense. They were kind faces though, like Wheedle's, and the man's voice made it something warm and welcoming. Except for the arm pulling, he decided he liked the Kavanagh family. *Anyone would love to belong in it,* he thought.

Then the men returned and pushed a large wooden box onto the table.

In the box lay an old man dressed in white, with hands folded on his stomach. His pale face smiled, and he had a thick swag of white hair.

The old lady in the chair stood, a flurry of hands helping her up. She leaned on the box.

"We are all here today to say goodbye to one of this family's great men, Samuel Kavanagh." She patted the arm of the resting man and her eyes with a gray handkerchief. "Samuel, you'll be sorely missed; that's the truth. There's so many who love you here."

The room resounded with a dozen yeas. Paddy Reilly's voice crooned over the top of the other voices.

"Shall we let the children pay their respects, and then they can get back to playing," a woman's voice suggested.

"That's the way, Meaghan," the old lady said. "Sing for the babies, Terry."

The man's voice filled the air again. *Sing?* the imp boy thought. Singing, like Beth had said? No wonder people gave food to hear it.

This time, the voice sang about a shawl from Galway. The imp boy swayed with the song, wondering if he could learn to sing. He breathed deep, smelled rich, warm odors; they were part of the walls, as if the old man had incensed them into the house—maybe from the leather polish and tobacco Nick mentioned. The house was full of such wonderful humanness.

"Come on," Henri said, and pushed toward the coffin. The other children filed past it. They shoved and heaved each other, half interested in fleeing and half interested in seeing a dead body in a box. The children Henrietta's age scurried for the door; the imp boy heard their brays of heroic escape resound in the corridor. The older ones wept for the man and stooped down to kiss his forehead.

The imp boy considered the old man. He seemed peaceful enough. The uneven smile on his soft, loose face suggested a lingering kindness. He wondered what regrets the old man had to sigh about. Henri tried to pull the imp boy away, but he wanted to have a long look. This was the man whose sigh had made him. His sigher, Daniel had said. He could also smell Nick and his mother behind him. He couldn't turn around.

The old lady smiled. "Samuel, look at both of us, all these babies and grandbabies, even one or two great-grands." She winked. "We've done well, Samuel; there's no doubting it. There's not a low-class one in the lot, 'cepting maybe your Nicholas, and he'll come good soon."

"Hey!" Nick yelled. Everyone in the room laughed.

"Look at them all." The old lady gave a tear-bleary smile. "Look, a couple of the younger ones remained. Here's Henrietta, my darling. You doing right by your ma?"

"Yes, Granny."

"And who are you, young fella? I can't see you through all that hair. Stand up and greet Great-Aunt Colleen."

A murmur of questions traveled around the room. No one could place him.

"Ethan's first?"

"Haven't seen him since the christening."

"Mom, it's the boy from the..." Nick began, but he was drowned out by a man's booming voice.

"Not mine," the man said.

"Oh?" Nick's mother whispered.

Then the imp boy found himself eye to eye with Great-Aunt Colleen. She stopped, her yellowed eyes growing moonlike as she stared. Her skin had grayed beneath her peach rouge.

"Samuel?" the old lady gasped. "Is that you, Samuel?"

The imp boy said nothing.

"Someone here tell me this boy's yours. Please." Colleen choked and drew her handkerchief to her neck as the papery skin on her hands tightened.

Nick raised his voice. "He was at the chocolate shop."

The imp boy turned and looked at Nick and his mom. A man stood with them, an older Nick with a beard. Nick's mom was pointing, and the man stared at him too, then closed his eyes and opened them into another stare.

"You can all see him?" Great-Aunt Colleen asked.

Assent buzzed.

"Give me the picture of me and Samuel, when we was young." She turned, and it showed effort. "The one over there. By the vase."

The picture passed from hand to hand, not on a direct route to Great-Aunt Colleen but in a circle to any set of hands and eyes wanting it. The few children left in the room did not hide their surprise.

"It's him."

"Can't be."

"The spitting image of Grandad."

"Could be twins."

"When was this taken, Ma?"

"The year of the great gale. When we lost the boat. I was ten. Your grandfather twelve." She turned back to the imp boy. "Don't leave us, spirit; we can all see you. You are most welcome. Is it you want to be buried in Irish soil? Is that why you're here to haunt us? You were mischief itself till the very end, Samuel."

The room hushed as it waited for him to answer.

He heard Nick whispering, "It's okay, Mom."

Henrietta grabbed the imp boy's hand. "No, Granny, he's not a ghost."

"It's true, Ma, I changed him myself. He showed up all mucky, so I put him into some of Jimmy's clean clothes. I assumed he was one of ours, and there's so many . . ."

The room chatted again. "Certainly looks like a Kavanagh," a voice said.

"Where'd he come from?"

"Good question."

The imp boy could hear Nick's mother crying. Hard.

Great-Aunt Colleen's frail hand quieted the mob, her pink and raw knuckles trembled. "Hush now." She turned to the imp boy. "Do you have a name?"

He wondered what to say. The one she'd given him—it felt good. It wasn't like the names the gargoyles had suggested for him, and it was nothing like "imp boy."

"Samuel." It felt right to say it.

"Your name is Samuel too?" Colleen said. "Well, flesh and blood you may be, but it would have been less of a mystery if you'd been my brother's ghost."

"D'you have a last name, Samuel?" someone asked.

Samuel. Someone called him Samuel. He'd called himself "Samuel."

The imp boy realized what he'd done and couldn't speak. He shook his head.

The room burst into questions. Where did he come from? How had he got to the wake? Where were his parents? People turned him around to have a look, and a sea of hands washed over him.

He found himself facing Nick and his mom and the bearded man, their faces as gray as gargoyles. His knees weakened under him and he swayed.

CHAPTER 10

He lay on the comfortable bed in his white shirt and gray trousers. An older man with an armband made of shiny black material had led him upstairs and told him to rest.

He could hear Henri in the living room asking to see him, and he listened to the confused conversation until someone yelled, "It's the old man's day, and he needs to be seen off proper." Then a different kind of frenzy and excitement continued until most of the people left.

He listened for the sounds of the house. He could hear everything. His gargoyle-keen ears enjoyed the creaking floorboards as they ached in the hot day, and the sea breeze fumbling at the curtains in all the rooms facing the boundless blue water. Soft sounds came from downstairs. No longer the cacophony of too many people squeezed into a small room.

His ears hurt less with fewer voices in the house, and his chest didn't rattle so much. He could think about Spigot and Wheedle and ponder where Daniel had taken them. He bounced on the mattress and ran his hands over the soft, fleecy cover—so much nicer than sleeping on dirt. The shiny edging of the bedding tickled his skin. On the opposite wall, under a picture of a ship, sat a side table, like the one downstairs, covered in photos. The imp boy sprang from the bed, smiling at the way it dipped and lifted under him, and looked at the photographs.

None of them had the old man in them. They were of younger people: men, women, and children. Some showed the faces of people he'd seen downstairs. He found one of Nick, his mother, and the man they had been talking to. He tried to recall the members of family Daniel had listed. Father? They all smiled at the camera. The mother held a much smaller human, with a round face and a patch of dark hair. Its hand touched the mother's cheek. He put his hand to his own cheek and returned the photo to its spot.

He knelt on the floor to put his ear to the carpet. He heard the chewing of bugs in the walls and a scatter of beetles outside in the vines. He jumped when the mother's gentle voice spoke out, traveling from the living room.

"How in the world did he get here? We saw him on Church Street. You know how far away that is?"

"It's obvious, can't you see for looking?" The imp boy recognized Great-Aunt Colleen's tone. "He's one of the little people and followed you here. That's why I took him for a ghost."

The mother sighed. "I wish you wouldn't say that."

Then a man spoke. "She's not joking."

"You've not told her then, Richard?" the old woman asked.

"Aunt Coll..."

"The Kavanaghs are one of the grand old families, and many of us are gifted with second sight. I've always known when something is otherworldly, Richard, and so have you."

"Aunt Colleen, there's enough going on without starting on that."

"You do too, Richard, and I've told your Michelle many a time."

"She has," said the mother's softer voice.

"And so I have," Colleen agreed. "I see things; things that shouldn't be there and sometimes people that shouldn't be there. I know what they mean. That wisp of a girl in green's been here today. She was with your father on our last visit too; near scared the life out of me. I saw her put the shroud on his shoulders, and I knew I wouldn't be seeing him alive again. There's no lie in that. When a banshee's about, death's not far behind. She's been a-keening today. Someone will have seen her."

Michelle's voice crooned. "Aunt Colleen, we're all grieving. It's natural for people to imagine..."

"Don't patronize me, girl. I've still got all my faculties. I've seen what I've seen. Make of it what you will."

They quietened and waited for the anger in the old lady's voice to seep out the walls.

The imp boy heard Nick's voice break the silence. "I saw a girl in green in the backyard, when I came looking for you."

"Nicholas, really..." Michelle said.

"No, Mom, really. A seriously pretty girl. She was hard to miss in that dress."

"With vivid red hair?" Aunt Colleen asked.

"That's right."

"You're not the first Kavanagh to see her. Won't be the last. Am I right, Richard? That girl is the banshee that haunts our family. She shows herself to those she wants to see her. Give her wide berth, Nicholas, she'll sing you away. Though there's no reports of missing boys for a while now, the fear should never go. Banshees have taken beautiful boys from our family for centuries. Remember Uncle Eamon? Disappeared for six months; came back addled."

The silence thickened until a fragile note burst into yells; and a baby, not far from the imp boy's room, woke and fussed.

"I'm sorry; I have to see to Beatrice." Michelle's feet padded bread-soft up the stairs.

"Nicholas, go make yourself useful," Richard said.

The imp boy listened to the low grunts and claps he couldn't understand. Then to footsteps, some treading upstairs, some to the kitchen.

He returned his attention to the conversation between Richard and Colleen.

"She's a good girl you've got there, Richard, and she's lucky to walk in just one world. You and I know better though, or if you don't now, you used to. That boy upstairs has a touch of the other on him, no doubt about it. Whether he's a changeling or a spirit or whatever, he's not all human. I can see the look on Michelle's face. She's not telling herself the truth about her heart."

"Don't do this to her, Colleen. Everything . . . stop it. He's just a lonely boy," Richard said. "It's an odd coincidence he showed up looking so like family . . ."

"And the spitting image of your father."

"Nicholas looks like Pop," Richard said.

"That boy is identical," Great-Aunt Colleen said. "And how does Nicholas looking like your pop make any of this more natural? Your boy and the one upstairs could be brothers."

"I'm sure there's a rational reason for that."

Feet climbed the stairs, and Nick came in with a cushioned tray and used his bottom to close the door. It shut with a satisfied click. He looked at the boy kneeling on the carpet.

The imp boy stood, feeling his cheeks burn as if he'd been caught stealing.

Nick gave him a quick smile. "Hello there. Come and sit back on the bed. I brought you something to eat." When the imp boy resettled, Nick placed the tray on his legs, and the under-cushion molded to them. Colored food in a bowl sat next to something white and steaming. He recognized lettuce, but not the red fruit on top of it. A liquid fizzed in a glass to the right of the dishes. "You don't look hungry. Mom's worried you've been starving on the streets. Or worse, living on chocolate."

"I've had pie and sandwiches."

"Pie and sandwiches? Well, salad, chicken, and lemonade might be a bit strange then."

The imp boy nodded.

Nick sat on the chair. "Where's your family?"

The imp boy framed a few answers in his head before saying, "Daniel looks after me."

"Who's Daniel?"

"An angel. My angel."

"He's a good person to look after you."

"Yes."

"Is he nearby?"

"No. Daniel flew off a while ago."

"Flew?"

The imp boy flapped his hands to show Nick "flew."

Nick laughed. "He's a *real* angel?"

"Yes."

"You live with an angel?"

"Yes." The boys watched each other. The imp boy looked away first. "Thank you very much for the food."

"Fine." Nick stood. "Eat quickly. Dad has to take Aunt Colleen back to her hotel, but she'll want to talk with you before she goes."

"Okay."

"Look, I brought the tray up because Mom and Dad are all over the place about you. They've been through a lot, right? A lot. You say your name's Samuel, and it makes everything worse." Nick's face pinked beneath his dark hair. "What is it really?" He glared.

"I don't have one."

"Then why did you answer to Samuel?" Nick studied him, but the imp boy couldn't speak. The other boy's hard look made him feel awkward.

The imp boy stared at his food. "She called me Samuel, and it's a nice name, not like Gutter or Slimeball."

Nick sat down again. The red faded. "Yeah, they would be horrible names."

The imp boy picked at the white stuff. He worried Nick might see his eyes wetting.

"Well, okay. Um . . . you dig in," Nick said, and left.

The imp boy waited for the door to click and ate, tasting every flavor on the plate. Sweet. Sour. Salty. His heart beat sadly inside him, and he returned his attention to the people downstairs. Nick's footsteps headed for the living room. Michelle's tread followed them down.

"Well, whatever he is," Nick said, "he's smart. He tells a good story. How old do you think he is? Like, ten?"

"He looks the way you did when you were about eleven or twelve," Michelle said. "Remember how small you were?"

"I was never small. Ever."

The imp boy thought Colleen had something in her throat, but he realized the sound was a dry cackle. "You were a nugget," she said.

"He looks eleven, twelve . . ." Michelle's voice faded out, and quiet settled in the room below until she said, "Someone's fed him."

"Yes, an angel, he says."

Michelle whispered. Her voice was so soft, the imp boy felt sure the others wouldn't hear her. "Twelve."

Colleen laughed. "I wonder what angels feed a soul. Has he existed all this time on manna, do you think?"

113

"Samuel. He says he's Samuel. He seems a good boy." Michelle sighed. "Samuel. He really looks like a Samuel."

"Michelle?" Richard said.

"I know, not possible." Her voice ached with sadness.

"Don't you be falling in love with him too quickly, girl, he could be a shape-shifter for all you know. He's taken off his pelt and come to land to win the heart of any woman who'll give it. He'll look however you want, doesn't have to be a young beau. He means to crush you."

"He's twelve, Colleen!" Michelle said, and exhaled. "Or at least he looks like he could be."

"Have you taken to him in such a short while? Guard your heart, girl; guard your heart."

Richard spoke. "Why don't we ask him where he's from?"

"Who says he'll speak the truth?" Colleen asked.

"I'm sure any boy raised by angels is likely to tell the truth, don't you, Colleen?" Michelle said.

"Don't take that tone with me, young lady; I'm not too old to recognize sarcasm."

The imp boy put the tray down and shuffled off the bed. The good food sat in his stomach like dirt. He had to answer their questions sometime.

His room stood at the top of a wooden staircase. A once blue carpet clung to each step but did not protect the house from the pad of his bare foot on wood.

He followed their voices back to the living room. Some things had changed. The coffin had gone; the bedraggled furniture had been put back into place. The pictures remained, as did the cloth-covered mirror and the sleeping clock. Colleen sat in the chair, and Michelle sat next to Richard, a baby on her lap. The little pink bundle lying belly-down across her legs breathed softly, the air around her twinkling. It sparkled more than chocolate wrappers.

Nicholas sat on the opposite sofa, his arms spread wide, legs dangling over each other with elastic ease.

"Hello," said the imp boy.

The conversation stopped. They turned to him.

Colleen lifted a white eyebrow, which wrinkled her forehead like crêpe. "Hello, boy."

"Samuel," Michelle added.

"Hello."

"Not your name, is it, boy?" Colleen asked.

"I don't know," he said. "I don't have a name yet."

Michelle sat on the sofa an arm's length away; she knotted the baby's wrap inside her fist, worrying it as she watched him.

Richard leaned forward to speak, but Colleen raised one hand to stop him. "You're not human, are you, child?" she asked.

"No."

"What are you then? Some sort of omen of death in the form of our Samuel?"

"For goodness sake, Colleen . . ." Michelle said.

"I'm impkind, but I'm not sure what type," he said. "That's why they didn't name me. I don't suit a gargoyle name."

"Well, he's got a good imagination." Nicholas laughed.

Colleen cast a baleful look at the young man. He shut up. "I know your mother says she doesn't have the sight, though her behavior this afternoon gives lie to that, but it's on you, Nicholas, so there's no excuse for disregard. And it's strongest in you, Richard. Don't tell me the boy doesn't make the hair stand up on the back of your neck."

Richard rubbed the nape of his neck.

"He's in the chocolate shop and now he's here. What explanation do you have?" She challenged Richard and Michelle with her gaze. "More importantly, does he mean us harm, or no?" Colleen said.

"For crying out loud!" Michelle's voice erupted, and the baby cried. Michelle patted the child's bottom.

The imp boy stared at the silvery light around the infant. It moved in shimmering waves. Light, sparkling light. It shone out of her. He wondered if it was her soul, like Daniel had described.

"Why are you here?" Colleen asked.

"Daniel brought me here. He says I came from this family, and if I'm going to belong anywhere, it's here." He felt his cheeks grow hotter.

"Your angel said you belong with us?" Michelle's voice cracked.

"Oh, you're wanting to believe now, aren't ya?" Colleen cackled. "You poor girl."

Michelle reddened.

"Look me in the eye, boy. D'you mean us well, or d'you mean us harm?" the old lady asked.

The imp boy took a deep breath and eyeballed the old lady. "I mean you no harm; I'm looking for a place to belong. If you like, I can leave when Daniel comes back."

"No, darling, no." Michelle grabbed his wrist and unsettled the baby, sending blue light spilling onto the floor.

"Do you have somewhere to stay with Daniel?" Richard asked.

"No."

"Come here, child," Aunt Colleen held out her arms. He walked to her, and she pulled him into her generous stomach. She sniffed him. "You smell like you could be one of the good ones. Samuel is a strong name, and you look like my Samuel. Do you like the name?"

"Yes."

"Then Samuel it is."

"Thank you."

"We really have to call the Children's Services," Richard said.

"Well, I think that's a mistake myself," Colleen said.

Richard rubbed his eyes with a rough hand.

"She's right. It's been a long day," Michelle said. "Can we think about it in the morning?"

Richard shook his head. "We shouldn't." Michelle's mouth dropped to a frown, and he sighed. "Okay. Maybe one night to unravel this mystery. I'd love to know how you got here from thirty miles away."

"I would like to know too," Michelle said, "but I'm tired." Her eyes shone and threatened to spill. The imp boy touched his face; he remembered his tears from his first day. Tears came with pain. "We've given you the third degree, but you must have questions of your own. Would you like to know our names?"

"You're Michelle," the imp boy said. "Richard, Nicholas, and you're Great-Aunt Colleen."

"See?" Colleen said to Michelle. "Now, how'd he know all that?"

"The baby is called Beatrice," Samuel said.

"Yes, this is Beatrice." Michelle patted the baby's padded bottom.

"She shines. May I touch her?"

"Sure. Don't scare her though."

The imp boy placed his hand on the baby's back. On cue, the tiny creature laughed.

Her laugh helped make me, the imp boy thought. *Beatrice's laugh.*

"It's time for me to get back to my hotel. I've had an exhausting day," Colleen said. "I've farewelled one family member and greeted another. It's a lot for an old woman. I hope the tea is made when I get home."

"I'll drive you there." Richard got up.

The baby continued her low, dreamy giggles. The imp boy watched as multicolored sparks flew from the infant. Michelle gazed at him.

Richard maneuvered his aunt out of the blue chair, and she ascended with arthritic grace and leaned on her cane.

"Will I see you tomorrow, Samuel?" she asked.

"I don't know, Aunt Colleen." He gave a crooked smile.

"I'm going to feed Beatrice," Michelle said. "Why don't you let Nicholas get you a drink . . . Samuel?"

He turned to see Nicholas peering at him. The young man's eyes gleamed. When he stood, the imp boy only came to his chin. "Come on," he said. "Samuel."

The imp boy followed Nick to the kitchen. He peered over his shoulder as Michelle took the sparkling Beatrice to the bedroom.

"What are you looking at?" Nicholas asked.

"She's so shiny."

Nicholas furrowed his brow. "You are weird, aren't you?"

The kitchen appeared bigger emptied of the guests, but shabbier and less alive. The curtains had yellowed over the years, the color imps liked, not the sunny hue he admired.

"I'm Samuel," he told himself.

"Yep, that's what everybody agreed."

"I'm getting used to it."

Nick opened a cupboard and found some glasses. "You know, generally, I think Great-Aunt Colleen's completely bonkers. Pa would go on about the Good Neighbors and the Little People too, but you . . ." Nicholas poured Sam a glass of water from a cracked glass jug. "You don't sound like your average twelve-year-old."

"I'm not twelve."

"Then how old are you?"

"I was made yesterday, I think. I'm not sure; the sleeping throws my ability to count."

Nicholas's thin smile slipped away. "We really do look like brothers. I read on this website once that said if you stand in one place long enough someone will come along who looks just like you. Is this something like that?"

The imp boy didn't reply.

"Or is Great-Aunt Colleen right?" Nick rubbed at a point on his forehead like the thought hurt. "Let's get outside, it's stuffy in here. You go—I'll get the drinks."

The front yard blazed in natural color; flowers threatened to conquer the sky. Lilies, delphiniums, and hydrangeas in white and blue surrounded brazen roses. The floral scent of each assaulted Sam's nose, and he blinked, trying to smell the individual aromas. He surrendered and breathed in the perfume of the garden. He sneezed.

A violence of green caught his eye, and he spun. In the space between the dark shadow of the trees, a girl in a venomous emerald dress stood on the other side of the garden gate. She made his skin prickle. Her hair shone with warm color, and her eyes were the same striking hue as her dress. She looked young but smelled ancient.

Her mouth opened into an "O," and she stared, pondering him before speaking. "My name's Maggie, but what are you? You're not a boy."

The imp boy held still. How did she know that? He sniffed again and trawled through his hatchling knowledge. Her smell was wrong. Obviously, not a mermaid. Maybe a shape-shifer? Then he caught it, a fairy smell overlaying the cold scent of moors and weeping. He sneezed again. "Are you a fairy?"

Maggie laughed. "Do I look like one?"

The imp boy nodded. "You're very lovely."

"What a darlin' thing to say, but, no. It's the Kavanaghs' own banshee I am."

"Does that mean you're a monster?" he asked. "You can stand in the light. Like me. Am I a banshee?"

"Not a banshee, no. You're a riddle, you are."

"A riddle? What kind of creature is that? I've never heard of those."

Maggie laughed, and the air glittered. She leaned over the fence and tweaked his cheek, making his skin flame. "It's magic that helps me stand in the light." She took a silver box from a pouch at her waist. When she opened it, he saw it contained a sparkling powder. "Magic can make all sorts of things happen. I can show you a world these humans can't. Why don't you come away with me?"

"Come away?"

"It'd be so merry, don't you think? But before we do, it's only right you tell me your name."

"We're calling him Samuel." Nicholas trotted toward them across the garden, and blushed as Maggie gave him a fresh girl's smile, full of promise.

The imp boy frowned. "That's not my name. Great-Aunt Colleen mistook me for a dead man."

Maggie laughed. "Be Samuel anyway. It'll grow on you. Don't you like it?"

He thought for a moment. "I like it very much."

"It fits, doesn't it? Play with it until it's part of you. Come on, say it aloud."

The imp boy inhaled. "Samuel, Samuel, Samuel." He grinned; it did sound good.

Nick was watching Maggie with a dazed half-smile. "I saw you before . . . I mean, I thought I saw you in the backyard."

The girl faced Nicholas, but her gaze never left the imp boy's face. "Because I wanted you to see me," she said. "Why don't you come on a journey with us? It'd be so diverting." She shook her head and something fell from her hair.

Nicholas, distracted, scurried through the gate into the shade of the arbor and picked up a mother-of-pearl clip. It caught the sun and glittered. "You've dropped something." He handed it to her.

"There, he's mine," she said. Nicholas beamed like a fool. "You do know about a banshee's comb, don't you, Samuel?"

The imp boy thought. "If he picks it up you're allowed to enthrall him." He frowned. "You don't need to do that, do you?"

"But it's magic, Samuel. Don't you like it? Let me show you what else the dust does. I don't like to waste it, but you're worth it." She took a pinch of powder and blew it at Nick. A trail of gold traveled from her fingers to his nose and mouth. Sam smelled fairy magic. It brought on a flurry of sneezes. One, two, three.

"How do you like him, Nicholas?"

Nick didn't blink. He sounded distant and tired. "I'm worried he's going to upset my parents. They're barely coping with how panicky Beatrice makes them feel." Nick blushed at Samuel. "I . . ."

"I don't think he meant to say that out loud to you, Samuel. What else don't you mean to say, Nicholas?"

Nick slurred. "Dad keeps rubbing his neck. Mom says he's got a sixth sense; that's how he managed to avoid the accidents at work last year. He hasn't stopped rubbing his neck since Samuel got here."

"Where's home, Nick?"

"Not far. We live in Brighton."

Something mean shone in Maggie's eyes, but she smiled and it disappeared. Nick made a gargling sound, looked wide-eyed at Sam, then peered at his shoes.

"I don't like what you're doing to him," Sam said. "I think you should go."

"Oh, I see." Maggie chuckled. "Don't want to share your toys, little Samuel?"

Nick groggily dipped and raised his head. "Sam?"

"You're magicking him, aren't you?" the imp boy asked.

"Oh, Samuel, of course I am. And so are you. You might not have a little box of fairy dust, but you yourself enthrall them all. Even that mother's feeling your otherworldliness, and she's frightened she cannot take another blow. I've come a-mourning lost Kavanaghs for centuries, and I've seen her broken almost beyond repair. You're going to have to spend a bit of time getting to know them before you use your playthings so cruelly. It'll be fun though. You could destroy the whole family without a drop of blood spilled. You'll let me have this one though?" She touched Nick's shoulder.

"Nick?" Sam stepped in front of him. "I couldn't do that."

"Greedy boy. I've been watching him for days, longer than you've been alive." She leaned forward and whispered. "The fairy dust gives me privileges, but I can tell you all about it on the way home." She grinned and looked at Nick's docile face. "All about banshees, all about magic. All about the Kavanaghs, if you're so inclined. It's why I understand the attraction. I keen for them, and I take some pleasure in their grief. But this generation is all kindness and comfort. So dull. Where's the bitterness? Where's the anger? The resentment? You'll get bored with it soon enough, darlin' Samuel. Now back in the Dark Ages, human anger was brilliant. It cut like claws." Maggie gave him an encouraging wink. "Come with me, let's see if we can't get that back." She reached across and turned down his jutting collar, patting his shirt. "You're a monster like me, but you can walk outdoors in daylight with not a speck of dust on you. We could have so much fun."

Nick rocked on his heels and tittered.

"I think I should get Nick inside. He doesn't look well."

"Oh, Samuel, I won't get between you and your fun, I promise."

Sam grabbed Nick's hand. "It was nice meeting you," he said, and dragged at the older boy's arm. Nick brushed at his face, shooing away invisible flies. Gold tendrils flew from his mouth and evaporated into the air. His vague expression cleared, and he stared at Maggie, no longer dopey, but his eyes twinkled.

Maggie sighed. "Oh, you naughty imp, you wasted all that dust. It's not easily come by, you know. Although he'd have awoken soon."

"Do you live here?" Nicholas blushed, and Sam smelled the boy's musky scent rising with it. "Most of Pa's neighbors are old."

"No, this is not my place. It's to home I go now. Sam's home too; you should ask him about it. If he ever feels like it, we could take you there. You could come right now, if you liked."

Nicholas stammered. "Right now?"

"Look at him, Samuel. He doesn't mind I'm not natural. Do you, Nick? The hairs on your arm tells you, the smell in your nose lets you know, and you're overcome by unreasonable reason and will believe what you want to believe."

Nicholas strained out a high noise.

"Samuel, don't be selfish. We could break and bamboozle him together."

Sam shook his head. He had no idea what those words meant.

She sighed. "As you wish, my darlin." If you want to be greedy, I won't stop you. For now, but we'll talk again soon."

The banshee put the comb into her hair and turned away.

"Wait, where are you going?" Nicholas called.

"Don't worry, my lovely, you'll see me soon enough." She put a pretty finger on the end of Sam's nose. "I'll be back when you're bored of them, my lovely lad. There's so many more games to play than you imagine." She blew a kiss to them both. Nick's eyes glassed over.

They watched her walk away.

"Maggie. She's gorgeous." Nicholas wandered back into the house.

Sam agreed, but she made him uncomfortable.

CHAPTER 11

Nick dreamed up the stairs. Sam watched him went then turned and went into the living room. He sat down in the old blue chair. The sky outside had darkened, and he shuddered. He wondered if Daniel had taken the gargoyles to a safe place yet and if he'd come back.

He listened to the house. Michelle sat in the bedroom above, sniffling and sighing. Richard had left and taken Great-Aunt Colleen with him.

They'd talked about calling Children's Services. Sam could guess who they were. He knew imps didn't like the police, or pest control, or anyone in the investigative services. He suspected Children's Services were like those.

The tiny sound of Beatrice patting her mom's cheek came from the room above. All thought of ogres and banshees fled;

Samuel hurtled upstairs to see the shining baby. He knocked on the door and stumbled into the room.

Beatrice lay in a portable cot next to a moldering wooden bed slumped to the floor. Michelle stood smiling over her, and Beatrice beamed. Her fists opened, sparks intensifying.

"Are all babies this beautiful?" Sam stroked the baby's foot.

Michelle went to touch his arm but pulled her fingers away as if they burned.

"I believe so," Michelle said. "She likes you."

Beatrice reached for him.

"Do you think I could hold her?"

"You might drop her; she's not as light as she looks."

"I could sit."

"All right, on the bed, Samuel." Michelle savored his name like a toffee.

He jumped up and wiggled back into the pillows. She laid the baby on his lap, then put her hand to her throat. A thin line bit between her eyebrows.

Beatrice giggled as Sam touched his fingertip to a sparkle and it erupted.

Michelle followed the baby's gaze to where the sparkle danced in the air. The crease in her forehead softened. "I wonder what she can see."

After too short a time, she took Beatrice from his arms. The fluttering light followed the infant in a tangle of deepening pink as her mother held her.

"Is that what love looks like?" Sam asked. "It's pretty."

Michelle put her hand to her lips, and her eyes dampened.

She finally touched him, stroking his hair. "You're a deep one, aren't you?"

Another hurdle came during dinner. Sam knew pie and sandwiches, but he had no idea what to do with the lumpy liquid in the bowl. Michelle called it soup. Did you pick up the bowl and put it to your mouth, or did you drop your face into it?

He waited and watched Nick take a silver tool. Nick caught him staring and mimed scooping the liquid into his mouth. Richard grabbed a beige rock from a basket on the table. Sam copied him. Despite its color and size, the rock was soft and light and smelled a bit like pie and a bit like sandwich. He watched Richard rip it in two, then spread yellow stuff on it with another silver tool. Sam copied him and ended up with a melting blob on his shirt. He stopped picking up things and sniffing them—the square of white fabric folded next to his bowl, the two white containers, one with salt but the other full of something that made him sneeze—when he realized Michelle was watching him.

Sam listened as Richard discussed his father's habits and remembered his parents' fights, their dances in the kitchen with tomato on their faces, and singing ballads off-key when Pop had had a touch too much port. Nicholas talked about fishing with Grandpa and the old man's habit of living with no bait because the living felt so pleasant. Sam liked the memories they'd accumulated by themselves; nothing dumped in to make them useful, just gathered moment by living moment. They knew the old man so well, and Sam pondered again what regrets he'd had that were enough to make a last sigh.

Nicholas mentioned the lovely girl at the gate.

"I . . . I think she's a bad one," Sam said. "You shouldn't see her again if you can help it."

"You know a lot about girls, do you?" Nick replied, and rolled his eyes.

This made Richard laugh mashed potato across the table, some out of his nose.

Sam laughed and stopped to blush, until he realized Michelle and Nick were laughing too.

Wonderful, he thought. But a bit strange as well. He remembered the talk of Children's Services, and the bread in his mouth became dry and tasteless.

He caught Richard looking at him.

"Maybe it's time for bed. We've all had a long day," Richard said.

"We could put Sam in with Nick," Michelle replied.

"Seriously? No," Nicholas said. "Nothing personal, Sammy." He mussed Sam's hair.

"I'm with Nicholas. Probably not appropriate," Richard said. "You know. The Services."

Each Kavanagh found something interesting on the floor to study.

"I suppose." Michelle's eyes took in the dirty dishes. "Today's been exhausting and Beatrice didn't sleep well last night."

"We'll do it all in the morning."

"But . . ."

"It'll all get done. We have a boy to order about. Two boys."

"What about the rollaway in the back room? I have no idea when Pop last used it," Michelle said.

"Sam and I can figure this out." Richard scuttled Sam upstairs to the back room to find a rollaway bed propped against a wardrobe so covered with dust even its vertical surfaces had a light coat. "Sorry."

Sam shrugged. He slept on dirt.

Richard found him a nightgown (an oversized T-shirt with the fading face of someone with purple hair and the word "Elvis" printed underneath), then tucked him into the bed.

"Thank you," Sam whispered.

Richard leaned forward as if to kiss his cheek, stopped, and shook his head. "Goodnight, Samuel." He left the room.

Nicholas slept in the next room, his low breathing deepening to snores.

"How is he?" Sam heard Michelle's voice in the room next to Nicholas's.

"He's odd," Richard replied.

She laughed.

"What do we do about him?" Richard asked.

"I know Aunt Colleen's crazy as a rabid dog most times, but . . ."

"We want to keep him, right?"

"You too? That's a relief. I'd fight to have him. It feels right." Michelle's soft laugh carried over her words. "Colleen's right about me falling in love with him. Why're you looking at me like that? You think I'm crazy too?"

"I never had problems with love at first sight, remember?"

"He belongs with us."

"I'm with you one hundred percent, especially if you keep that expression on your face."

"Sorry?" she said.

"Your this-is-the-way-it's-going-to-be look. I haven't seen it in a long time, you know?"

"I'd lost my fight."

"No, you hadn't. Here it is. Besides, I agree, we were meant to have three kids."

"He's not a replacement, I know, but he's the right age. It makes . . ."

". . . The back of your neck prickle? No one can replace our own little Sam though. This one's his own new person."

Michelle gave a sharp sob. The warmth in Sam faded. If she wanted him, why did it make her sad? He turned over; when her weeping weakened to sleeping breaths, he drifted away too.

A fuss in the kitchen woke him. Sam listened to the rest of the house. Nicholas snored, and Michelle mumbled and moaned in her sleep. Richard sat up next to her, whispering to Beatrice.

Sam padded down the bare wood floor and saw the stairs, the furniture, even the pictures on the walls in clear, green edges.

The fridge door leaned open with its light out, grumbling with exhaustion. Imps lolled over every surface of the room. Pixies, brownies, a young goblin sat on the edge of the table swinging its legs and giggling while a puck handed food from the fridge to a couple of bogeymen. A sprite sat in the sink washing its hair with Fairy Wash while a crew of miserable-looking brownies washed, dried, and put away the dishes.

Three more brownies peeked out from under the fridge, and then the pantry door flung open to reveal a dozen pixies stuffing their faces with chips and nuts. One had an electric-blue ribbon around its neck.

Maggie stood out against the dour brown and rag-covered imps with her folded arms and venomous dress.

"Hello again. What are you doing here?" Sam asked Maggie.

"The dishes," moaned the brownies at the sink. "Not willingly. We're compelled to."

"This is why I live in a house with a maid," whined the wiper. "Can't stop cleaning if there's a mess. Wouldn't be in a dung hole like this if . . ."

"Wish I'd stayed home. I'd be watching reality TV in the basement."

"Lotta good you are," Maggie called over the top of them. "You're s'posed to show him the pleasure in mischief. None of this cleaning business."

"Ooh, there's cake and blue cheese," yelled a pixie from the fridge. "Let's eat!"

"Now that's more like it." Maggie clapped her hands.

The pixies skirmished over the snacks; packets tore open and rippled chips flew. The brownies squealed in horror. The imps converged on the table, writhing and eating, like a rat infestation.

"Why don't you get in there, Samuel? There's goodies galore in this house." Maggie pulled out her silver box and blew a finger of dust into the air. The powder encircled the cleaning brownies in a golden spiral and lifted them off the draining board. "I could keep you in dust for centuries and the world would be our playground. Wouldn't you like that, Samuel? What creatures couldn't we torment?"

The brownies squealed and giggled, reaching for invisible handholds as Maggie's hand waved, and they turned over and over. The pixies squeaked in wicked pleasure at the sight.

Sam laughed.

The brownies fell. One plopped into the sink next to the shampooing sprite. The others hit the bench and somersaulted onto the table.

"What delights do you long for, Samuel? What are you after? Gold? Jewels? Power?"

"He don't want none of that." The goblin grabbed his hands and jigged him around the table. The other imps clapped and Sam heard music, a frenzy of invisible instruments played in his ears. "He just want to dance and do mischief and lark about, like all us new-mades. Don't you, Sam?"

The goblin let go of Sam's hands. They both reeled back laughing as the imps linked arms between the plates of food and swung each other.

"Well, Samuel," Maggie asked. "Is that what you want?"

Sam clapped along with the magic melody. "I don't know. I think I want..." He chuckled as a bogeyman fell into the French onion dip and white cheese covered its face. He grinned at Maggie. "I have a name now. I think the only thing I want is a family."

Maggie swept him into her arms and twirled him around the kitchen. Dust floated around them, swirling and playing the furious music. "We are your family, Samuel. We have always been. You're pretty as a lamb, but you're monster through and through. Come away with me; come away with us."

The music sped and the dancing frenzy on the table died down. Some of the imps settled to eating dips and shoving sweets into their gobs, then sat up, making a symphony of belching, burping, and farting. They stared at Sam. The goblin's eyes peered over the edge of a dip bowl, its tongue licking it clean, and brownies grinned as the pixies devoured the last of the chips with their greasy little mouths.

"So, is he coming with us?" an oily-faced pixie asked. "You said he'd come."

"You will, won't you, Samuel?" Maggie said. "Ask me for anything, anything at all."

The music played on, but only the sprite on the drainboard danced. The rest of the imps quietened, all leaning forward to hear him speak.

Sam looked at his eager audience. "Could you . . . ? Do you think it's possible? I would like Bladder back in one piece."

"What's that?" a pixie asked. "What's a bladder?"

"He's a gargoyle. An ogre took him from me."

"We'll find you a dozen to replace it," Maggie said.

"I don't want a dozen, just him."

From the bedroom, he heard Nick mutter, ". . . Green . . ." Then the older boy rolled over in his sleep.

Two pixies dashed down the stairs. "There's a baby. All fat and juicy up there," they cried.

The sprite stopped spinning, and the invisible instruments shrieked and ceased to play.

The goblin tongue held in midlick. It had cleaned half its face. It drooled. "Baby?"

"Pixies, you can't trust them around the babies, can you?" Maggie laughed and kissed Sam on the mouth.

He pulled away. "You mustn't touch the baby!"

The little dancing goblin tilted its head. "Why's that then?"

"Because . . ." Sam started

Maggie jumped in. "Because she's his, not yours."

"Well, it's not really about . . ." the blue-ribbon pixie replied.

"Hush, Nutty-Arm," Maggie said. "If Samuel says the baby's his, the baby's his."

The imps studied Maggie with bewildered faces.

"I don't understand," said the goblin.

Maggie reached for Sam, taking his shoulders and turning him to face her. She studied his expression.

"Ooh, he's jealous of his sweetmeats," the goblin said, and laughed.

"Just putting away the last of the trash," the brownies said.

"Leave it!" the pixies wailed. "For crying out loud!"

"Normally thin pickings in this area. This has been good," the blue-ribboned pixie said to another. "We'll have to come back."

"Pixies. Such light-fingered little rascals. Don't worry about them; they'll behave. You're not to touch his toys. Shoo!" Maggie waved her hand again, and the pixies, brownies, and bogeymen ran for the fridge and slid under the pantry door. The rest of the imps dashed into corners and up the walls, disappearing into cracks like cockroaches. "Come with me now, my darling?" she said.

"I think I'd better stay. Just for now." He opened the pantry door. The space seemed empty. He moved the bin and checked behind it.

"If not just now," she asked, "when?"

Sam stared up the stairs as Maggie watched him. He heard Beatrice whimper, and Sam remembered her beautiful sparkles. He also remembered he looked like the Kavanaghs. They might not be as much fun as the imps, but it was worth investigating more. He also didn't trust the pixies not to return if he left. "I don't know."

Maggie sighed, kissed him again, and vanished.

He looked over the kitchen and saw the room, neat and shiny. The brownies had even dusted the windowsills, but there were no snack foods left.

CHAPTER 12

Nicholas, in slippers, shuffled into the kitchen. "You did the dishes. I knew I was gonna like you." Then he opened the creaky fridge and saw the bare shelves. "I don't suppose you want breakfast though?"

"You did the dishes?" Michelle said behind him, the baby dangling in her arms.

Nick nodded in Sam's direction. "But he was hungry. At least he left us some eggs." He pulled out a carton, flipped the top, and grinned at a dozen bald domes. "Scrambled?"

Beatrice's rose-colored lights wriggled toward Sam. The boy tapped them back one at a time. Her small hands flexed open and closed, catching rebounded flickers.

Michelle fixed a kiss on Nick. "I'll take you into town this morning and buy something you want. Samuel needs new clothes, and if we hand him over without a good spit and polish they won't consider us...I mean, they won't think we've taken care of you." Michelle patted Sam's shoulder.

"Yeah, the vision of him in Dad's old Elvis shirt is a bit much," Nick said. "Mom, do you mind getting me that Bad'un T-shirt while you're there? You know the one, right?"

"The red one?" She frowned as he sighed. "I take notice."

"Last winter's anorak says not."

Sam wondered why she laughed.

"You want a new shirt to look nice for that girl?"

Nick flushed.

"Not for Maggie?" Sam groaned.

Michelle folded her arms. "Stop scowling. It'll happen to you soon enough."

"I'm never going to be in thrall to a banshee."

"Ouch," said Nick. "Harsh!"

Michelle stroked Sam's cheek. "You'll understand one day."

"Where's Dad?" Nick asked.

"Beatrice kept him up all night so I let him sleep in. We'll get out of the house and give him some peace."

Sam smiled. A morning with Beatrice would be a treat, and moving might keep them all a bit safer, until Daniel returned.

"I'll look after her," Nicholas offered. "I'd rather not hang out with you and Sam looking for Spider-Man T-shirts. I can watch TV and stick Bea in the rocker."

"Who's Spider-Man?" Sam asked.

Michelle pressed her lips together. "She'll need a feeding and be put down for a sleep."

"Well, what if she goes to sleep while you're out, won't you want to come home anyway?"

Michelle patted Beatrice's diaper. Blue sparks flew from her bloomers. "I suppose we won't need to be gone more than an hour. We could shop in an hour, couldn't we, Samuel? I could get this one a pair of jeans too."

Sam gave her his best unknowing grin.

"Go on," Nick said to Sam. "Work your magic on Mom. Whatever you're doing makes her happy. Talk her into getting me a gift card. I don't wanna end up with mom jeans." Nick chuckled. "And Mom, get him something decent 'cause that look's not working for him. No collars. Let him look normal."

Sam giggled when the car vroomed to life and vibrated around him. Michelle laughed and leaned over to help him wind down the window. He had seen vehicles moving, even this one, but it tickled being inside a car with all its rumbling and humming.

"Why'd you bring that awful old backpack?" Michelle asked. He still wore Elvis, but he'd put on the pants Daniel had given him. Michelle brushed her hand over one dirty knee.

"It's all I have. And if I have to leave . . ."

"Oh," Michelle said. The word sounded like it couldn't quit her throat, and she avoided looking at his face. She stared at his bare feet instead. "We'll get you some sneakers too."

As they drove away, he put his head out the passenger side window to smell the salt air and watch the whitening coast disappear and little white shacks shove up against each other to hide the sea. The car puttered along, quivering on slight bends. They headed west, tracing the road along the seashore. Boats bobbed away white and sheeplike, huddling in threes or fours as waves trembled in. Magnificent white birds—seagulls, Michelle said—moved up and down between the boats.

"The world is a wonderful place," he said.

"It can be."

He looked at Michelle's face; a tear gathered on the lower lashes of her eye. Sam marveled at how it magnified the hairs. It sailed over and down her cheek. She saw him watching and rubbed it away.

She seemed to cry a lot.

"Do you miss the other Samuel?" he asked.

"What? How did you know?" Her eyes threatened storms again.

"It was his..." He'd heard someone say the word, what was it? "His wake. Yesterday."

"Pop? You mean Pop?" She didn't wait for his answer; she drove the car up to the curb and they sat with it rumbling under them. She pinched her nose, high across the bridge. Sam mimicked her. It hurt. "I thought you meant the other 'other Samuel.'" She laughed, but it was high-pitched and didn't make Sam think of happiness. More frightened pixie.

"The other 'other Samuel'?"

Michelle put her head on the steering wheel, and tears coursed over it. "Oh, hell."

Sam had no idea what to do. He put his hand on her shoulder, like Daniel would, willing it warm, wanting something to pass between them. It didn't, but she reached up and put a damp hand over his.

"Samuel was our baby, Nick's little brother. We lost him twelve years ago, not long after he was born. He was weak and sick, and then he was gone." Michelle's voice thickened and muffled. She stopped talking and pinched her nose again. "When I saw you in the shop, you are the way I imagine he'd look. I wonder all the time, you see? I think, he'd be starting high school soon, or I wonder if he'd like skateboarding, like Nick, or whether he'd be more of a reader. What would his favorite food be? Would he be quiet or loud?"

Sam studied her face. She was smiling, which confused him. Her words sounded so sad. He said what he'd heard everyone say at the wake. "I'm sorry."

"No, I'm sorry. I should have realized that you meant Pop. But with your stories about angels and . . . belonging with us . . ." She put her lips together and exhaled hard. "Samuel, would you really like to belong with us?"

I *would*, he thought, *although that wouldn't be safe for you. I wish Daniel would come back and take me far from you, and I wish the monsters would all forget about me and let me stay here without bothering me anymore.* He thought all these things and knew he wished he could, and when Michelle looked at him with pink eyes he said the truth. "Yes."

Michelle burst into noisy sobs and threw her arms around him. "We'd like that too." She stroked his hair and wet his T-shirt, soggying Elvis. He held her. It warmed him. He felt her heart beating.

"Why did that make you cry?" he asked.

She laughed as loudly as she'd sobbed. "Oh, Samuel," she

said, and touched his cheek, starting the car again without answering his question.

Michelle drove at the road with ferocious focus, and Sam studied her, thinking over her words. She said she wanted him to belong too. A heat built around his heart. He'd felt it before, from Daniel. The angel called it "hope."

They drove a little longer, then parked along a road of red bricks. No cars drove up it, just people in groups or idling alone, smiling in the sunshine.

Michelle grabbed his hand and headed toward gleaming glass windows filled with red pots and pans, blue balloons, and pink cake piled upon white. Some teenagers passed them and sniggered. Sam guessed it wasn't normal to hold an adult's hand, but he liked it and gripped harder. Michelle only let it go inside the stores so he could try on T-shirts, shorts, and a couple of hoodies, and her eyes grew damp when he showed her.

She remembered at the last minute to grab a pair of sneakers, and they got thrown into the bag. The girl in the store let them have everything because Michelle had a square of plastic.

They walked past a sweet shop. Sam stared at the bars of chocolate in the window, thinking about Bladder. Michelle bustled him inside and bought him a couple of bars. He shoved them into his backpack.

"Time for a quick cup of tea, and then we'll head back," she said in the tea shop. She slung her handbag over a chair and watched Sam as if he might disappear; then with an abrupt swivel she moved toward a sign saying "no table service, order here." While she was away at the counter, her bag buzzed like insects wanting to escape. Sam jumped. It buzzed again and again, then stopped.

Michelle returned, struggling to put her money away. "There. A few moments to catch our breath before we head home."

"Thank you." Sam wondered about the insistent sound of her bag, but when she opened it to put her purse into it nothing flew out.

Michelle ran her fingers through his hair. "We'll keep the clean clothes until you've had a bath, eh?" She watched as he ate a cookie and drank half a cup of tea. "Are you telling the truth about your angel? I half believe you. He brought you where you belong." She caught sight of the tearoom clock. "We've been away long enough. It's time to head home."

She chatted in the car and asked him whether he could read and write. Sam knew he could read. He didn't know about writing.

The car climbed the hill to the house. The sun hit a tranquil blend of brickwork and flowering plants. Ivy covered the walls under intertwining branches of trees; an occasional boxy two-story house broke the greenery, but most of the houses hid behind vine-wrapped stone walls.

Sam wound down the window and breathed. The streets reeked of fairy magic; it hung in the foliage and swung on the gates. People and dogs on the roads wore it in hair and fur.

When they turned down the street to the house, cars cluttered the way. Two vans were parked along the curb. Michelle paled when she turned into the driveway and saw a police car. She parked and ran without closing her door. Sam clutched at his pack and chased her in.

A police officer stood on the doorstep, staring at the far corner of the garden. Two men and a woman in dark jackets were working within a small area of trees. Between them sat an empty baby rocker encircled by a mauve toadstool circle. A *pixie trap!* He should have stayed with Beatrice, Sam thought, not left her alone in the house while he'd gone off enjoying himself with Michelle. He'd assumed the pixies wouldn't have been silly enough to steal a human baby.

Michelle grabbed his hand, crushing it. She balled her other hand into a fist and dug it into her chest.

"Mrs. Kavanagh?" The young police officer stared at Michelle. "Mrs. Kavanagh?"

"Where's Beatrice?"

"Come inside. We'll explain everything."

Michelle lurched forward, her legs shaking. Sam held her hand tighter to stop her from falling.

In the living room, Richard sat on the sofa, his head in his hands, as Nicholas answered a young police officer's questions. When Michelle and Sam came in, Richard jumped up and reached for his wife.

"I tried to call you. Several times."

"What's happened to Beatrice?"

Nick's eyes were swollen plums. "Dad . . ." He groaned. "Dad was asleep, and Beatrice fussed so . . ." He looked around him. The officer stared at him, nodding for him to finish. ". . . For some air, just for some air." Michelle sank to the sofa. "She was in the carrier, then she was gone." He looked at Sam, focusing on his shoulder. His eyes dulled, and he couldn't seem to close his lips, as if he were concentrating on something too hard to understand. "Really just there and then . . . not there." He put a hand to his head and rocked himself.

"We're checking all the neighbors along this road first, and the surrounding areas . . ." the officer in charge said.

"Checking the neighbors?" Michelle's voice shook in a high note. "What . . . ?"

"Not just that; we've contacted Child Rescue Alert, and they are sending someone to go over everything."

Michelle gazed at them all, turning from face to face, including Sam's, as if the solution would appear on one. Sam thought she looked lost and lonely, even though they all filled the room. Then she sobbed into Richard's shirt, and he held her. They shook together.

"He says . . . he says . . ." Richard couldn't finish.

Michelle looked to the policeman.

"It looks like it could be an organized abduction, ma'am." The officer in charge put out his hand. Michelle stared at it numbly. "I'm Sergeant Trelawney," he said, tugging an imaginary forelock, "and this is Officer Teague." Michelle's dazed gaze took in her face.

"From what the experts outside have told me, the blanket and bottle were removed, which suggests whoever took the baby means to look after her. There's a chance a ransom may be requested."

"A ransom?"

Richard held Michelle's hands. "The detective here seems to believe Pop's death brought this on. The house is worth a lot, and the kidnappers think we have money."

Her eyes brightened. "Okay. We give them everything. We will, won't we, Richard? They can have everything."

Sam knew pixies wouldn't ransom anyone. He felt the tea-shop food slurry in his stomach. It was his fault this happened to them. He should have left the moment Maggie appeared.

"We'll do everything we can to get your baby back, ma'am. Who knows, one of the neighbors may have heard her crying and come to collect her."

"Her name is Beatrice."

The sergeant flipped his notebook as if confirming this. "Beatrice, yes."

"I was with her the..." Nick turned to Sam, his expression pleading to be believed. "I'm so sorry, Mom. I'm so sorry."

"If it's a ransom it could be over quickly?" Michelle grabbed Richard, shaking him to confirm it. "It'll be over quickly, Nick. Don't worry." The smile on her face made Sam uncomfortable and he stepped back.

"Is this your son too?" The sergeant pointed his chin at Sam.

"Yes." Her eyes lit on him. "I mean, no."

"He showed up at the house yesterday afternoon, during the wake. We don't really know who he is..." Richard trailed off.

"You didn't think to call Children's Services?" the officer asked.

"Teague . . . ," the sergeant warned her.

"Yes, we did, but it was so late last night and . . . so much happened yesterday; we didn't know what to think. He looks like a family member." Richard shook his head. "Do we really have to go into that now? Our daughter's missing."

"We just wonder if his presence might have anything to do with that," Teague said.

"He's been with me all morning," Michelle said. She stopped and studied him, putting a hand over her face. "Please, Sam, please. You didn't have anything to do with this, did you?"

Sam peered at each face in turn. He had brought this down on them.

"Distracting you, perhaps?" The sergeant stared at Sam. "Son?"

Michelle cried.

"Yes, it's my fault, sir." Sam's eyes burned. "Pixies took her because of me. It's my fault." Sam bawled. His stomach ached, his head hurt. Every awful emotion he knew to feel filled him until he felt sick.

"Take it easy, son, you're sounding a bit hysterical. Doesn't sound like you're to blame at all." Sergeant Trelawney stepped closer.

"I'm so sorry. I'm so, so sorry," he said to Michelle. She reached for him. Nick stared at Sam, the dazed expression lifting for a moment.

"Come on . . . Sam, is it?" Officer Teague moved to touch his shoulder. "Calm down. If you were in town with Mrs. Kavanagh, we're sure . . ."

Sam saw Trelawney and Teague stalking him from both sides. He'd been hunted from the moment he was made, and he knew what it looked like.

He ran.

He dashed from the living room, down the corridor, and

through the open front door. He swung his pack onto his back so it rattled and bounced as he ran.

Trelawney and Teague yelled after him.

Michelle called, "Sam?"

He ran past the investigators searching the garden.

The police officers' yells grew louder as they broke free of the house, and Sam bolted out of the garden. He did not think where to go. His bare feet bashed against the hard sidewalk.

A huge *ee-awwi*ng sound started behind him. A monster pursued him; it flashed red and white lights. He ducked down a path between houses, hearing the chase behind him.

"Down there, down there!" someone yelled, and he looked ahead to a green expanse. He would have nowhere to hide out there. He jumped the fence next to him.

A grate was set against the inside of the fence, underneath the end of a drainpipe. He looked at it. He knew where Beatrice would be, and he was the only one who could bring her back. He slid between the bars of the grate, like a monster, as slick as a pixie, his body snaking into the darkness.

"He went down here!" Teague's voice yelled.

Sam stepped back into the darkness between the human world and the monster world. Had they seen him slip into the grate? They couldn't follow him, could they?

"He must have gone into the Downs."

"Can't see him."

"Stay here, he might have gone into one of the gardens. If you see anything . . ."

Footsteps pounded past him and softened as they hit the meadow.

Sam panted. He looked between the bars. The day above was beautiful and he felt wretched. His heart hammered in his chest and ears. No matter what those poor humans did, they'd never find Beatrice again, not unless the pixies brought her back, and did pixies ever return the things they stole? Sam considered the darkness. If he followed it he'd find The Hole. He had to find those pixies. He had to get Beatrice back before her sparkles faded out in that horrible place.

CHAPTER 13

The bars of the drain cooking in sunshine smelled like blood, but the scent faded as he moved farther in, and the temperature lowered. Sam wondered which direction the pixies had taken Beatrice. He knew it wasn't down this particular dark cavity, the old stink of goblins and trolls seeped from the walls, but there was no human smell. Still, all tunnels led to one place, The Hole, and he was sure the pixies had taken Beatrice there. If he hadn't been forced to run, he might have tracked her from the Kavanaghs' house, but it was dangerous to go back and start again. The police were hunting him in the lanes and fields above his head.

He climbed deeper into the gloom, and when he turned to catch a last touch of daylight, he could no longer see the opening behind him.

It was dark. Sam could still see, he had a gargoyle's eyesight, but there was more to this darkness than a lack of light.

He descended into its inkiness, dropping a few feet to land on his bare feet.

He rested, explored his backpack, and checked his two bars of chocolate and the sleeping bag. He found something else under them and smiled. A sandwich. The last Daniel had given him before they left the cathedral. It looked a bit squashed.

"Thank you," he said into the darkness. The walls did not echo his words.

Then he walked for a long time, following the shafts and the ogre stink ages away. He walked over debris and tunnel floors smoothed by centuries of footfall. Pixie footprints and the clodding marks of trolls patterned the ground. With each step, he hoped he could find some trace of Beatrice.

In one tunnel, he found a burlap-dressed human skeleton. It had been there so long, its smelled only of dust and dirt. The dark holes in its skull stared at him. Sam felt sorry for it.

"Hello," he said. "Are you lost?"

The skeleton did not answer. Sam wished he knew its name and where it belonged. He had the horrible thought that a monster had kidnapped this poor human and been turned to ash, leaving the person to wander around in the monstrous dark before starving to death. It hadn't occurred to him before, and he wondered if Beatrice was lying in these catacombs somewhere with a pile of ash next to her.

If the souls did that, it would be as bad as letting the ogres eat people. Beatrice would only survive if they weren't that stupid. Sam hoped they weren't.

The gray tunnels sucked him farther. When he heard the thumping of pickaxes behind stone walls, Sam stopped and listened.

"Tommy-knockers," he guessed.

Sam sniffed, and rot greeted him. In the distance, the sounds of the monster hive hummed and growled. He was close to The Hole.

One step closer to finding Beatrice.

"It's my fault she's here," he said to the walls.

A troop of dwarves with coal-blackened faces stomped out of a hole at Sam's right—the tommy-knockers he'd heard. Sam stopped again. Thunderguts had sent pixies to find him. Were other imps looking for him too? He knew they wouldn't eat him themselves.

One peered at him, yawned, and strolled after its pack.

Sam relaxed, but reminded himself to be careful in the future.

He followed the tommy-knockers to a cobbled entry. When they had gone through, he peered inside. He was high above the Great Cavern. The murderous bellowing clicked into sudden volume, and he watched thousands of ogres and imps traveling below on their diabolical business. He sniffed, but with the overpowering reek of ogre paddies, he could barely make out the troll sweat and pixie fear, so the gentle scent of baby was undetectable. Nonetheless, the Pixie Cavern was in here somewhere, and someone there might know something. His heart chilled, the opposite of the way it felt when filled with hope. But it was all he had to go on.

The tommy-knockers climbed down into the great mass, using their picks to steady their descent. Sam shuddered and followed them into the murky, mucky space below. All the imps and monsters were on their important business, scurrying about, ignoring the doings of other panicked creatures as they worried about Thunderguts's moods and orders. Nothing looked at him; nothing cared. The multitude would give him better cover than an empty corridor.

Sam dropped into the rabble, knocking over a brownie, which took off at full speed. Goblins loomed over him, and hundreds of pixies shuffled at his knees and waist. Each face was a map of intent. He stayed with the company of pixies and followed them into a tunnel which had "To the Dunjuns" chalked over its entryway in bony white.

Sam tucked in his head, pushed up his backpack, and moved with the press. He hoped this pack would lead him to more of their kind, to the Pixies' Cavern where he might find some information on Beatrice. He swayed like a troll as the push of the mob shoved him onward.

Still the creatures shuffled directionless and frenetic. He continued hunching, hoping they wouldn't look his way. Sam saw plenty of dark entrances leading off the main corridor and wondered where they led. Many of the black mouths swallowed up imps, while other doors vomited yogurt-white pixies and brownies back into the great crowd. He still couldn't smell the baby; the bare hints of human scent seemed ancient and long gone.

When the pixies made a left, Sam followed them.

"Hey, you!" An ogre with tusks and one good eye leaned

against a wall next to a dark entrance. It called and pointed over the mob.

Sam hunched into the ground, waiting for its huge claw to fall on him and jerk him into the air, but the great brute flicked at a pixie clutching a small brown paper package. "What you got there?" the ogre asked.

"Nothing." The pixie shook so much, the wrapping crackled. "It won't interest you."

"Likely story," the ogre said.

The ogre plucked the package from the pixie's arms and ripped through the paper, then held up a small gray-green tunic. The crowd had slowed, squashing Sam against the wall. All the pixies' eyes, round and wide, watched to discover the package carrier's fate. Sam stared with all the others as the ogre studied the package and the pixie shivered. Hundreds of imps gaped at the pair, pressing at them, like water around a rock, pooling around the prodding, poking bully and its victim.

"Get out of here! Go home!" Sam hunched farther down, his bottom on the hard dirt. His heart rattling. He looked around, but no one was talking to him. The ogre flicked the tunic at the sobbing pixie, then raised its arms. "Don't the lot of you know it's guards and prisoners only in the dungeons? What you trucking useless stuff about for?" He aimed a kick at the package-carrying pixie, and the imps turned to scamper back the way they had come. Sam would have followed them, but his feet were stuck to the floor, and if he didn't move, the ogre would see him.

It's *fear, just fear*, Sam thought. No time for fear. He had to find Beatrice.

The pack attempted to reverse, but a few trolls and goblins pushed on, wanting to get farther down the dungeon corridor. Five pixies and a goblin a head taller than Sam exchanged blows in front of him. The goblin seemed to think Sam was in the fight too and shoved him backward. Sam fell, expecting to hit the wall, but he found himself landing with a solid thump inside the entrance to a side tunnel. He could see out to where the imps squabbled. A pixie in a top hat sailed into the tunnel and plopped next to him, but it sprang up without paying him any mind and threw itself back into the fray. The ogre who'd started it all guffawed, and the goblins sent a few more pixies flying.

Sam turned his head to try to peer farther into the thin corridor. He was met with, not complete darkness, but flickering flames high up on the inner walls. He smelled the hint of a human, newer than before and as gentle as fresh air. It came from a long way back in the tunnel. He crept toward the aroma, sniffing as he went, aware that anything nasty could be ahead and that he had lost the protection of the crowd. He would be easily seen, but he had to follow that scent.

Torches sputtered in the blackening corridor. Flames licked hungrily at metal rims, and tar drooled to the ground beneath.

Behind him, the one-eyed ogre giggled and grunted, the battle noises fading, before the monster's footsteps got louder. He was following Sam into the side tunnel.

Sam scampered in farther, listening as the ogre trailed him.

Then ahead, out of the gloom, came the slapping echo of mighty, flat feet.

Ogres in both directions, Sam thought. *I'm trapped.*

He scaled the wall and clung onto the ceiling. His backpack was hanging down. A large ogre could brush its head against it, even if it didn't see him first.

The ogre coming from inside the tunnel was a short one, but if it looked up it might have been surprised to find Sam there. It had sharpened tusks, an enormous skull, and bulbous nose, and one arm was dragging by its side. It swaggered down the corridor, and as it did, the one-eyed ogre galumphed down the tunnel toward it. Matted feet smacked the earth. One-Eye passed under Sam and stopped.

"I was coming to get you," One-Eye said.

"Any news?" Tusks asked.

"Won't be long now. Thunderguts says a coupla things ain't gone quite right, but he's got a plan."

"He's always got a plan."

The two chuckled.

Tusks spat up something solid. One-Eye leaned over to pick it off its toe. It squelched. Sam held his position and his breath.

"Finished?" One-Eye asked.

Tusks grunted. "Someone I ate. Didn't agree with me."

"Well, they never do," One-Eye said.

The ogres laughed a horrible gutter-belch of noise.

"Come on," said One-Eye.

The pair took off back the way Sam had come.

When the ogres were far enough away, he let his breath rasp out.

They hadn't bothered to look up. Sam guessed, when you're the biggest, most frightening thing in the room, you don't check your surroundings. Sam scuttled along the ceiling, increasing the distance between him and the ogres.

The last turn plunged Sam into a somberly lit, stone-lined pit. Stairs spiraled down its sides. Vicious hooks and manacles hung from the walls, too high up for even the tallest ogre to touch the ground, although Sam doubted the hooks were for ogres. He dropped from the ceiling, rolled in the air, and landed on all fours. He smiled. He hadn't known he could do that. Behind him, voices drifted away. Ahead the snore of a heavy animal traveled up the stairs.

Sam held his shaking hands together and ran into the sepia darkness. His feet were braver than he; they took each step in a rhythmic stride as his parrumping heartbeat echoed off stone walls. The smell of human grew stronger.

It wasn't right though—too diluted. A dead body? He hoped not, he really hoped not.

At the bottom of the steps, a rusting gate stood ajar. Sam sized up the thin gap in the gate, then slid through. As his pack scraped the wall, the hinges shrieked.

"My name's not Tinkerbell," a rough voice called.

Sam stopped everything—moving, breathing, daring. Sweat gathered at his hairline.

Snores started again. Sam blinked and slipped free of the gate and, with the last of his courage, tiptoed toward the human smell.

The ogre guard's snores filled the space between four small, black-barred cells, and the thick smell of blood crammed up Sam's nose. The great creature's bottom smothered a suffering three-legged stool, and mounds of fat from its backside cascaded down the sides, legs bowing under the weight. The ogre's convex nose draped over its chin. Twin horns—stained a deep, rotten red—stuck out of its forehead. It drooled onto its potbelly, its tongue lolling all the way to the top of its shorts. From underneath the stool, a twinkle caught Sam's eye, as if a tiny piece of sunlight had caught there.

The ogre stank. It sleep-belched, and the pungent copper smell eddied off its breath.

Sam smelled the remnant of fresh air clinging to its breath. There was a whiff of sunshine, but whatever it had been hadn't been human. This wasn't the scent he had followed. It was an animal smell. Sam felt sorry for it. The poor creature was gone, and all its sunshine with it.

The gruff voices of ogres echoed into the stairwell, followed by flat, meaty footfalls descending the steps. The ogre muttered in its sleep. It burped again, and Sam backed farther into the dark space of the cells.

Sam looked around and realized they were empty. Their doors hung open. He slipped along the short corridor and looked into each as he passed. Dirt floors furnished with misshapen rocks and rotting wood. The human smell came from the last one, subtle but slight. The touch of a fingernail or a hair in a brush, not a whole person.

Sam peered back at the guard. Its mouth hung open, black liquid pooled on its bottom teeth. The candle on the table next to it died. Ogres had good nighttime eyes, but a gargoyle's eyes were stronger, and in this black hole even Sam struggled to see.

He trembled to have the huge brute behind him, but he

dashed toward the farthest end of the short corridor and slid down into the dirt.

As he moved he felt a sharp red pain shear up his arm. A splinter stabbed deep into his palm. When he pulled out the jagged stone, he felt a second hot wave of pain, and his blood plopped out onto the filthy floor. In the half-light, the liquid swelled warm and black in his hand. He looked at the broken piece of gray stone sliding between his blood-oiled fingers.

Bellowing laughs came down to the cells. Sam huddled in the corner, hearing his own heartbeat and studying his hand. He'd sliced his palm. Black fluid seeped from the wound. He felt weak, as if his energy was leaking out of the small, pulsing hole. He pressed his other palm over it and wondered how to slow the leak. When he pushed his hand to the wall, his blood prevented it from sticking. He couldn't climb to the ceiling.

Ogres smell blood better than anything, Sam thought. He wished he didn't know that. He stared at the ogre sleeping on its laboring stool.

The wheezy mass of the guard snored on as two ugly monsters moved toward it. Sam put his torn hand to his mouth.

"Grumblebum! You sleeping?" an ogre voice demanded. It took up the doorway. Sam shuddered when he saw the massive, neckless body, all covered with rigid muscles. There, red-eyed and regal, his stone fist hanging in Sam's eyeline, stood Thunderguts.

"Never said I liked coffee," Grumblebum the guard muttered.

Thunderguts turned toward Sam.

Sam waited for the ogre king to discover him. He pressed at

his hand, slowing the escape of the blood. His head lightened but he held still, his muscles aching.

The king turned back toward the sleeping guard.

"Wake up, Grumblebum," Thunderguts said.

The ogre grunted and opened one bloodshot eye.

"How's the torturing going?" the second ogre demanded. Sam trembled as he saw that it was the ogre from the cathedral.

Grumblebum slurred as he spoke. "Broke him three times. He don't know nothin', Snide."

"Maybe we should get 'Bum here to put the gargoyle back together. Bring it back topside. Use it as leverage." Snide's voice rumbled in his chest.

"And where will you take it? Our prince is playing fast and loose with some humans right now. The crone says wait till he's bored," Thunderguts said.

"He sounds like a little monster," Snide said. "Spoiled brat needs to come home."

The three ogres laughed.

"Anywise, you don't think he's interested in the gargoyle?" Grumblebum started.

"Gargoyles are sniveling, conniving sun-dwellers with no more self-respect than humans," Thunderguts said. "They run at the first sign of danger. If our little prince is half what I think he is, he won't spare another thought for that trash."

Snide's shoulders slumped forward, and Sam stared at the ogre's lowered back. He burned with the effort to remain still.

"I've waited many years already," Thunderguts went on. "It's taught me patience. In the end, he'll seek us out. If the crone's right, he's just trying to find out what he's here for."

Sam shivered at the mention of the crone. He thought of her bony hands reaching for him on Hatching Day. Her kiss. And she knew about the Kavanaghs?

"Like we all done when we was hatched," Snide said. "Time we nab him, then?"

Thunderguts turned to Snide and put a claw on his back. "No talk of nabbing. Let him come back in his own time. He may look a bit odd, but he's still just a monster."

"Tasty-looking, in'he?"

Thunderguts chuckled. "I smell blood in here, Grumble-bum. You been eating human?"

"Nah, I'd be off me nut blathering if I did that. I'm not stupid. Was a cow. Always makes me sleepy," the guard mumbled.

"Smells glorious. What breed was that?"

"Friesian, I think."

Thunderguts laughed. "Come on, 'Bum, tell me more about this delicious-smelling cow and where you got it. Then I can go and find out if there's any more news of my little monster."

"What about the rock?"

"Fed up with thinking about it," Thunderguts said. "Leave it to rot."

Snide dragged Grumblebum up and staggered toward the exit, leaving Thunderguts looking back at the cells. A frown passed over the ogre's face before he issued a guttural sigh and walked out.

The gate screamed as Thunderguts left.

Sam staggered up. The thick blood was clotting in his

palm now. He looked at the sliver of rock that had hurt him. It was gargoyle gray. He studied the ground where it had lain. It must have been flung there from one of the cells.

He had to have another peek at those odd-shaped rocks. As the ogre tread faded into the distance, Sam peered through the bars at them. Pieces of granite spread over the dirt. He squinted, too dark for him, but as he stepped closer, he saw Bladder's head lying upside down in the corner. The lion's stone eyes stared at a spot somewhere near Sam's foot.

Despite the pain in his hand, he raised a quiet cheer.

Sam began.

Bladder's torso lay twisted. His shoulders faced up, as did his belly and back legs. A fixed howl sat on the gargoyle's face. Sam wondered what agony Bladder had suffered before splitting apart. He pulled at the head. It was the heaviest piece, but he propped it in the dirt next to the body. He would put it on last. Bladder might start yelling as soon as he was whole. He didn't need the ogres rushing back.

The cherub wings, ornamental at best, had sheared off. Sam attached those first. A frying-pan sizzle crisped as each fastened, and raised scars formed along the ruptures. Sam liked the sound. He might actually be able to reassemble Bladder.

Sam stopped and listened for footsteps again, for anything slithering or stomping back to the cells. Then he took off his backpack; it was cumbersome and squeaky. Maybe too soft for an ogre's ears, but Sam didn't want to risk anything.

He put down his bag, but it wouldn't sit flat, so he pushed it aside and found a white stone lodged underneath. When he held it up, it looked unlike the other gray pieces. It glowed the gentle white of milk, and flecks of bright color ran through its surface. It created its own light. Sam sniffed. It smelled like Bladder, like gutter water and church roofs and a little like imp boy, as if it had absorbed everything in Bladder's life. Here was the slight scent of human Sam had followed. It had been his own smell.

It looked like part of a solid egg. One side was smooth and curved, but the other sides were hard angles and rough, still glowing, still white. Thick gold seamed one jagged edge. Sam looked around for more pieces like it. It felt incomplete. He remembered the tiny glow from under the guard's seat, and struggled to get it out from under the bloodstained stool.

He dusted off the new piece, similar in shape to the first, picked it up, and put the two parts together. They did not fit, so he turned them twice before he heard—softer than the sizzle of stone on stone but delightful anyway—a *shush*. The two pieces joined at the gold vein. Half a stone egg now.

Sam crawled back into the cell, hoping for a third piece. He scrambled to the back of the gargoyle and searched in the muck, where Bladder's poor torso lay in two. When he peered inside he realized where the egg belonged. He could see right into the gargoyle's innards, and the hollow inside Bladder shimmered in the same pretty tinted white. When Sam put his hand in, a third piece fell into his palm. He turned it twice against the first half before hearing the pleasant sigh of pieces joining.

He sat up, and scanned the ground for the last quarter and saw it under Bladder's claw in the corner. Sam picked up the segment. It fit the first time.

The egg hummed in his hand. It had joined at the gold, but four thick cracks ran the outer surface. Sam lifted the glowing egg, smearing its surface with a layer of dark blood. It pulsed stronger, throwing light to the walls and casting a golden glow around the cell.

He put the egg inside Bladder's leonine chest. The egg sighed and nestled inside.

Sam thumped down on the floor, his body deciding it needed to rest. He looked at the gash in his hand. The flood had slowed, but not stopped, and somehow he felt himself leaking out that little hole.

No, *can't stop.*

Sam got working. Maybe Grumblebum would come back to rebuild Bladder and break him again or, worse, throw him away. He pushed the two halves of Bladder's torso together, the pieces fitting with a sputter.

Then the feet. The first locked on with a satisfying hiss, but the second would not fix. The breaks did not match. A thin gap opened between them, and Sam glanced around for the sliver of stone. It lay next to his pack, black with blood. He picked it up and added it to the break; it hissed and fastened. Sam reattached the rest of the leg.

He struggled with Bladder's weighty head. He felt sleepy. Maybe he would rest before he put on the head. Sam sat down and closed his eyes for a bit. They flickered open, and he saw the great cat staring at him. Its lips pulled back, revealing lion's teeth and great suffering. He'd rest after Bladder was fixed. Sam grabbed the head. He struggled to put it at the right angle and panted as the scar sizzled.

Bladder sat up, wide-eyed and shaking, untwisting his big cat body.

Sam put a finger to his lips. "The guard's gone, but Thunderguts was just here, and there's ogres wandering up and down out there." Sam trembled and his knees felt rubbery.

"What did you do?" Bladder nudged his rough snout into Sam's hand and growled. It hurt so much.

"I'm sorry," he said. "It's my fault you got smashed."

Bladder shook as he raised his paw, all claws extended. Sam raised his arm in a feeble attempt to protect himself, as the stone lion slashed at his belly.

Material fell away from his T-shirt in strips.

"All right, around the wound, and then up the arm." The gargoyle wrapped the fabric about Sam's hand, and it went dark with blood; then Bladder wrapped cloth farther up, firm and fast.

"What are you doing?" Sam slurred.

"It's supposed to stop the blood. If we don't, you'll die. I think you will anyway. It's what happens to humans when they lose blood. Trolls and witches too."

Sam's heart throbbed in his arm. He didn't remember it doing that before. He glanced at his backpack, too weak to reach it. Bladder grabbed it, knocking Sam's head and sore arm with a solid shoulder, before shoving it on him.

"Climb on." Bladder lowered himself so Sam could get onto his stone back.

Sam fell rather than climbed.

"You on? Good. Let's get out of here." Bladder ran out of the cell, through the gate, and up the dungeon stairs. The sound of the crowd mixed with Sam's steady heartbeat.

"Do you know how much blood you lose before you die?" Bladder asked him.

Sam had no idea.

"Well, if you're not nearly dead, really hold on. I'm going up."

Sam stuck his hands to Bladder's sides. He could feel how weak he was—if he stopped focusing, his hands would let go. The gargoyle scaled the corridor wall and took off toward the exit, upside down.

Sam held on with the last of his energy. At the end of the corridor, he saw One-Eye with his back to the door. The brute was focused on something at his feet. Bladder stopped.

One-Eye bent toward the floor.

Getting his head into some poor brownie's face, Sam thought.

"Hold on," Bladder whispered, and shot forward up the lip of the exit to the wall outside. Below them, the crowd of monsters swept on.

One-Eye raised his body. "Mmmm, what is that smell?" he said.

Bladder ran toward the Great Cavern. Sam looked back. One-Eye stared open-mouthed at the pair. Sam lost sight of the ogre as Bladder raced through the entry. A greater mob moved on the cavern floor. Bladder stepped off the wall and onto a ledge.

"We'll do this upright from here," Bladder said.

Sam relaxed, letting his hands and feet unstick, and slumped forward, drained and weary.

CHAPTER 14

Sam moaned. His head hurt. His sliced hand lay on his chest bound in ragged strips of Elvis purple. Bladder sprang over and pressed boulder-weight paws onto his chest.

"Bladder . . ." Sam gasped. "Gotta breathe."

"Just checking you're alive, Imp."

Sam leaned on the wall and let the dizziness wash away. He could see the rocky ridges of a messy burrow and sighed.

"It's a gargoyle hideout. Sometimes we come here when ogres block the exits."

Sam looked around. There were chocolate wrappers and empty candy bags everywhere. A neat stack of cans and small boxes leaned against the wall.

"They been here though," Bladder said. "Look up."

Sam stared at the scratches and gouges taken out of the ceiling. Ogre heads had bashed against it.

"So we can't stay long, Imp. If someone goes back and sees me missing, and there's blood all over the place . . . We got you bottled up, so a little rest and we're off, alrigh'?"

Sam stared at his hand. Bladder had ripped up more of his T-shirt, and a few drops of blood stained the wrapping's surface. The T-shirt itself barely covered his belly, exposing the dimple Daniel called his belly button.

"It's a bandage," Bladder said. "Humans do them."

"How do you know so much about humans?"

Bladder squatted. "Films and shows. Like that *Accident 'n' Emergency*. Also I spent centuries up there, picked up a thing or two."

Sam nodded at him, encouraging him to continue.

"Most important thing to know is, they ain't nice."

"Monsters aren't nice either."

"True enough. It's a bad world."

Bladder put his nose up to Sam's own. Sam patted him. The gargoyle stepped back. "I was just sniffing you. Seeing how you're doing. We gotta go."

"I'm hungry."

"Seriously?"

"And I feel weak."

"There's no chocolate. Best I can do is a can o' cold soup or some crackers. Some twit from another pack got it in his head that we should try them." Bladder gestured to the stack of cans. "Din't have any myself but I heard about the faces what got pulled. Disgusting stuff."

Bladder fetched a can, pulled off the lid, and watched Sam use his fingers to scoop out the contents.

Sam took two mouthfuls, and his stomach stopped protesting.

Bladder stared at the door, his face set into sad cat lines.

"Are you okay?" Sam asked.

"You shouldna fixed it."

Sam's thoughts fogged. He didn't know what Bladder meant until he remembered the beautiful white egg. "I didn't really. It's still badly cracked."

"Maybe that's why it hurts."

"Sorry," Sam said. "What is it?"

"Nothing we talk about. It'll get every gargoyle mashed and pounded. At the mo' the ogres tease us for fun. If they knew we had . . ." Bladder snarled.

Sam remembered the beautiful stone pulsing inside the lion's chest. "Is it a . . . heart?" he whispered.

"Shhhhhh." Bladder turned with alarm to the door. "Don't say it out loud."

"How'd it get broken?"

"I s'pose that's what they do. Hurt to break; hurt to fix." Bladder ignored him and shoved his nose into Sam's soup. "Now eat something, so we can go home."

"I can't, Bladder."

"What? You must be starving."

"I mean I can't go back up yet."

"You can't stay down here; they'll sniff you out like you was some high-quality pâté."

"Pixies stole the family's baby."

"Family? What family?"

Through slurps of soup, Sam explained about the Kavanaghs and the disappearance of Beatrice from inside a toadstool circle.

"Well, that's pixies, that is. You know that?"

Sam eyes prickled, and he blinked back their heat. "I've got to find the baby, Bladder."

Bladder shuffled and revisited the chocolate wrappers lying all over the floor, nosing each one. He peeped at the boy. "You still leaking?" The gargoyle huddled next him. His face softened. "You are a sap, but thanks for coming to get me, Imp."

"My name is Samuel. They call me Sam," Sam said.

"You got named. Well done. Hmmm, Samuel? Not musical, is it? Eat now, Imp. I'll decide when you're well enough to travel. You're all emotional. Not thinking." Bladder watched him. "Come on, shovel in a bit more soup. Eating's supposed to make you pink things feel better."

Bladder stood next to the door and stared out onto the cavern below. Sam could hear sniggers carrying up from the floor and swallowed the last of the soup. It hurt going down. "You leave first, Bladder. No use waiting for me. I'll just have a rest and then I'll go."

The cat shook its mane.

"I'll miss you, Bladder."

"I thought if you ate something then you'd stop saying stupid things."

"If . . . if you could just point out where the pixies' cavern is, before you go. Then I'll be off."

Bladder stared at him and snorted. "You'll be mincemeat

within hours. And who knows if that baby's even alive? It don't take long for humans to give up in The Hole."

"I've got to try."

Bladder groaned. "You know that flying fluffball Daniel can't help us down here. He wouldn't even want to. No souls, no support. We're on our own."

Sam stared.

"Yes, I said 'we.' Wheedle'd kill me if I let you go off by yourself." Bladder grunted. "He's an idiot."

"Bladder, thank you."

"I'll help you if I can, but no more ogres, right?"

"No ogres. Just pixies."

"You are such a pain." Bladder turned his rump to Sam and moved to guard the door. Sam crawled forward, and Bladder put a paw over his mouth, signaling him to be quiet, hush, and they both crept outside. Then they stretched on the ledge, flattening their bellies against the dirt to watch the business of malice continuing way down below at the bottom of the Great Cavern.

The clusters of monsters and imps had grown. Brownies moved faster, if possible. The ogres returned through exits and aimed kicks at the defenseless. A few bogeymen waved their arms around, shrieking like apes.

In the middle of this scene, Thunderguts stood. Tiny as he was from a height, his massive body smothered his throne. He pointed and gestured at pixies and brownies, sending them skidding off on errands.

Sam watched the sea of moldy green and stagnant yellow. Even the touches of red and orange reminded him of blood and clay rather than vivid sunshine.

"Why do you think he wants me?" Sam asked.

"It would have been better if it was just for dinner, but I don't think so. You don't get this busy unless you got plans. An' he's not a blockhead."

"What's a blockhead?"

Bladder smirked. "What you are. Thick as two short planks, Imp." His claw pounded the dust. "If you're stupid enough to want to find this baby, I'm stupid enough to help you. But when we get out, we're never coming back into this dung hole, not even for Hatching Day. Don't think we'll be able to after this. You better take the rest of the cans an' stuff."

"Thank you, Bladder." Sam reached for him, but the gargoyle slapped his hand away.

"You're gonna get me smashed. Again." Below them, the mass of bodies washed over each other. "Come on then. It'll probably get us killed, and I'll hate you forever," Bladder said, but this time he didn't push Sam's hand away when the boy stroked the great cat's mane. "You really don't know anything, do you?"

Sam stared across the cavern at all the holes, big and small, some leading to whole other caverns and corridors to the world outside. Beatrice was hidden inside one of them. He knew that much.

CHAPTER 15

They climbed as high as they could, keeping in the dark of the cavern roof. Few imps had business in the higher regions, so the pair met nothing as they scrambled along. Bladder made Sam rest often, and Sam felt stronger, despite a light-headed giggliness and feeling like every important emotion had been shoved into his feet.

At last they sat on a ledge overlooking the entrance to the Pixie Cavern. A small waterfall ran from the darkness above the cavern and followed the outer curve of the doorway. Sam chewed a cracker.

"You know pixies don't trade in crackers or soup," Bladder said.

"I have chocolate."

"You what? And you never told me?" Bladder glared at him,

then chuckled. "Yeah, I wouldna told me neither. I can't believe I said that." He climbed downward. "Let's get on with it."

Sam put his face into the trickle of water, rinsing away dirt and lapping until his thirst died. Then he followed Bladder into the cavern entrance, clinging to the ceiling above gangs of sweet-faced pixies clambering over each other and up the walls. Bogeymen and brownies mixed with them, and neither Sam nor Bladder wanted to be among the hundreds of swarming creatures.

Minute colored globes lined the tunnel, half of which were broken while the other half flickered and fizzed. Sam touched the end of one, and it burned him.

"Fairy lights," Bladder said.

Sam gulped. "Made of fairies?"

"No, good grief. It's just lights, all right?"

Soon the corridor narrowed, and the fairy lights spread upward to cover the ceiling, forcing Sam and Bladder to drop to the floor. They stood out, being twice the height of most. The few leprechauns rambling about only came to Sam's shoulder. Everything else was knee-high. While a couple of brownies studied them, the rest chatted with friends or nibbled on food clenched in tiny fists.

Sam and Bladder stepped out onto the top of a road, and a small cavern rose overhead.

Fairy lights encircled the door to each burrow. Greater, whiter lights hung like daggers from the edge of each level. Glittering decorations wrapped lamp posts on the walkway. Their yellow light bulbs had been replaced by cheerful pink globes.

Small holes covered the contours of the walls, cramming imp dwelling on top of imp dwelling.

"It's pretty," Sam said. Bladder didn't reply.

Imps sauntered about. A few sat on a bench near a pond. Plastic water lilies covered the surface of its brackish water. Triangular, plastic trees, shoved hard into the ground, surrounded it. More fairy lights twinkled between their fake leaves.

Bogeymen slid around the edges of the cavern, hugging the shadows.

Sam and Bladder stopped on the sidewalk, blocking the route of an annoyed brownie. The imp growled.

"Don't let them see your fear. Keep it down," Bladder said.

"Huh?" Sam followed Bladder's gaze to his shaking hands. He steadied them before taking off his backpack and reaching inside for the chocolate. A few small faces turned and stepped closer at the flash of the purple paper, then with sneaking steps and gathering swiftness, pixies and brownies surged around him, piling out from doorways and shadows.

In moments, Sam couldn't move.

Bladder rammed in front of him and tossed his rock-heavy lion's head. Pixies scattered, leaving them in the center of a tight circle of imps.

"Come on, get on with the questions," Bladder said.

Sam held up the eight ounces of purple-papered sweetness and fat. Pixies, brownies, and other light-fingered imps gawped at it. Many "oohed" as if he'd performed magic.

Teeny hands reached high, but Sam held the chocolate above their heads.

"What do you want for it?" one asked.

A creature in burlap pants and shirt stared him in the eye and edged closer. "What does pigeon want? We can pay in dust."

Sam wanted Beatrice, so who would know where she was? He thought about who Maggie had brought into the kitchen. What distinguished any of them? They all wore brown rags. Then he remembered, "I'm looking for a pixie wearing a bright blue ribbon."

The crowd laughed. Something yelled, "I gotta pink-frilled leprechaun in high heels."

"I know the very pixie you mean. His name is Nutty-Arm," said a greedy-faced pixie, appearing from a burrow at the back of the cavern.

"Keep your voice steady," Bladder said.

"You taking advice from a gargoyle? That's gonna get you in trouble," the pixie said.

A couple of brownies laughed. "You tell him, Billygrabber."

"Scum of the monster world, gargoyles," Billygrabber said. "What you need with Nutty-Arm?"

"I think he might know who stole a baby from a family. I want to know what happened to her. I need to find her."

The word "baby" traveled through the crowd. A few gasped. Many burst into tears. Someone cried out "ash now," while more imps retreated to the safety of dark burrows. Other pixies' faces paled, and they raced toward the exit, throwing longing glances at Sam's raised hands as they left. The remaining crowd thickened and slithered around him. A murmur of voices spread through the crowd: "That's him; he's the one." Frightened pixies watched him from the eaves and wreaths of fairy lights. A few hid behind the artificial trees.

"Leave it, Billygrabber. Not worth your boots if the crone finds out about this." A group of pixies pulled at the pixie, dragging it a few paces.

"No, no," Sam called after it. "What's the crone got to do with Beatrice? Does she want to eat her?" Hunger had been on the crone's face on Hatching Day; maybe she was still hungry. Maybe she'd figured out a way to eat her without the sword knowing.

A groan rose from the crowd, and more of the imps scarpered, this time muttering "crone" and "baby" together. Even Bladder twitched.

Billygrabber chuckled. "Stay there. I'll get Nutty-Arm for you." It dashed off to a cave and returned dragging Nutty-Arm, shoving him in front of Sam.

Nutty-Arm bowed and smiled so much it made Sam ill. The pixie's jacket was the color of mold and the electric-blue ribbon still hung around its neck, a startling color against somber clothes. A snaky smile slid across its face.

"Here he is. You'll give me the chocolate, right?" Billygrabber said.

Sam lowered his arm to head height. It was enough— the imp sprang, clutched it, and ran away with the sweet treat. A few imps, bolder than most, had waited for this, and they squealed and scurried after the chocolate thief, a few blood-cooling squawks echoing from its direction.

Sam and Bladder were left alone with Nutty-Arm and fewer than a dozen others. No longer hidden in the crowd,

Sam recognized them from the Kavanaghs' kitchen: the sprite, brownies, other red-headed pixies, the bogeyman.

"I know you," Sam said. He studied the other pixies, the bogeyman's bland face, then he turned his attention to the three brownies standing with them. "And you. You're the ones who cleaned the dishes." He looked around, remembering the kitchen party. "I can't see the dancing goblin anywhere."

"Don't you worry about him, m'lord," said the tallest of the three.

"He's ash now, isn't he? Sam asked.

The imps' little faces paled.

"Can't be helped. Silly mistake. Anyway, the rest of us is here, and we is all at your service. I'm Cutpurse, and these are my comrades, Angler and Betty." The brownies bowed low.

"I want the baby back," Sam said.

Nutty-Arm tried to grin, but the effort looked painful.

"You know where Beatrice is, don't you?" Sam looked at Bladder. The gargoyle waved its paw in a "go on" motion. "Maggie told you not to. She told you she was mine."

"I know, I know." Nutty-Arm winked at him. "You're right—it was wrong. I'm sure I'll get my butt smacked."

A few titters rose from the group.

"Please, just tell me where she is, and let me take her home," Sam asked.

"He said 'please' to me," Nutty-Arm said. Its face pinked in pleasure. "Like I was a troll or an ogre."

"Nutty-Arm ain't got the baby no more," the bogeyman said. "There's consequences for baby-napping, even if you ain't the baby-napper. We ditched it."

"Shut it, Bogweed!" Cutpurse ordered the bogeyman, slapping its face.

Bogweed mouthed insults at the back of Cutpurse's head.

"Can you tell me where she is?" Sam asked. Bladder growled at Nutty-Arm. The pixie hissed in return.

"Well . . ." Angler started. "Don't do no harm to help, and Maggie did say it were his."

"Don't *do no harm to help*?" Bladder repeated. "Imp, pixies ain't—"

"That's right, she might still be alive," cut in Cutpurse. "An' if she is, maybe sending her back upside means the souls got no beef wivvus."

"Imp," Bladder said. "A word, Imp."

"Shut it, you fossilized dinosaur dropping," Angler said.

Bladder roared. Nutty-Arm's eyes widened.

"Let's go, Imp."

"But they just said they'd take me to Beatrice," Sam said.

Bladder screwed up his face. "Maybe they did, but I know I hate this many pixies in one place, an' I smell lies. Something's not right here. Pixies ain't this helpful."

"But we might be able to get her before something eats her," Nutty-Arm said, smiling.

"You're not usin' your noggin', Imp," Bladder said to Sam. "You ask a few questions of the pixie an' they act all nice. But these creeps run with a banshee. That makes 'em more dangerous than the normal kind."

"You're probably right." Sam poked his sore hand. "But I've got to find Beatrice."

Bladder's voice softened. "An' they ain't makin' any

demands. Since when have you heard of a pixie not hagglin'? Whatever's happenin' here smells off." Bladder put a claw to Sam's chest, then turned away. "Let's just leave."

Cutpurse leaped forward. "No, no, no, we do want one thing."

Bladder turned back. "That's more like it. Gold. Mounds of white chocolate?"

"We'll show you if you don't tell no one about this," Angler said. "If Thunderguts hears we've . . . well, there's consequences to baby-napping."

The pack of pixies and brownies nodded their innocent-looking heads, muttering in agreement.

"An' maybe if you had any more chocolate . . ." Bogweed started.

Bladder pushed in front. "He's already paying you in silence. An' I'm not going to hurt Nutty-Arm, no matter how much I'd like to."

Cutpurse eyeballed Sam. The face was cheery and round, a friendly face, but his eyes remained cold and stony, as dark as his hair, and light did not reflect in them. Sam wished the brownie would stop staring.

"Could you show me where you took her?" Sam asked.

"If you're happy to keep silent about our involvement in the incident, then we are happy to reunite you with your tot, all right?" Cutpurse said.

Sam nodded.

CHAPTER 16

The imps led the way out of the main tunnel. As they walked back up the slope, Cutpurse clicked his fingers and a brownie ran forward with a pungent, flaming torch. They passed two small goblins, who stared at the group with wide eyes. The pair dashed off into the dark.

Sam's group had walked a long way when Angler turned into a side passage. It was so dark it looked like part of the wall and, once inside, the greedy blackness licked at the torch flames. Sam shuddered. The sparks gave off a dim light, illuminating little ahead. Even the walls were too far away to be seen.

As they walked, the pixies giggled and Cutpurse often stared back at Sam and Bladder and gave cute waves. Bladder made Sam hang back a safe distance.

Sam studied the cave roof. "How old are you, Bladder?"

"Around eight hundred years or so. Give or take a decade."

"That's very old. Will I get that old?"

"Who knows, Imp? I've known pixies and brownies last many, many centuries. You're as pink as they are."

"What about humans?"

"Nope, they're weak and sappy creatures and don't like to let each other live long. Or anything else, for that matter."

"I don't understand."

"Gargoyles live upstairs most of the time, right? We survive humans if we're careful, but they destroy buildings with big machines. These days at least they pick and choose with their bulldozers, but I remember the Blitz. Wheedle's only a coupla hundred years old, a bit young and gormless, but the Blitz made him even harder."

"What's the Blitz?"

"War. One of the big ones. Humans loved it. They dropped bombs all over London. We didn't stay at the cathedral then. Daniel moved us down to Brighton, the busybody said it was to keep us safe. But it was too late, we'd seen the destruction. We'd seen what his precious humans was like. Heavy boulders dropping out of the sky. Beautiful buildings, ugly buildings, cathedrals covered with families of gargoyles. All of this done so humans could hurt each other. Death means nothing to them. They're all the same, Imp. Every single one of 'em. Don't become them." Bladder patted Sam's arm.

"Families? You said 'families of gargoyles.'"

"Did not." Bladder shook his head at Sam's gaze. "No, I didn't! I said 'packs.'"

Sam continued. "I don't think the Kavanaghs are like those humans. They care about each other, and Grandpa Kavanagh's death meant something. When Beatrice got taken they were . . ." He struggled for the word. ". . . Devastated."

Bladder turned his head away and didn't answer. Sam reached out a hand to pat Bladder's ruff. The stone felt warm.

The tunnel grew snug, and the brownies turned to offer sly smiles. Bladder sneered at the swaggering imps.

"Not far to go now," Betty said.

"Don't talk to us," Bladder replied. "Just keep walking."

Sam and Bladder halted, and Sam pulled his backpack around to rummage. He found the other bar of chocolate, ripped open the wrapper and put three squares in his mouth. The instant energy woke him. Bladder stared up at him, and Sam dropped two rows into the gargoyle's mouth.

"Hey, look at that. Cuban heels." The gargoyle sniggered.

Sam looked ahead to see Betty and Angler in the flickering glow; each wore thick-soled boots adding inches to their heights. The cloistered tunnel of dirt muffled the clicking. Sam's own footsteps were swallowed entirely.

Cutpurse's eyes shone in the torch. "It's not long now, is it, Nutty-Arm? A few hundred more paces and we'll be there."

Sam smelled the stink of wet dust and of something long abandoned. He trudged on.

Angler and Betty slid back to walk beside Sam. "Why do you want this one baby so much?" asked Betty.

"So I can take her home."

"Don't tell them that," Bladder said.

The brownies looked at each other. Angler spoke first. "I don't understand. Why'd you need to take her..." The brownie stumbled over the word. "...Home? You could play with her here."

"Because she matters to the Kavanaghs. To her family."

Betty frowned. "Why's that matter to you?"

"Because..." Sam stopped. "I want them to be happy."

All the imps peered at him, and Cutpurse laughed. Even in the barren place his snickers filled the dark.

"Is he addled by his time with them, do you think?" Cutpurse asked Betty. "Humans are awful."

"I told you not to talk to us," Bladder said, then looked to Sam. "But he is right."

"Exactly," said Betty.

"Exactly," said Angler.

"Who cares what makes them happy?" Bladder asked.

"They're nastier than they appear on the surface," said Cutpurse. "They need to be culled like feral animals."

"Stop it!" Sam said. "Stop it, all of you."

The imps smirked.

Betty whispered, "He's even odder than he looks."

"Come on then—just down here," Cutpurse said.

The group walked on. Nutty-Arm was shivering.

The tunnel mouth opened onto an old, empty cavern—a ghost town with hollows leering down on them. A few lights here and there shone with a reddish tint.

"What used to live here?" Sam asked. The dirt echoed with his question.

"Succubi and incubi," Bogweed said.

"Were they horrible?" Sam found himself whispering. Cold soaked into his back and bones.

"They sucked souls from humans."

Sam shuddered. "It's an awful place then?"

"If I had a soul, it might be," Bogweed replied.

Angler and Betty tittered.

The place looked a little like the Pixie Cavern, though most of the lamps were broken, and those giving light had a tinge of red to them, like blood mixed into the yellow miasma. The walls climbed rough and earthy, and the dome above rose so high the light could not pick out where the roof finished. This place felt dead.

Sam stared up into the darkness and imagined the incubi and succubi's dead eyes boring into him.

"Why did you bring Beatrice here?"

Cutpurse pointed ahead. A dead well sat in the middle of the cavern, a dark-bricked thing. The canopy had rotted away, although its skeleton remained. The wood may have been ebony; it was dark to the core.

"Nothin' comes here anymore, not even ogres. Right, Nutty-Arm?" Cutpurse said.

"That's right."

Sam stared at the pixie. A wide smirk stretched across Nutty-Arm's face.

"How could you put her down that awful dark place?" Sam said. Even Bladder shuffled away. Sam's voice sounded as cold and dead as the cavern.

"Is his little lordship, Sir Ogres' Nip, unhappy? I am truly sorry." Nutty-Arm bowed. "What can we do to make amends?"

Sam took a few steps toward the well and peered into the blackness. He heard Bladder behind him.

"Imp! There's something goin' on here. I knew I shoulda trusted my instincts. They've been all too helpful. Come on. It's not worth it," the gargoyle begged.

Sam turned and glared at Bladder. "Beatrice is not worth it? Well, maybe you're not worth it either. Why are you even here? You don't consider me part of your pack."

The mixed monsters cackled between the gargoyle and the boy.

"Watch them, Imp," Bladder said. The gargoyle growled as Cutpurse, Angler, and Bogweed stepped closer. The trio encircled the gargoyle, and picked up stones and began chipping at his mane with them. "Imp! Pay attention!"

"Just . . . leave me alone, Bladder." Sam strained to make out any movement at the bottom of the hole. "How far down does the monster live?" Sam asked Nutty-Arm.

"I'm sure it's not far, just lean in and have a look." The tiny pixie shook its sweet curls.

"Beatrice?" Sam called down the hole.

Bladder screamed as Angler and Betty pushed Sam over the wall and into the well.

CHAPTER 17

The blackness swallowed him, blinding his gargoyle eyes. He could have been floating; no wind blew up to create friction. It was only when he reached out and smacked into the wall and the force threw him back against the opposite side that he developed a sense of dropping. He put out one hand. It grazed the wall at high velocity, and he howled. It slowed him a little, and even as he screamed, he put out his other hand. His palms burned, and his face hit bricks as he dragged down the walls. He stopped, dangling in rough darkness, yelling at the pain. His voice drained down into the space below.

He had no idea how far he had fallen.

If Beatrice had hit the bottom, she would have died.

"I'll take you home, Beatrice." He felt the words vibrate in his throat, but they slurped away before he heard them.

His back ached under the weight of his bag. The stones pinched and pricked at his raw hands. It gave him something to feel, so he focused on climbing and his steady heartbeat, at the rhythm inside his head.

"Beatrice?" The darkness gobbled his words.

Sam had no idea how long he climbed down. His legs shook by the time he touched the bottom, and his hands had gone beyond pain into numbness. He couldn't move his fingers, and his thumbs were stiff and sore. He dropped to the ground, wanting to sleep but, as tired as his arms and legs were, he scrambled around, sniffing for Beatrice.

No sign of her; no sign of anything. He touched the rounded wall to where the base of the well opened into another tunnel, feeling its low-slung roof against the backs of his hands.

Sam stooped and crawled inside, his backpack scraping the dirt above. He pressed from wall to wall.

He sat down alone in the darkness, leaning against blackness, his chest rising and falling, the sound of his breath darting away down the unexplored part of the tunnel. He closed his eyes. Beatrice was not here. What was he supposed to do?

Sam imagined Michelle's eyes the color of plums with crying. Sam thought of Richard when he last saw him, his waving arms and feverish nods as he talked to the police officer.

He wondered what they said after he left. "Yes, officer, it'll be that boy's fault. We don't even know his real name. He helped someone take our baby. Then he tricked Michelle into taking him to town, the one person who would have protected her."

Sam's chest ached. What else could they think of him? He arrived, Beatrice disappeared and he followed soon after. They must hate him.

Bladder must hate him too. Sam remembered hours ago, days ago maybe, the last thing he'd said to Bladder had been cold and unfriendly. Sam's only friend, who'd tried to warn him. And he'd left the gargoyle with those vile pixies. Sam hoped he'd got away. Maybe Bladder would think Sam had behaved too human and be glad he was gone; he wouldn't have to bother with the annoying little imp anymore.

He wailed, and his wail sucked away as dirt and dust from the tunnel roof pattered onto him. Silence smothered everything. When he didn't have the energy to cry, he held himself and his raw hands. And wondered about the absolute emptiness.

Maybe there was a reason for it. *Maybe I am dead,* he thought. *The pixies pushed me into the well, and I died. I wouldn't know, of course. I don't know what happens when you die. My hands hurt, and my shoulders are sore, but other than that it feels the same as before. Maybe this is how death feels.*

He wasn't cold. Sam didn't know if the dead could hear their own thoughts. Maybe you sat where you were until someone came along to tell you that you were dead. If he slept, he might be asleep when they came. He could wait a hundred years and miss the one person who passed.

Sam found comfort in the idea of being dead. He didn't have to do a thing. Nothing could hurt him, he was no use to the ogres, and he would never have to find out if the Kavanaghs hated him. Maybe if someone told them he'd died they would be a bit sorry about it and not angry anymore. They would hold a wake for him.

Sam's sigh danced off. It was an awful place to be dead though. It would be nicer to be dead somewhere with sunshine.

Whatever I do, I can't just sit here, he thought.

"All I want is Beatrice," Sam said. The words escaped before he heard them.

He crept on. It became a tight squeeze pulling himself and his backpack through the tunnel, the ceiling above pressing down on him until he slid along on his belly. If it got any closer he would be stuck, or maybe he'd be forced to retreat and climb back to the succubi's cavern.

He pulled himself forward and realized something had changed: his arms felt space, his pack sprang free soundlessly, and he could slide his legs out of the tight area he had thought would be his silent, lightless grave.

Sam stretched his arms, feeling his shoulders and elbows crack. He stood and extended his back, reaching his hands up to loosen every squashed and distorted muscle. Did dead imps ache? He contemplated the idea. The relief was the first pleasure he'd felt since the fall.

The windless, soundless, dark space gave him no sense of his surroundings. He put his arms forward, lengthened his spasming muscles and stepped out.

His joints jolted as he fell forward into nothing but air.

His scream slithered away into black space. He dashed downward; his body hit three times and smashed against a ledge as he plummeted. His heart thrummed like a squirrel's.

Sam's bag padded his fall, but the contents shifted and pulled him sideways, and he rolled into the walls of a new cavern.

In the absolute darkness, explosions of light and pain fired behind his eyes.

When the sparks subsided, Sam looked around.

The darkness was complete. The silence too. Only the smell of old bones and dead things gave him any sense of this cavern.

A bony hand clamped over his mouth.

"Found him," hissed a haggish voice. Despite its grating quality, his ears were hungry for sound. Light stung his eyes, and he cried out.

Fingers clutched at his legs and arms. A hand muffled his screams.

"Hush, fool boy," a voice said. "And stop wriggling. It no use; we no muscle to harm; we just hair, eye, tooth. You can't fight."

The speaker lobbed Sam into the air above its head. A second pair of hands caught him and forced his hands behind his back. Sam felt groggy and dizzy, but his head didn't hurt as much as his shoulder. He stopped struggling as strong finger bones manacled his arms and legs.

Snarking giggles cradled him. The smell of ash seasoned the air; somewhere a fire died.

His kidnappers bore him along at a lolloping speed.

They entered a burrow that stank of sweat and old food. A strange fire was dying in the center of the cave. After such absolute darkness, everything shone in the morsel of light. Red, gold, and molten blue.

One of the creatures clutched him from behind, while the other darted about in a tangle of limbs in front of him. She was a bony hag with sunken eyes and skin like gnarled wood. She had hair as white as ash, and Sam was sure he saw a mouth on the crown of her head spitting out hair, puffing and pfaffing as the strands tumbled back and caught in its yellow teeth. She threw a cord at Sam's unseen captor, then piled kindling on the fire, which cracked like thin bones as the flames caressed it.

The light flickered in the lanky hag's face, and she knelt and blew on the fire. A flare licked the other twigs. Sam thought it roared like a crowd, laughing as a thin voice called out from the fire, dark and lonely. White sticks snapped as the flames twisted.

"Fuel," said the fire maker, and ran to find more bones to keep it going. The bones she dragged back were huge—heavy and white and thick. *Even bigger than an ogre's would be*, Sam thought.

Sam's captor wrenched off his backpack, and he could hear rummaging; then a claw reached around and tied the rough cord around his ankle.

Sam wriggled harder and yelled out.

"No one hear you, lad," his captor said. "The dragon-fire draws every sound and light and traps it down here. We hear you hours back."

Sam's voice shook as he asked, "What's dragon-fire?"

"Fire from dragon bone, of course." The voice behind him tutted as the lanky hag shoved a bone into the heart of the fire. "Long, long ago some crawl here to die in cave; leave skeletons full of dragon dreams. A dragon is greedy thing, boy. Even its bones long for song and sky and gold. Dragon magic draws all precious to it. All sound and all light it draw. Even down here in dark."

She pulled at Sam, wrenching his shoulder, whacking his head as the lanky hag took the rest of the cord from his captor and tied his wrists and ankles together.

Disturbed voices came from the fire. Ogre yells, pixie screams, the lost call of someone wandering in the dark. The flicker of flames formed a face for a moment, then faded as the bone beneath it cackled.

His captor shuffled forward and grabbed at a thin stick living in front of Sam's foot, and now at last he could see her. She looked more dry and shrunken than the other witch, shorter than him. And she had chicken legs.

"My name Baba Yaga. You hear of me?"

Sam shook his head.

"Bah! Thunderguts, he not breathe my story!" She glared at the other. "What we do with boy, Yama-Uba?"

A lipless, too-wide grin spread across the lanky hag's face. "Stew?"

Yama-Uba ran off to the back of the cave and lugged a huge black pot toward the fire. Sam looked at his cord. It was a combination of different hairs plaited together to form one long rope. Silky blond hair, frizzy brown hair that irritated his wrists, and a lot of red hair. Pixie, he guessed.

"She say 'no', remember?" Baba Yaga said.

Yama-Uba dropped the pot. A flood of black water washed over its lip and darkened the earth beneath it. "Bah!"

"Who said 'no'?" Sam asked.

Baba Yaga smirked and sucked on a small, white bone.

"She get pixies to pretend send us baby so you come. Trap you here. Baby never here." Yama-Uba licked her lips. "Would be sweet."

Baba Yaga peered at Sam. "You know *who*."

Sam's headache returned, his shoulder throbbed. He groaned and pulled his knees to his chest, making himself as small as possible. He shivered, the fire incapable of warming the cold in him. "The crone?"

Baba Yaga laughed. "O, Moya Solnishka! Dah! Yes!"

Yama-Uba sniffed at Sam, then turned to Yaga. "We not eat? You sure she say? It is the more nice taste. I am hungry."

Baba Yaga swung her heavy head. "You see what she do with one who disobey? You think she any less slice you? She queen of everywhere. She know everything."

"Bah!"

The fire spat and dimmed. Yama-Uba rummaged through the sticks and bric-a-brac at the back of the cave. She came to the fire, and the flames reached toward her. She laughed and the sound broke into sparkles over the flames. Her cackling sent rainbow-colored smoke curling from the cave entrance out into the wider cavern.

"Hate coloredy smoke," Baba Yaga said.

Sam sat up, pushing his wrists and ankles together. The cord didn't loosen. He looked at the small bone between Yaga's lips. "You haven't eaten a baby recently?" He watched Baba Yaga's face, expecting a cruel laugh.

"Baby? Not stupid me. No. Ash too much for baby. Sometimes I think we too far down in dark for notice, so am tempted, but, hmmmm ... risky."

Yaga and Yama screeched and giggled.

Sam sat up, pushing his wrists and ankles together. The cord didn't loosen.

Sam rocked himself. His eyes filled with tears, but there was a chance. He was trapped but alive. Beatrice might be alive too. He sniffed to check if they were lying and could find no trace of human or fresh air anywhere. She'd never been in this horrible place.

"Oh, more cry? We hear blub-blub as you come through tunnel and blub-blub as you fall. Enough already!"

Sam snorted back his tears.

Yama licked her lips and smiled at him again.

"Why does she want me?"

Baba Yaga crunched her bone. "She come before and say Great Cavern want boy. When he fall here, we not to eat."

"Maybe this one's not the one she want," Yama-Uba said, then sat up. "He little monster-u, but look like he taste like boy." She waved her arms around the cave roof, gesturing at nothing. "We have plenty salt."

"How many boy-monster you think in Hole, Yama? Huh?"

"Maybe we eat you, maybe no." Yama touched Sam's leg. The tip of her tongue stuck out of the side of her mouth.

Yaga flicked Yama's hand away with a pointed nail.

Yama-Uba plopped on the floor, her stick legs in front of her. She thrust out her bottom lip. The long tongue from her crown surprised Sam as it poked from Yama's head and licked the air. Yama crossed her arms and stared at Sam. He wondered if she knew she was drooling.

Then both hags seemed to tire of him. Yama-Uba threw another large bone onto the fire. It ignited and flared blue.

She turned and joined Baba Yaga at the doorway.

Sam knew he had to get away before the crone arrived. He shuffled closer and let the fire warm him. His cords hurt as he studied the hearth. There were stones, some round and curving but a few sharp and nasty. Just what he needed.

Baba Yaga watched him, her eyes flickering as she nestled in the doorway wall.

"No escape for you, lamb chop," she said.

Sam curled around and rubbed the cord against a toothy rock. The strands of hair broke easily, but there were thousands of them to get through. He pushed toward the fire, hoping to break more, but the flames gave out a gentle warmth, making him sleepy. He was so tired.

He thought of Beatrice. He wished he knew she was all right.

The fire breathed. A soft, gentle breath, like a sleeping baby. An image flickered there.

"How long will she sleep?" Thunderguts's voice asked from the flames.

"As long as the siren's song holds," Snide's voice replied.

"Good. Every time she wailed, I drooled. It's dangerous having one so close."

Sam stared at the fire, a golden-red baby flashed there, her face mucky with dirt and her eyelashes moved by pleasant dreams.

Sam yelped and fell back. He had been thinking of Beatrice and she had appeared in the flames.

What had Yaga said? *Dragon-fire pulls all precious things toward itself.*

The most precious things to him were the Kavanaghs.

The heat scorched him and licked toward him, leaching secret treasures from his heart and showing them in flames. Michelle's sudden face bloomed in the yellow tongues, just as he'd imagined her, her eyes swollen and fire red.

"Our baby's gone," she told Richard.

Then the red tongues exploded into a single huge face: Great-Aunt Colleen. Her orange eyes turned blindly toward Sam. "Who's looking at us? Who's out there? Is that you, boy?"

The dragon-fire ate the image, and the old lady was gone. Sam sobbed on the cord biting into his wrists. Beatrice was fine, but he'd not just heard and seen, he'd hurt too.

Baba Yaga snored in the entryway.

The dragon bones cracked, and the fire licked them, subdued and shrinking.

Sam returned to scraping at the tear-wet hair with the stone. He needed to get far from the cave. Beatrice waited for him.

Yama got up, and Sam rolled over onto his elbows and knees, his face on a smooth boulder, so she couldn't see how far he had got through his restraints. He tried not to think, and he didn't look into the fire. "Not toast boy." She dragged him back from the fire by his waist, his face scraping on a rock before she dropped him into the dirt. "Maybe when the crone get what she need, we can stew. Be many patient."

Sam's mouth had filled with mud, but at his eye level, so close it should have stuck and blinded him, was a charred piece of bone. It looked as sharp as the shard from Bladder's leg. He wriggled around to it, watching Yama-Uba busy herself at the fire, licking her slobbery lips.

Yama threw another dragon bone onto the fire, casting light into the whole cave and illuminating a stack of tiny pixie skulls decorating one wall. She sniffed him, her tongue slithered out, and she licked the side of his face. Then she scuttled off to a dark corner, returned with pots of salt and some herbs, and sprinkled a handful of each into his hair.

"In case . . . ," she said.

She returned to the darkness and Sam knew he didn't have much time. He shuffled closer to the bone fragment and twisted it in his fingers until its jagged side rubbed at the cord. Crack, crack, crack. Hair after hair fell away. He moved the bone up and down in the space between his knees, breaking a few more hairs each time.

Yama rattled something metal, and Sam heard a soft "shick shick shick" of something cutting again and again through a solid lump. Yama hustled back and threw onion pieces on his back.

The fire spluttered the noise of sure footsteps.

"She here now," Baba Yaga said from the entryway. "That her." Yama screamed, and Sam almost cried aloud, but he continued wearing down his rope.

He heard the steps and turned to look.

Maggie's face peered in the doorway.

198

"Maggie! Maggie!" Sam called. It wasn't a face he'd hoped for, but it also wasn't one he'd feared. He laughed. "Maggie! Thank goodness. You have to help me!"

Maggie handed Baba Yaga the bone torch she was holding and entered. She carried a burlap sack over her shoulder. An animal writhed inside, the bag muffling its complaints as she dropped it.

"And happy I am to see you too," Maggie said. A grin lit her beautiful face.

"They said the crone was coming."

"Did you tell him that?" Maggie glared at Yaga and Yama.

Baba shook her head and hugged her arms. "Yama say 'you know who' and he yell 'Crone.'"

Yama squealed and glared at Yaga.

"He's a bit too clever for words, isn't he?"

"I have to get away before the crone comes," Sam said. "I think she's been hunting me since I was hatched."

"That she has." Maggie smiled and pulled her hand toward her, as if dragging dark air into her chest. She shrank a little, her face dried, and the color in her red hair leached from the tips and deepened at the roots until they turned a blood-red so dark they could have been black. Even her clothes decayed and frayed to rags in the same moments. Her dazzling green eyes simply faded.

The crone was as emaciated as the first two, but while the others hunched and scrambled in the dirt, she stood tall.

"Samuel," she said. "I would say that this is a pleasant surprise, but you are easily led. It's a shame you had to go and make me set a trap for you in the first place."

"You're the crone? The one who tried to catch me on Hatching Day?" Sam said.

"I hate being called that. It's so impersonal." The crone came closer, bending over with an aged groan to stare into his face. "Oh, Samuel. I never meant you harm, in either form."

Sam studied the creature. It was hard to see with his chin in dust. She held herself with regal arrogance: her grayed head and her hands, although clenched in painful talons, moved with grace. Her voice, though croaky and aged, was still Maggie's. Her eyes were pure hunger.

"She eat you," Yama-Uba said.

"Yama, remember your place." Baba Yaga kicked Yama-Uba's leg.

"Aach!" Yama-Uba groveled in the dirt. "We eat?" she begged of the crone.

"I'm sorry, my darlin', not this one," Maggie said.

Drool hung on Yama and Yaga's bottom lips, but they both nodded. Yaga sneered at Sam, waving him away before hobbling to a corner. She pointed her hairy backside at him and pulled a brown animal skin around her shoulders.

"Don't be like that, darlin' sister. I've brought you something else." Maggie kicked at the sack on the ground, and the contents groaned.

Yaga scuttled over to undo the rope at the sack's neck and felt inside; the bag howled, and she pulled out a bright blue ribbon. "It pixie. Maybe not as delicious as real boy, but do."

Maggie laughed. "I'm in a good mood today. Don't be so worried, ladies. When he..." She pointed at Sam. "... Does right by us, there'll be babies for everyone."

Yama-Uba cheered and ran to get a cooking pot. "Pixie do till then."

The bag squirmed and squealed.

"Let's go outside, Sam."

Maggie pushed her hand deep into the dragon-fire. She didn't scream as it licked over her arm, and she pulled out a brightly flaming dragon bone. Then she picked up Sam by the shirt and carried him out of the cave.

As he spun in her hand, light as a fairy, Sam watched the dragon-fire illuminate the ceiling. He saw Yaga hit the bag with a heavy frying pan; it grunted and stopped wriggling.

Outside, Maggie put Sam onto a rock. As soon as she set him in place, he pushed his wrists between his knees so the breaking cord didn't show. She reached out a clawed hand and smeared dirt around his face.

"I'm amazed Yaga knew you for a boy. I've not seen one so grimy and gritty in centuries. You could have stepped right out of the Dark Ages, Sam. Is that not a lovely thought?"

"Maggie, why do you look like this?" Sam asked.

The crone stared down at her rag dress. "It's my true form, and for centuries I have preferred it. Pretty is not anything a creature down here wants to be. You see how put upon the pixies and brownies are, and they're little more than cute. The glamour I keep for the humans. They like pretty things."

Sam wished he could think of more questions to ask her so that he could work at his cords. A few moments more, that's all he needed.

The cavern looked empty, but sounds of a nearby skirmish

flickered from Maggie's dragon-fire torch and something that could have been a voice calling his name.

"What's that noise? It sounds near," he said.

"Ogres squabbling, I expect. Thunderguts has commanded every Great Monster in The Hole to gather in the Ogres' Cavern. Ogres, trolls, goblins—every man jack of them is making their way there. And Baba Yaga loves chaos above all things, so the sound of all those monsters moving has been drawn to her dragon-fire. Dragon-fire draws the heart's desire. If you yearned for the sound of hummingbird wings, they would echo through these flames as loud as drums." Maggie turned and stared at Sam's face. "Now, it's time to stop this tomfoolery. I brought you down here so you could under-stand our plans. You forced me into trickery, you know, because I couldn't drag you away from your toys up there. So I brought your most precious toy down into The Hole."

"My toy? You mean Beatrice?" Sam stared at Maggie. "It was you who had Beatrice stolen?"

"Of course it was, Samuel. Nutty-Arm played his part well enough—his only role was to trick you into the well, where you could not escape. He wasn't supposed to have you pushed down, though. That was bad of him. You could have been hurt. I don't want you hurt. Don't worry. He'll make a fine snack for my sisters."

Sam went cold. Maggie had tricked him, and she probably had more tricks to come. He felt his cords; thinner, but not thin enough. Maggie wasn't his friend, and she wouldn't help him. He'd have to escape by himself.

He wished he had one friend.

"Sam? Sam?" a voice called from the dragon-fire.

Sam wondered who it could be. Maybe it was Daniel wandering about way up there under a light-filled sky. He ached for a real friend, and the fire had sent him a real friend's voice.

Maggie frowned at the flames.

"What does Thunderguts want with me?" Sam asked.

The crone turned, and Sam saw the contours of her cheekbones and her clear jawline. Even without her glamour he could see hints of the young Maggie. "We're his pack, you and me, and he has a plan. You have a much greater destiny than playing with humans. We've been waiting for a creature like you for centuries. You belong with us, Sam. Come and see for yourself. Your little Beatrice is waiting there for you, too, Sam." Maggie patted his leg. "All snuggly and safe. So no more of your tantrums and silliness. Your king wishes to see you. You're a special breed, Samuel, but he gets impatient with your delays."

Sam nodded as the stone broke more hairs. Of course the king wanted him, either to eat or to figure out how to make more like him. He kept his movements so tiny she didn't notice. Break. Crack. Break. The hairs came apart in twos and threes.

"If I come with you, will you take Beatrice back to her family?"

Maggie's answer was not an answer. "I know you have a soft spot for Kavanaghs, little prince, I'm the same myself. I've mourned for them so long, and I understand how a capricious imp could grow too fond of one or two toys." She tweaked his cheek, just under the eye. It hurt, and a tear leaked out. "But enough now." Maggie put a taloned hand on his shoulder. "Let's set the world to rights, shall we?"

The voice from the torch called "Sam" once more. For all Sam knew, the speaker was a thousand miles away, flying in a sunlit sky.

"You have a great destiny, Samuel . . ."

A stone missile hit Maggie square in the head and shoulders. The rock was almost as big as the crone herself. She crumpled under its weight and lay still.

"Bladder!" Sam yelled at the uncoiling stone cat.

"You okay, Imp?"

Sam rubbed his shoulder and head. "I'm good now!"

"Let's get you out of here." Bladder's eyes widened at Maggie lying on the ground moaning and the hags bustling inside the cave. "They planning to eat you?"

Samuel rubbed sharp bone against the cord, splitting more hairs. Maggie groaned under the gargoyle.

"They've all been working for Thunderguts. The crone too."

"That's the crone? Well, I'm rubble. She's his oldest ally."

"So much noise out here. What happen?" Yaga yelled from the cave door. The bony beast scuttled forward on all fours to stare at Maggie lying flat on the ground. "She dead?" She pondered the crone's still form, fixed her eyes on Sam, and licked her lips. The old hag rushed back into the cave. Sam heard a pixie scream.

"Come on!" Bladder said.

"Gotta get untied." Sam bent double and jumped to get the bone, furiously rubbing at long strands of hair. "I won't be going anywhere like this."

Baba Yaga came crashing out of the cave with Yama-Uba at her side. Yama carried the frying pan, and Yaga had a fiery dragon's bone in her hand. Yama strode straight for Sam, drool wetting the front of her ragged dress.

Bladder leaped, his stone body clanged against the frying pan, and Yama dropped it. Sam desperately broke hairs.

Baba Yaga turned on Sam, and Bladder jumped between them.

"Here, Kitty, does kitty like fire?" Baba Yaga cackled as the torch crackled.

Bladder laughed. "Seriously? Kitty's made of stone and don't care one way or the other."

Bladder opened his jaws wide, clamping down on the burning end of the torch. Flames flickered from his mouth into his mane, turning it into a golden halo.

Sam rubbed the cord against the bone. Friction burned his sore fingers but chewed through the hair rope.

"'Urry uk!" Bladder said around a mouthful of fire.

Bladder whacked Baba Yaga around the head and knees with the unlit end of the torch. His mouth glowed red. Yaga screeched at him, her lanky arms whipping around to protect her face and chicken legs.

Sam heard the victorious snap as the last of the threads frayed away, and he cheered as the rope uncoiled from his wrists and loosened at his ankles.

Sprinting, Nutty-Arm fled the cave, soaked and smelling like soup stock. A piece of cabbage covered half his face. He slipped toward the cavern edge, away from the fighting.

Bladder choked as he poked and hit at the furious hag, but his eyes widened as he looked to Sam's left. Sam caught the movement too. Yama was crawling toward him, her claw clutching the frying pan.

Sam scuttled back and flung himself to his feet. He ran past Bladder and shoved a solid fist into Yaga's chest. They both leaped over Maggie, who still lay in the dirt like a corpse. Yaga took a few steps sideways. Yama collided with her, and they collapsed in a clatter of limbs.

"Un! Un!" Bladder's words were still muffled around the burning torch. Sam grabbed the white end of the dragon bone and pulled it from the gargoyle's mouth. Bladder spat as they sprinted from the hags. Their steps were echoed by a patter of tiny feet.

Sam looked over his shoulder. Yama and Yaga were two shadows in the distance. Maggie lifted her head, and Yama screamed.

CHAPTER 18

Sam scanned the scene behind him. He couldn't see the hag's cave, and their dragon-fire had vanished. He thought they could risk a rest. As he sat, his body reminded him he had a sore shoulder.

"It's that sleep stuff, is it?" Bladder asked.

Sam would have liked to sleep, but since he'd seen Beatrice's face in the fire, all he wanted to do was to get to her. He tried to stand, but his wobbly legs mutinied. "I could rest for a bit," he replied.

Bladder grunted and sat.

Sam hugged the hard shape next to him.

"Ooph!" Bladder said. "What you doin'?"

Sam let go of him. "I can't believe you came for me. I

thought you'd leave to find Wheedle and Spigot. I've caused you so much trouble."

"They're all right. It's us down here that needs help. Especially you, the runt of the litter."

"I was mean to you. I said . . ."

"What, you? Don't be ridiculous! Wheedle says ruder things to me before sunup each morning." Bladder laughed and shook his mane. "But you made me owe you, see? I'm paying a debt. And like Wheedle always says, pack looks after pack. They stick together. You don't drop someone because he's a bit stupid. Especially if he risks himself putting you back together."

"Well, I'm sorry." Sam squeezed him.

Bladder purred for a while before shaking him loose. "That bogeyman, whatzisname? Bogweed, tried to pick me up and throw me after you, an' I broke his toe when he dropped me. Then I chewed on the big brownie—I took a chunk out of his leg and ripped his jacket, caused a lotta howling." Bladder chuckled. "Must've shocked 'em to see me go in the well by myself. I knew the fall wouldna kill'd ya, but had I known how far down it was, I might've thought twice." Bladder stared at the dragon-fire. "When you weren't at the bottom I knew you was alive, so I kept on coming."

"You called my name?"

"Course I did. Who were you expecting?" Bladder harrumphed. "The flying fidget? Sorry to disappoint you."

"It's just you've never used my name before."

"Yes, I have. I remember it felt weird. I'm hardly going to call 'Imp, Imp' down here, am I? Everybody would answer. Now stop talking. You obviously can't talk after a walk."

"I'll be all right. You're here." Sam wanted to laugh. "How did you find me? You couldn't have heard or seen anything."

"Sense of smell, Imp, you really do stink."

Sam chuckled so hard his shoulder and head hurt again.

Bladder turned and spoke to the darkness, "You don't have to sneak around over there. We could hear you even if we didn't have dragon-fire."

"Are you going to eat me, good sirs?" Nutty-Arm asked.

"No," Sam said. Bladder made a disappointed face at him.

"Why not?" the pixie asked.

It was a sensible question; everyone else wanted to eat him.

"I don't like the taste of pixie," Sam replied.

This seemed to reassure Nutty-Arm, and he stepped into the light. When no one jumped to eat him, he trotted closer to the flame, plopped down, and warmed himself. Despite Sam's reassurances that he wouldn't eat the pixie, the drying herbs and vegetables on his clothes did make Nutty-Arm smell tasty.

"Will they come after us, do you think?" Bladder asked. Beyond the circle of dragon-fire the area was unbroken dark.

Nutty-Arm blinked. "You bought us some time, good sirs. They can't hear us. If we didn't have this dragon-fire torch, they could, but now we're out of range of the bigger fire, our torch will draw sound and light to us. We'll be silent to them." The pixie hugged his knees. "Although this torch isn't strong enough to draw from very far away, we're safe enough here."

Sounds zipped through their small bubble. Sam peered around the circle of light. He could see the dirt at his feet and a stretch of ground littered with stones and bone fragment. "Where's here?" Sam asked.

Nutty-Arm didn't answer. He shuddered and stared into the darkness until Bladder poked him. "Oh, you're asking me, sir? Valley of the Hags, I think. The old ones who lived here once have been hunted until those two hags are all that's left. They tend to eat their new-mades."

"Well," Bladder said, "it's no point climbing back up the well, even if we could find it. An' your hands look like mincemeat. Do pink patty hands still stick? If they don't, how do we get out?"

All three of them sniffed. They were assailed by too many smells, too many nasty rotten aromas.

Sam and Nutty-Arm both shrugged.

"Maybe if we find the Cavern wall, we can follow it around until we find a tunnel out. There's gotta be a tunnel out, right?" Bladder asked.

"Dragon-fire draws the heart's desire," the pixie said, echoing Maggie's words. "Ask the flame, sirs, it's a small one, but powerful enough. It remembers being free. Freedom's a heart's desire. The flame will help you see or hear anything you want, if you ask."

"Show me?" Bladder shoved his snout between the flame and Nutty-Arm. "And no tricks."

The pixie pushed his hands into his armpits and sighed. "What's Cutpurse saying? I want to know."

The flame spat and the sounds changed to a sad, small collection of pixie voices.

"This looks a good place," Cutpurse was saying. A door creaked, and footsteps sounded on wood.

"How long we going for?" a small voice squeaked.

"Forever, Betty," Cutpurse replied.

"They're leaving the Pixie Cavern?" Sam asked.

Nutty-Arm nodded. "They think Maggie made me a meal for the hags 'cause I messed up. An' it'd be like her to put the rest of the pack on the menu. They're just getting out of her way." The pixie's face twisted with longing. "I want to be with 'em."

"Flame, Wheedle, and Spigot, I want to hear them," Bladder said.

The flames crackled, but no sound came.

"Maybe they're too far away," Nutty-Arm said. "It's only a small fire."

Sam stared at the flame. "Is Beatrice all right?"

The sound was gentle, the softest breeze. Sam blinked for a minute, wondering if he was listening to the wind rustling a single leaf or a tunnel guiding a whisper-soft draft. Then he realized, it was baby's breath. He smiled. "That's all I need."

The flame hissed like a snake.

Nutty-Arm watched them with round, hazel eyes.

"Yes, sir," Nutty-Arm said. "Now, Flame, give us noises to where we needs to go to get outta here?"

The clashing yells of huge beasts filled their circle of light. They jumped. The flames sputtered toward the sound.

"If you want something too much, it'll distort, you know?" Nutty-Arm said. "It's dragon bones, remember that."

They followed the sounds of fighting until they came to a dirt archway. The flames flickered toward it even though a dirty breeze came out at them.

They stepped inside. "They sound close," Bladder said.

"No, sir, they're a long, long way away," Nutty-Arm replied. "You get a feel for the flame's noises after a while."

"How do you know how it works?" Bladder glared at Nutty-Arm.

"Traveled in the dark with Her Ladyship often enough."

"You're being too helpful. Again."

Sam picked up the torch. "He won't get out if we don't."

Nutty-Arm crooked his thumb, pointing it at Sam. "What he says."

They walked upward.

Sam realized his backpack was behind them, in Baba Yaga's cave. He groaned.

"What?" Bladder asked.

"I'm hungry and . . ." He tasted the top of his mouth. He wanted to drink the juice from a cold can of soup. He wanted a drink. Was there a word for that? "Flame, is there any water on the way?"

The flame gurgled and flowed, trickling ahead. He heard water rushing. Sam hoped it was near.

By the time they were on it, the water sounded like a waterfall and Sam almost collapsed with need.

The "waterfall" turned out to be a tiny trickle down the cave wall. It flowed over the stones from a gap in the rock above. Sam put his mouth to it and lapped at the cold, cold water. Near his knees, Nutty-Arm did the same. They turned around to see Bladder looking bored.

"Well, you look better," the gargoyle said.

"I'm still hungry."

"Me too," Nutty-Arm said.

"You don't need to eat any more 'n' I do," Bladder complained.

The pixie shrugged.

Sam didn't think his legs could lift another step before they saw wall torches and their natural light stretched toward them. Some of the light sucked down the corridor passing them, the pull of Baba Yaga's magic still stronger than their one small torch, but knowing they were close to an upstairs exit made Sam feel better. The gargoyle and pixie strolled beside him, no more tired than if they'd gone for a walk to the park.

When violent shots of ogre argument zipped through their dragon-lit cocoon, near and explosive, the pixie screamed.

Bladder shuffled forward.

"Look, sirs." Nutty-Arm shook as he pointed at the torches on the wall.

The glow trickled down the corridor, but it didn't shoot away like Sam's torchlight had.

"The Yaga's magic, it's starting to fade," Bladder said.

In the distance, noise gathered naturally.

Nutty-Arm raced off up the corridor, his pattering feet echoing in the flame.

"Good riddance," Bladder said. "You didn't have to eat him, but we could have killed him, at least. He's the reason you're down here. He took your baby, remember?"

Sam hadn't forgotten. "I'm going to get her back."

"What? All this time spent tryna avoid Thunderguts and now you're gonna walk right up to him for a baby? 'Sides, she don't belong to you."

Sam peered at Bladder. "It doesn't matter. I owe the Kavanaghs. Like you said, pack looks after pack."

Bladder sighed. "That lot aren't pack. I think you're taking gargoyle codes and putting them on humans. I don't know how loyal they'll be. I keep telling you, they're weak. Codes mean nothing to them."

"Maybe. But I want to do for them what you'd do for me. Even if they want nothing to do with me afterward."

Bladder scratched at the ground. "An' it don't matter how revolting, stupid, or useless they are, you have to look after them."

Sam considered this, then said, "Is it possible to belong to two packs?"

Bladder trotted next to him. "Oh, yeah, if you want. Look at Nutty-Arm's group, all sorts in that pack." Bladder sighed. "But, come on!" he said as Sam scratched his mane. "Those humans won't be loyal just 'cause you save that little one. You can bet on it. You won't belong to their pack no matter what you do."

Sam recognized the stink of ogre paddies in the tunnels and saw the hungry torches along the walls. Far-off sounds carried back the noise of ogres dim-gurgling in the distance.

Imps hustled by, wearing the panicked expressions of those in service to Thunderguts. Their rushing told Sam this place was all business and murder.

A pair of ogre guards' voices boomed ahead. Bladder shot up the wall and pulled into the dirt, disappearing into rock. Sam pressed himself flat and hunkered in the dark.

When the ogres moved on, Sam reached up, digging in the ceiling to find Bladder. He sighed out his relief when his hands stuck to the surface, and he found he could pull himself up without it being agonizing. The gargoyle poked out his head.

"You know I can't go in there," Bladder said. The ridges of his mane paled.

"I know. I think it's time for you to go upstairs. You've done enough."

Bladder peered down both ends of the passageway and licked his lips. "I'll just come a little farther, okay?"

The tunnel narrowed as they moved toward the noise. An uncountable number of ogre voices shook the corridor.

"Why're so many of them in there? Big monsters don't like getting together. Too many fights."

Bladder pulled in his head when the next patrol arrived. The great brutes walked in single file. They shoved and pushed, and the lout at the rear staggered and fell to get in front. In the cramped space, the brute kicked Sam and cried out.

"S'matter, Brutus?"

"Stubbed ma toe on a rock."

Sam bit into his knuckles to stifle his scream. If Brutus thought he'd kicked a rock, Sam felt he'd been kicked by one. He rubbed his shin.

The ogres' voices faded. Bladder giggled a little too high. "You're a rock."

"They don't seem very smart." Sam stared down the passage after them.

A brownie scuffled past, small, wide-eyed, and squealing. Trolls' yells bellowed after it.

Bladder whitened to quartz.

"Don't worry. It's better if you go upstairs. You can tell Daniel I'm still alive," Sam said.

"I'm sorry. I can cope with most things, but I can't do another smashing."

Sam kissed the stone lion's nose.

"I don't want to go," Bladder said. "It hurts inside, like my . . . you know . . . is going to fall apart again. I can feel the cracks coming loose."

Bladder leaned in so they were cheek to cheek. When a scream echoed in the tunnel, he took off up the wall, disappearing into earth. Sam was alone.

CHAPTER 19

Sam hid as a troop of ogres thumped by, their faces intent, the last one blubbering and chewing its knuckles. He trailed them to the rotten light at the end of the passage and stopped. Head after ogre head moved into the gap in the wall and disappeared downward. Sam followed them in, first peering behind himself to see if any other ogres were coming before stepping through the opening and looking down.

He was high above the Ogres' Cavern. It was a horrendous sight.

Below, thousands of monsters carpeted the base, encircling a stone podium in front of a black rock. The monsters closest to the rock watched it with pained and anxious glances. One goblin skirted it as if its surface was hot to the touch. *What is it?* Sam wondered.

Blacker than the rock, and right behind it, was a small cave entrance.

Sam studied the bare, smooth tiers of the cavern. No burrows lined it: nothing lived here. The only hole to hide in was a single cave behind the rock. It must be where they had hidden Beatrice.

Sam dodged as three ogres shot through the door he'd come in by and tumble-climbed toward the spreading gathering.

"I don't like being near that sword," one said.

"I ent eaten no one. It's got no call to get at me."

"But we're . . ."

"Shut up," said the third. "Don't talk about it."

Ogres, goblins, witches, imps, and all creatures of the darkness overflowed the tiers. He could see monster head after monster head leaning from the heights, a bestiary from the cavern's depths to its ceiling, and the violence roared. These were old monsters; even the few pixies he spotted in the crowd were wizened and hobbling. The place filled with their smells and sounds. Underneath it, the tiniest scent of sweet human.

Beatrice is here, he thought. *I've gotta get down.*

His arms and legs didn't agree.

Sam saw Thunderguts emerge from the crowd below and lumber across the stone podium and toward the small cave entrance. A few sparkles escaped from inside into the somber air.

Sam dug his hands into the dirt on the shelf and smeared black muck onto his face, hoping he looked a little less human and a lot more bogeymanish. If he hid at the sides and kept low, he might be able to avoid eye contact and any monster's interest. Besides, the crowd seemed more focused on the ogre king's odd behavior.

"Beatrice," Sam said to himself and climbed down, and when his legs shook, he said her name again.

Sam scurried along the tier above the monstrous heads, in the direction of the cave. He watched an ogre lobbing pebbles at an ancient brownie. The smaller monster threw its arms over its face and squealed, "Stop it!" It turned to look at the ogre and instead peered straight at Sam. "It's here! It's here!" it called.

A rush of movement hit him from the right, and Sam saw grimy goblin hands just before they shoved him. He fell the short distance to the cavern floor. Even that jarred his shoulder, and he had to clench his teeth to stop from crying.

His attempt at quietness proved useless, as the crowd peered in the direction of the brownie's shriek and thousands of hairy fingers pointed at him. A few sniffed and shook their heads, and hundreds of maws hung open, sharp teeth, drool, and bad breath decorating each one.

Yet not one monster moved toward him. Instead, they parted, creating a pathway to the ogre king.

Thunderguts's eyes lit with surprise and triumph. "Let him through, friends. My little monster, I see you came to me all by yourself in the end. The crone said you would."

A troll with piggy little eyes grabbed Sam's sore arm and yanked him to his feet. "Go on," it said. "Prepare for your fate." Hoorays and hurrahs moved dirt into clouds, and huge monsters stamped their feet. Hungry black and red eyes watched him, not a gentle one among them, and large heads and bodies loomed over him. They patted him. Some pushed him along the pathway. A troll rushed forward, grabbed Sam's hand, and shook it until his shoulder hurt, while smaller monsters clambered onto larger ones to get a look at him, clapping their claws as he neared.

Sam imagined the pain of an ogre bite, but guessed no one would be silly enough to eat him with the king watching. The only way to get closer to Beatrice was through the crowd, so Sam stepped along the quaking path toward the podium.

"YAH!" they roared, and he felt sick.

They pressed on him, blocking his way out, and he knew he would never see the Kavanaghs again, nor Bladder or the other gargoyles. He would die in this strange cavern.

Sam gazed up at the exit high above all of them, but a heavy hand stopped him.

"No chance!" a gruff voice said. "You're not leaving now. We've all come in here to see what you can do. Don't fail us." He saw eager faces and huge fangs exposed in carnivorous smiles. They pushed him to the podium.

Maybe he would see Beatrice at least.

Thunderguts trembled, stopped, and patted Sam's shoulder. His claw was cold. "It's all right, little monster, you're here now. Safe with us."

The ogre king wore the same hungry expression Sam had seen on Hatching Day, but he'd said, "*safe with us*." What did that mean?

"I know you're embarrassed for running from me. I can

read your face," the ogre said. "Too many hungry mouths and your survival instincts kick in and you run. It's a good trait in any self-respecting monster, but you know not to be worried now, don't you? You're a prince among your own kind." Thunderguts grinned. "You've got grit, like us; you're a warrior, and you're going to help us monsters live again in the world above. You've been made for a great destiny, little prince . . ."

A faint line of sparkles twisted from the cave entrance and danced behind Thunderguts. Sam didn't care about a great destiny. He stared at the lights. "Beatrice?"

The ogre king said, "The crone said you had a thing for babies. I must admit, I prefer something with more meat and less fat, but I guess we got time to get you and your dinner reacquainted. You do know, you can't eat it yet? No, no, no. But once you've done for us, it's all yours." The ogre steered Sam toward the cave, its heavy claw resting on the boy's shoulder.

As Thunderguts dragged Sam inside, the noise and chaos outside fell away, and the ogre king let go of his arm. A weak glitter retreated into the darkness, turning in the air so it floated before them.

Sam watched it weave its way back to a bundle against the wall. He clambered across the floor toward it, but the sparkles evaporated when he put his hands on the ragged pile. Sam opened a gap in a blanket to reveal Beatrice's tiny face. Ashy lashes lay on the baby's cheeks, and her dark thatch of Kavanagh hair stuck to her head, slick and shiny. Her thumb shifted between her lips, and a bubble budded in the corner.

Sam pulled his arms around the infant, and Beatrice's face sank into the dirty fabric of his T-shirt.

Sam looked at Thunderguts. "She's sick?"

"Dying, actually. And sleeping. The crone put some of that dust on it. The sound made us all hungry."

Sam put his hand over his mouth to prevent himself blubbering in front of the old ogre. "She's dying?"

"Monsterkind is their despair and misery walking around. We do something to their heads, and they die so easily." Thunderguts bent down and sniffed Beatrice. "For all their guff and nonsense, a human is just an animal clambering in the mud, readying itself to be eaten." The ogre king ran a finger over Beatrice's face and licked the tip. "You wouldn't believe something so fragile could be so dangerous."

Sam didn't understand. He shook his head.

"Souls, they've got souls. It's all right when it's just the one and it's your meal, but a lot of them together... deadly. It's why all those monsters back there can't look straight at the podium without whimpering. It's that sword. A sword made of human souls. We touch the sword that killed the Jabberwock and we turn to ash."

Sam gasped. The Vorpal Sword had killed the Jabberwock. The one made of souls he'd read about in Daniel's papers. He remembered. Thunderguts was talking about *that* sword.

Thunderguts ignored Sam's shocked expression. "Only a human, or something close, can touch it without suffering. Without a soul, that sword burns you up. We tried everything. Dragged a few humans down here to take it away, but they go mad before they die. The last human I got down here lasted just long enough for me to move her like a puppet." Thunderguts held up his stone fist. Sam looked closer—no, not a fist, there was a gap through it, where a small arm could fit. "A monster touches the sword an' turns to dust. But holding a human who's touching it will do this."

The ogre king didn't want to eat him, he just wanted him to move the Vorpal Sword.

"Then the crone suggested we hatch our own monster *with* a soul to get rid of the sword." Thunderguts flashed his fangs.

A small storm churned in Sam's belly.

"You're monster and human, all in one. Tough enough to be near the sword, touch it, and not fall apart. You've hardly even noticed its power, have you? We feel its hate and loathing like nobody's business." Thunderguts snarled. "But once you take it away, we'll all be free, and you can have anything you want."

Sam jerked his head back and stared at the ogre. "Anything?"

"You pick up that sword for us, get rid of it, then yes, anything." Thunderguts spread his arms. "So, do you want to get the revolution started?"

Sam looked at Beatrice. His goal was to get her out of here. He'd go along with anything until then. He stooped and gently picked her up, then stepped toward the exit.

"That's the spirit," Thunderguts said, and chuckled at his own joke.

Sam followed the ogre back out into the cavern.

CHAPTER 20

A delighted bellow lifted the dust. Sam hadn't expected that and couldn't help smiling in response to eager faces. They were grinning at him. They were cheering for him. Maybe he could ask for anything. He wondered if Thunderguts would keep his promise. Maggie had said they were pack. And pack looked after pack, right?

Anything you want, Thunderguts had said. Anything? A home. Somewhere for Bladder, Wheedle, and Spigot to live with him safely. Perhaps he could be with the Kavanaghs too. He looked down at his dirty, bare feet. Shoes. He'd like shoes. Shoes would be great.

Except to get them, he had to do what Thunderguts had requested.

The ogre king stepped forward. "Monsters all, our time has

come! Too long we have endured this misery!" Thunderguts waved his arms around the dais as if the misery somehow surrounded him at the podium.

The crowd cheered.

"For centuries, the sword has held us back. For centuries, we've been kept from our castles, our keeps, our dungeons, our torture chambers, and forced to take to farms and forests for food. This sword stole our simple pleasures. Humans walk fearlessly in the dark, and we no longer enjoy their terror. After Jabberwock died, the sword trapped us down here. Its power compels us. And if we hunt upstairs it makes us pay, and pay dearly, with ash and dust." Thunderguts whispered the last sentence, but his voice carried. "We want to hunt again, don't we?"

The beasts salivated. And bayed. Thunderguts let the mob roar out its frustration.

When the howl died, the beasts griped and stared at the dais, shuddering.

"But at last there is a way forward," Thunderguts said. "We remove our destroyer. Our liberation is here." He pointed at Sam. The monsters raised their claws, celebrating them both. "He can break the curse on us, free us from this shackle."

Thunderguts walked to the black rock and reached and pinched his fingers together in midair.

"Don't touch it!" a goblin yelled. Something screamed, high-pitched and terrified.

Thunderguts exhaled and took a tiny piece of the rock. Sam watched it bend and pull, and then he realized, it wasn't rock, but a rough, black fabric. With a quick twist of his huge wrist, Thunderguts pulled off the black cover to reveal a chiseled white shard sticking into the luminous stone beneath.

The crowd moaned. Sam watched as monster after monster held its head and cradled it as if the rock had brought on a crowd-wide migraine.

It was beautiful, that's all Sam could see, a glowing rock the same color as the one inside Bladder. It didn't move.

"It won't do anything to us if we bide by its rules. Friends, you have no reason to fear it. No soulless monster's going to eat a human just yet."

Nervous laughs shook the cavern walls. Dirt fell, and ogres threw out punches as if startled. Sam watched a battle break out between two ocher ogres. Thunderguts roared, and a reverent silence fell. Huge monsters blinked and stared at their king and gaped as he circled the white rock. It sparkled and shone. It sang. Thunderguts pulled Sam toward it.

"Look at him. He doesn't even flinch at it."

Claws waved at Sam, giving him the thumbs-up. They whistled; they stamped their feet. The monsters' confidence built seeing how close Sam stood to the sparkling stone.

"Anyone seen the crone?" Thunderguts yelled. "She should be here for our triumph."

Sam stared at the chaos and dirt, and the lamps. The light of each had grown stronger since the removal of the cover, shining golden, a little burst of sunlight. He noticed the monsters moving away from the lamp posts.

"Here I am." The banshee hobbled forward.

"You're late," Thunderguts complained.

"Had a nasty accident with a rock, and I can't heal the way I did once." Maggie grinned, her ancient face creasing into a smile. "But, darlin' Samuel, you came to us. I knew you would. You were smart to run. When I woke, Yama was still holding the frying pan, an' you'll be happy to know, I took three of her toes for threatening to eat you." Maggie peered around Sam. "No gargoyle?" She smiled. "Of course you didn't leave your Maggie for a moldy pebble. Did you smash him the way he smashed me?" She leaned forward and traced a calloused fingertip over Beatrice's face. "And you've finally got your plaything back. They look so delicious when I'm like this." Maggie gave Sam a withered frown. Her sagging eyelids lifted. She reached into her dress and pulled out her silver tin and sniffed the powder. The age faded away, and young Maggie stood before him. The crowd made disgusted noises. "You prefer me like this, just the way I prefer them when I'm glamoured. Come to my arms, my Samuel." She said and reached for him.

Despite everything, Sam felt something of the weight of his journey fall from him as Maggie pulled him into her chest and held him. Beatrice slept on between them, and the noise of the cavern died away. He closed his eyes. She stroked his face and kissed him just above his eyebrow.

"Oh, sweet Sam, so this is what it's like." She cooed. "We could be a family, perhaps. After this."

"Family?" Thunderguts scoffed. "Whatever makes the princeling happy."

Sam rested on Maggie's shoulder and closed his eyes as she sang him a lullaby. It sounded ancient and lovely. "Is it magic?" he whispered. "Are you magicking me?"

"No, Sam, this is us," Maggie said. "You're my own boy. It's the soul that makes us like this."

Sam wanted to sleep in Maggie's warm arms, but the word drifted from him. "Soul?"

"I carried it in me for twelve years. It took twice as much fairy dust to contain it, such a powerful little thing, and to keep the sword from knowing I'd stolen it. Without the dust it would have pulled me apart."

Maggie rubbed her soft, young cheek against Sam's.

Sam looked up at her. She cradled him against her shoulder, and it did feel right, smell right.

"Which soul?"

"The soul inside you, of course. The baby laugh makes you look human, sure enough, but you *feel* human thanks to your soul. I breathed it in you when you'd scarcely opened your eyes."

"When you kissed me?"

"That wasn't a kiss, Samuel. It was a gift." Maggie pulled her shawl about him. "I gave you a soul, my dear. You're the only monster ever to possess one." Sam drifted. The Kavanaghs would be okay without him, the gargoyles too, maybe. He could stay forever with Maggie. She wanted him. Someone actually wanted him.

Thunderguts"s rumbly voice drifted in. "Yeah, you're the first one it worked on. We tried making other half-breeds before you, but all of them exploded."

Sam was dreamily aware of Maggie glaring at Thunderguts. Her voice continued soft and smooth.

"But something happened when the old man sighed

his last, something peculiar: the baby laughed," she said. "Then when the nugget didn't want to leave an' looked fierce different, I knew it was special. It would work. Had to really; otherwise your little soul woulda kill'd me."

Sam gazed sleepily around the cavern. Maggie trailed her fingers over his forehead, and he smelled her misty scent. He snuggled closer to her chest. She was so warm. He'd longed to be held like this since his first day. He yawned.

"We're bonded, you and I." Maggie chuckled. "You're as good a thief as I; you even stole that name back. Those Kavanaghs named the baby I took the soul from 'Samuel Kavanagh.'" Sam opened his eyes and stared at Maggie's face. She kissed him on the nose. "See, you are my own Samuel."

"Samuel Kavanagh?" Sam had a vague memory of the baby Michelle said she'd lost: the other "other Samuel."

"Mmmm," she said, and pulled him in again, he didn't want to move.

He put his head on her chest. Maggie had no heartbeat.

"Any time now would be good." Thunderguts's gruff voice broke through Sam's sleepiness.

Maggie smiled at Sam. "It's to work, my darlin.'" She pulled Beatrice from his arms. The baby's tiny sparkles reached back for him.

Maggie took Sam's hand and strode forward. No longer stranded in a shuffling and wounded old body. Her dusted figure did not shudder, though a few of the larger ogres winced as she approached the white stone spike.

The ogres and trolls retreated, some violently, pushing those behind them back and back, so the ones at the rear walls let out crushed *oofs*. Sam wondered what the sword would do to him.

The blade glistened in the moldy dankness, and Sam stared. It was so like Bladder's heart, milky white, with a rainbow trapped in its surface. Parts reflected blue and pink as others became whiter.

Thunderguts leaned in. "You'll do right by your pack, won't you, little monster?"

Sam gazed at Maggie; she brushed fingers across his cheek. "Make it a world for our kind."

"Our kind?" Sam stared blearily at Maggie.

"Pull out the sword, Sam."

The edges of the sword gleamed.

"Samuel?" a tiny voice called from the rock.

"Quickly, my little prince," Thunderguts said. "Take it."

"Get it away from us," a voice called from the crowd.

"Take it back upstairs, as far as you can with it, where it won't hurt us anymore. Up where it won't be able to keep tabs on us," Thunderguts said.

Sam remembered exploding monsters, crazed humans, the ogre king's own stone hand. His legs wobbled. "What if it kills me? Like it did the others."

"You have a soul," Thunderguts said. "You'll be fine, little prince."

"Give us back our dark spaces," Maggie pleaded.

Sam's mouth dried. He looked at the sword. At Maggie. At the dwindling sparkles around the baby she held. "If I die, will you make sure Beatrice gets back to the Kavanaghs?"

Thunderguts glanced at the baby and frowned as he peered at Sam's face. "Why would you care . . . ?"

"If that's what you want, my darlin.'" Maggie rocked the baby. Sam reached for the sword. The air tingled under his fingers.

"He can hold it; he has to." Thunderguts panted. "You'll be the prince of all monsters!"

Sam had no choice. He touched the hilt with one finger. Warmth moved to greet his skin. The mob moaned again.

He pulled it away and wiggled his fingers. He hadn't turned to stone, nor fallen to ash. Maybe he hadn't touched it with enough skin or for long enough. Eager eyes watched him study his fingertips.

Then a single light popped from the blade and hovered in front of him. It grew into a pale human shape a little shorter than he. Close up he could see features.

Thunderguts cowered away from the shape. "Take it, take it up, Sam. Don't let any more souls escape. Get it away from us." The ogre king moaned and dropped to his bulbous knees.

Sam studied the transparent shape of a serious little girl inside the white light. Her pale-blond hair and light blue eyes gleamed. She wore a gray-rag dress and a metal collar.

"Sam, the room, the light's getting too strong. You must contain the souls until you're outside," Maggie said. "Grab the sword. Control them for us. Have them do your bidding." She pushed his arm toward the hilt.

Sam grabbed the sword, and it clung to him as much as he clung to it.

Another light popped from the edge of the blade, and a woman with a blue tattooed face appeared. "Leave!" she said. "Your kind doesn't belong here. Take the baby and go."

"Get it outside," Thunderguts yelled. "The light hurts."

The sword's power filled the air around Sam. He felt thousands of souls moving inside it. Their courage, their determination, lifetimes of will and energy.

"Go. Get Beatrice out and leave us down here," the blue-faced woman said. Hearing the baby's name wakened him. Thunderguts and Maggie called her "it" and "this." The woman floated toward Sam. "Above all, do good. If we have learned anything from shepherding these monsters, it is to do good, to protect the weak."

Sam waved the sword, and the monsters in the crowd pushed back again, crushing even more of the creatures at the rear.

Maggie alone seemed unworried by the blade, a gauze of fairy dust surrounding her. Sam sneezed.

An old man appeared. "If the sword is returned to the surface, there will be no one to control the beasts. Put it back. Wherever we are, we are trapped in the sword. At least down here, we can do some good."

"Put it back, Samuel," a younger woman's soul said. She stood tall, dark, and sun-dyed, with skin the color of soot. "Then run, boy, run far from here."

Sam looked about him, at the monsters shrinking from the sword in his hand, but ready to murder him if he tried to leave without it. "Please, stop talking," he said to the souls. "I can't think."

Maggie smiled. Sam looked at her firebrand hair shining, a blast of color in the cavern, but despite her bright coloring, she gave off no light. Not like Beatrice, not like the sword.

He turned to put the blade back into its setting.

"No!" Thunderguts said. "Take the sword now!" The ogre leaned forward to grab him, his living claw almost on Sam's shoulder. He stopped. Sam still had hold of the sword. The ogre's eyes lit on the bundle of rags in Maggie's arms and he snatched at Beatrice. "Take it, or this thing stays here forever."

"And after you've taken the sword, do you think they'll have any use for either of you?" the young woman's soul asked. "She'll die and you'll die before you see another day."

". . . Or you'll die before you see another day," Thunderguts echoed. The prince-maker had gone, he was only an ogre after all.

Sam groaned and stepped away from Maggie and Thunderguts. The crowd groaned with him.

"Why don't you just all go now?" Sam screamed at the souls. "Then they don't need me."

"Is he ranting?" Thunderguts asked Maggie.

Sam stared at Beatrice's face. His whole purpose had been to save her. If I could complete that task at least, I will have done one thing right.

The blue-tattoo woman leaned over Beatrice and seemed to touch her forehead. Beatrice cooed in her sleep and sparkles exploded into Thunderguts's face. The ogre king grimaced.

Maggie studied Sam, her face gentle with concern. He knew it was an illusion caused by fairy dust, but even with

Thunderguts's threat and the souls' refusal, he didn't want to disappoint her.

He tried to shove the sword at her. "Please, just let me take Beatrice home first. I promise I'll come back."

"No," Maggie said, and waved a hand at the monsters. "They'll not let you."

He looked at them all. Thunderguts's meat-rich breath stank.

"Samuel, take it and get out of here," Maggie said. "You can have everything you want. Just do this one little thing for us. For me."

Sam howled. In this whole time, he had always been able to decide. He had chosen to reassemble Bladder, he had resolved to follow the pixies and brownies, even though it had been a bad idea, and even in the emptiness of Yaga and Yama's tunnel, he had determined to keep moving. And every single step had been driven by his decision, his ultimate purpose, to save Beatrice.

But no matter what he did, he knew the outcome. There was no right answer. No matter which path he chose, Beatrice would die. They were trapped.

Sam held the sword high above his head. All that power and he couldn't do the one thing he wanted most. The mob of monsters cheered.

Sam screamed and smashed the sword down onto the rock. It broke, and sharp pieces flung through the air.

The shards captured the dying glimmers of lamplight as lanterns dimmed, the sallow light thrown across the cavern. The pieces clattered down upon the white and stony ground, and the rock and sword faded, as ashen as a goblin's face.

A gasp lifted from the crowd of monsters desperately trying to avoid the splintered pieces as they landed. Then everything went quiet.

Thunderguts stepped forward to look at the broken weapon. He leaned down and hit a small piece with his stone fist. When nothing happened, he put Beatrice on the ground and touched a sliver with a living finger. Still nothing. The ogre's maw opened, his jaw falling to his barrel chest. Then he chuckled. He threw back his huge head, and a laugh rattled out of him into the gray air above.

The crowd roared its approval.

"He did it, the princeling did it. Who knew it was so simple? Come to my arms, my beamish boy."

Thunderguts gathered Sam to his cold, damp chest. Sam surrendered to the embrace and smelled the ogre's carrion breath. When Thunderguts completed his gruff hug, he dropped Sam and turned back to the ogres.

Sam grabbed Beatrice off the ground before any monster could take it into its head to eat her.

"You've freed us, Sam. You've freed us." Maggie smiled and opened her arms, but he stepped back toward the cave and watched the brewing crowd. Heads bobbed and stretched to look at the broken sword.

He wondered what creature he'd have to avoid first, but none of them were interested in the baby. They had forgotten Beatrice and made confused faces. Sam heard one whisper, "But where'd the souls go?" "Gone," a stooped troll replied. Others giggled.

And then the monsters rushed the walls.

The crowd around the dais looked up, and the excited conversations carried. While Thunderguts's triumphant laughter filled the cooling cavern, ogres, goblins, pixies, crones, bogeymen, brownies, and all the rest climbed. The ones on the highest tier reached the exit quickly, while those below fought for a place on the wall so they could escape and get upstairs, where they could consume thousands and thousands of human lives.

What have I done? Sam thought.

The sword lay silent, except a single piece, which rattled.

Lights peeled from it one by one and circled Sam, floating over his face and brushing his cheeks.

The monsters got busy climbing, shoving, falling, and cheering, all desperate to be the first one to break free from The Hole, to start the hunt. None of them noticed the tiny floats of light.

Even Maggie fixated on the breakout and clapped as ogres and trolls and imps of all kinds swarmed up the sides of the cavern.

Only Sam saw the first shape re-form. A sliver of the sword glowed, and the soul of the little girl in the ragged dress grew from it. She stepped toward Sam, blew him a kiss, and dogged the heels of a younger ogre at the back of the horde. The creature was busy cheering, but Sam saw its ravenous expression. The soul tapped the ogre's shoulder and the joyous, drooling beastie turned. Its triumph solidified as its face became stone, and after a flick of her finger, the statue dropped into an ash pile on the floor.

The brutes wanted out, to be free in the world above, so the ash pile went unnoticed.

Sam looked to the sword again, the pieces glowed and shrank as souls formed out of them. A young woman soared up, diving toward the dark ceiling, illuminating the walls above. A few brownies at the top threw their arms over their faces and melted on the ledge. A bunch of bogeymen behind them screamed and tripped through the ash piles with shrieks of disgust, their speed increasing from eager to panic. The soul of the young woman turned into a golden bead, and she disappeared through the roof.

A group of children's souls, a dozen or so, formed out of a single, broken splinter of the blade. Sam heard their laughter in his head as they burst toward three ogres on the lower tier and turned a dozen goblins to dust.

The monsters on the floor screamed, and those above who had not noticed beforehand began gawping at the bawling and watched fleeing monsters kick an ash spray of goblin debris. The whole swarm looked down.

Maggie turned to Sam, her beautiful face confused.

Then a larger sword piece melted into thousands of souls.

Their brightness burned Sam's eyes. He heard thin yelps behind him but could not turn from the faces of ancient spirits floating up to the cavern roof and lining the ledges. There were so many they doubled over each other, faces upon faces upon bodies blending like waves of water. They sailed up into the ceiling, out of the exit, through solid dirt.

The group of monsters around Maggie stampeded past her.

The screaming continued. Ogres rushed for the exit, several trying to enter together. The larger ones pushed smaller ones out of the way and flung them a dozen stories to the ash-covered floor. They shrieked as they fell.

Thunderguts watched it all. His stone fist raised above his head, his laughter gone, as he roared to the roof. Dust and ash fell on him. He turned and snarled, but his gaze looked beyond Sam, to where lights continued streaming out from the broken blade. His eyes widened in animal terror.

Thunderguts ran, but a bright orb zipped over Sam's head, toward the ogre king. It settled an inch in front of his face, then nipped forward and tapped his snout. The king whined, high and horrible, and his feet locked to the ground. From his toes up, his sallow body turned gray. The change moved faster, his solid calves, his boulderish knees, his thighs, belly, chest. As the change hit his neck, he thundered and his face fixed in a yell, which turned to stone. The glow of souls filled the space from wall to wall, and the force of heat and light disintegrated Thunderguts into an ash statue, his face growing brighter until he glowed from inside.

Then his hands crumbled finger by finger; the great flaps of his ears fell apart, arms and mountainous legs dissolved. His mouth remained open in an angry bawl as an explosion burst through his last scream.

He wasn't the only one. Ogre statues littered the floor, in many positions of misery and fear. They collapsed as monsters fell against them, slipping on the ash piled between them. One raced into the wall, both hands over its face, and erupted into a cloud.

Sam looked around the walls. He had to escape before the exits became filled with brutes.

The dash of joy had turned to one of panic as all the beasts tried their best to move away from the dissolving sword, so the wall above the cave was a clear road to the top, the one patch of rock free from fleeing monsters.

The soul of a woman with bright hazel eyes gestured for Sam to follow her. "Time to leave, Samuel." She tried to pick up the black cloth, but her fingers passed through it. "For the baby."

Sam nodded, and ripped a couple of strips of fabric from the piece, and strapped Beatrice to himself, tightening knots to hold her to his back, and he climbed. His hands were still raw from the fall down the succubi's well, but he felt the pain as a distant annoyance. The woman's spirit followed beside him. She looked a bit like Michelle, her soft eyes watching him as he ascended. He looked down at the sword as the last pieces shrank and melted away into individual souls.

"Look to me, young man," the woman's soul said.

Sam's feet carried him farther up the wall, under the main exit. But here the clutter of escaping monsters filled it like mud in a sewer drain; he knew he could never hope to get out while they fled. He waited underneath and clung on as a party of souls flew by him, capering around him, laughing, celebrating, brushing past him with golden kisses. An ogre threw itself back in terror, plummeting many feet below, causing a huge cloud of ash to powder up from the cavern floor. The rest of the monsters backed away from the doorway, letting the souls claim it.

One foolhardy bogeyman dashed forward: a soul, a young man with wild matted hair, reached out and touched it. The bogeyman blew away as wind from the tunnel gusted its gray powder into the polluted air.

The other monsters hung back, mostly brownies and pixies, Sam noticed. There were few of the Great Monsters left to climb. Some of the remaining imps had even descended the way they'd come.

The souls waited for Sam to move to the door.

He gave a last glance back at where the sword had lain. He no longer saw any glowing pieces on the floor below. The last few souls floated upward and dissolved two ogres who huddled on the third tier. A few shivering pixies and brownies huddled in the shadows on the cavern ground.

Maggie had not moved from her spot. She stared after Sam. He had the strangest impulse to wave to her.

"Come on, Sam," the woman said. "It's time for all of us to go home."

Sam clambered up through the doorway. The last of the souls turned into beads of light and floated by him upward to the cavern roof.

Sam twisted Beatrice around to his chest and ran into the tunnel.

CHAPTER 21

"Sam!"

A lion's face peered in from the top of the door.

"Bladder? Bladder!"

"Come on."

"Yes, they're all . . ."

". . . On the move. Let's go!"

They plunged inside the exit tunnel, hearing confused voices of patrols echoing in the corridors. Guards had heard the yells from the ogres' cavern, and already someone had reported seeing hundreds of piles of ash everywhere. Had the sun got underground? Panicked voices spread the news. They ran forward faster than Sam and Bladder could, each monster asking another what had happened.

A cluster of pixies argued about the noises. "Did you hear the screams?" asked one. "Let's get out of here."

Bladder motioned to Sam, and they fell in with a thickening swell of imps.

Huddles of impkind rushed together, broke off and escaped down smaller side tunnels. Pixies ran by them asking the whereabouts of Thunderguts. The afternoon's batch of droppings had arrived, they said, and they needed the ogre king. But the crowd pushed on, running from roars building in the rear. The charge gathered brownies, leprechauns, and a few tiny trolls.

The mass turned into a larger tunnel. Sam pushed against them, inching to the side. The hubbub of bodies pulled at him; he staggered on, unable to slow as Bladder bustled above him on the ceiling. An army of small ogres joined in, looking around for guidance from the old ones, but there was none to be had, and they cried out in confounded roars. Sam swam from clumsy, meaty paws swinging near Beatrice's head. The stampede noises grew louder, and the weight of terrified bodies flowed onward. Where was Bladder now? Sam sought the gargoyle, but he'd lost him in the throng.

The surge drove forward toward the ledge overlooking the Great Cavern. Sam fought the flow, but as the widening cavern entrance opened, he knew he would plummet with the others if he did not escape. He saw a few quick-witted imps, light and fortunate, jump from the doorway onto the vertical face of dirt outside. Sam hurled himself sideways after them and, as he threw himself, hoping for solid earth under his hands, Bladder grabbed his shirt and wrested him up the rest of the way. The gargoyle pointed to the tier above, and once Sam's feet found the ledge, the pair ran in the direction of the gargoyles' hideaway.

The cavern floor far below them gagged with imps and monsters, crushing and pushing. Sam saw a few anxious trolls below them, maybe half a dozen. A few smaller ogres too, little bigger than Sam himself. The huge monsters, goblins, trolls, all those others, had gone. The souls had thinned the herd.

"Stop gaping. Inside, inside," Bladder said.

Sam slipped into the hideout. The baying continued but grew no nearer. He unstrapped Beatrice and laid her gently on the stony floor.

Bladder bared stony fangs at him. He was grinning.

"You should have left, Bladder, it was safer," Sam said, panting.

Bladder shook his head. "I would have lost you for good then. What if you died?"

Sam flung his arms around Bladder's neck and buried his face in the stone mane. It felt soft and warm like sand under his face.

Bladder tolerated the hug. "Will that thing cry if it's hungry? They do that. It'll get us killed."

"I don't know. She's asleep right now, but when the spell breaks . . . she could wake any time soon."

The gargoyle fell back on his haunches. "Then we need to get out now. Straight up! To Mên-an-Tol."

"Mên-an-Tol?"

"It's one of the old places. A door. Where humans would bring changelings way back. It's a long, old climb, but at least we'll be safe up there, and it's centuries since it's been used, so it'll be quiet. If we're lucky, it might even be easy to open."

"Might be?" Sam said.

Bladder studied his face. "I can't think of any other way out right now. Using a corridor will get us killed. I saw what happened down there, and there's enough left alive that will make sure everyone will know what went on. Word will spread. There'll be big, bad monsters looking for you and that baby, an' they'll all be out for blood."

Sam walked to the door. He looked at the floor and saw the hubbub of bodies boiling together in excitement and anger. Yells and moans buzzed the air. Imps moving up and imps moving down covering the stairs and walls.

Everything above disappeared into black ceiling.

"I will stay with you, Sam," Bladder said, "no matter what."

"You really think it's our only choice?" Sam felt tired. He didn't know if he had any climb left in him.

"Sorry," Bladder said. "We can't stay here."

Beatrice shuffled in the dim light, proving the gargoyle's point.

Sam hoisted Beatrice and followed Bladder out of the burrow.

They climbed up into cold, sticky black.

Even in the dark, the cavern went on; ledge after ledge littered with hole after hole. When Sam's arms got too sore, the pair sat down to rest on a ridge. This high up, the mass of monsters and imps below blurred into puddles that gathered, separated, then gathered again.

"Let's have a look then," Bladder said.

"A look?"

"At the baby."

Sam turned so Bladder could see Beatrice and her popping, sizzling sparkles.

"You did all this for one of those?"

"For this particular one," Sam said.

Bladder sniffed her. "'Cause she's pack. Each to his own, I guess." He grinned at Sam. "She makes you do good things, don't she?"

"Her. And the Kavanaghs. And you."

"What? No," Bladder said, but he was purring. He realized what he was doing and covered it with a cough.

They climbed more ledges, trudging up endless black levels past murky-eyed burrows.

Sam shuddered.

"Don't think it, boy. Nothing lives here anymore." Yet the gargoyle scurried away from one entrance, and something rotten scratched inside.

The dark thickened, but Sam felt he could climb forever. He had Beatrice; he had his friend. Even if that was all he had, for the moment it was enough.

"Time to rest now, boy."

"No, I'm fine."

"You're slurring. You feeling... what's one of them things you feel again?"

"I said I'm fine."

Sam stepped onto a ledge. Something screamed far below. Bladder darted up the wall, and Sam lurched up after him, guided by the sound of Bladder's tapping feet. The earthy face ran smooth except for a few short, distant ledges and then it curved gradually toward the middle.

"Getting close to the top," Bladder said.

"Good. I have to get out soon. I need a drink."

Their hands, feet, and claws pattered like water against the walls. Sam tutted and his dry tongue held to the top of his mouth.

As they climbed the final bend into vaulting space, Bladder cheered. Beatrice burbled in her sleep. Below them black space dropped into nothingness.

Sam licked his mouth again. He wanted water more than anything. There definitely had to be a word for that.

They scrambled faster, and Sam forgot his mouth.

Beatrice's light was dimming.

"Sam? Sam?" Bladder's voice drifted in from the distance.

"What?"

"You have to rest."

"Not now. So close."

"You don't smell right. You're not well."

"I just . . . need a drink."

Bladder looked around. "I can't get you one. I don't know where I'd go and . . ."

The world blurred.

"There's a ledge, three, four paces that way . . ." Bladder was saying.

Sam's hands slid from the wall, his bare feet slipped, and he fell.

CHAPTER 22

"'At 'akes 'ree 'imes I saved your 'ife."

Sam screamed at the pain of being dragged onto the ledge by his hair.

Bladder spat strands back at him. "It's lucky you got that much fur, but it tastes awful."

Sam touched his sore scalp.

"Look," said Bladder, "we're here, but the way is definitely filled in."

Sam looked past the ledge and into a circular cave behind it. There was an obvious difference in shade: black earth around, brown earth choking up the middle. The faintest smell of air.

Sam touched Beatrice. She sent out clear pink sparkles. She was waking. He couldn't take her back down there again, and he couldn't stay here.

Bladder chuckled. "Check these out!" He showed his claws to Sam. "May be made for rending and slicing, but they're useful for digging too. Good thing we don't have to rely on your little mitts."

As Bladder dug through the hardened dirt, Sam wondered what the creatures below thought of the earth falling on them. If Maggie was down there somewhere stomping and yelling, they might think she was shaking the ceiling onto them. He was impressed by how fast Bladder's claws tunneled and coped with the occasional slap in the face of Bladder's swishing tail.

"What are all these ropes for?" Sam asked.

"Ropes?" Bladder glanced at the dark tendrils that had appeared as he shifted the earth around them. "They're tree roots, you nitwit. They mean we're close to the way out."

Beatrice's sparkles lit the way three feet ahead, revealing mud, clay, and more of the tree roots curling through the tunnel Bladder had excavated. His stone tail wagged as his fat stomach and forepaws worked against dirt.

The dirt fell with an abrupt plop, and Bladder led them into a cool, dark space. Three white rocks sat near the opening. One was strong and circular, with a hole running through it like a stone tire from a stone car. Rough, green vegetation sprang up everywhere.

Sam groaned. Above him spread the expanse of another endless cavern, lit by an odd silver orb like a small, weak sun.

"Who lives in this cavern?" he asked. "It's dark. Except for that. What's that?"

"That's the moon, you lug," Bladder said. "It's nighttime."

"We're above ground?" Even though every part of him ached, Sam thought he could run. The tiredness slipped away.

"Seriously mentally deprived," Bladder said to a rock. "And I almost thought he was getting there."

Beatrice stirred. Sam stroked her head and quieted her, then looked up at the sparkles above and grinned. "Bladder..."

"The twinkly things are called stars," Bladder said.

"Thanks."

"It doesn't take much research, you know? Documentaries. A quick internet search..."

"I meant 'Thanks for everything.'"

Bladder sat down on his dirt-covered haunches and purred. "You're welcome. I wouldn't be out here if you hadn't come back for me." Bladder rubbed his head on Sam's legs. "Although you did get me banged up in the first place."

From the other direction, the smell of fire filled the air; perfumed as if spices had been thrown into its flames. It invited Sam to investigate.

"Come on, Bladder. Just a little bit more."

Bladder's butt wiggled between the carved white stones, and together they followed the smell.

Sam stared up at the stars again—a delicate spray of lights dotting the gorgeous black expanse, gathering together in swirls of hot white. They could have been souls spread out against the all-spanning sky, which went on and on like a cavern roof but glittered with light and energy. Real endlessness, more precious than a world of leprechaun gold.

The smell of incense grew stronger. Beatrice threw a lively

burst of pink sparkles around Sam's head. She was awake and laughing at him.

"Hello, little girl."

"Bada."

"You bet."

They saw fire burning and smelled food. A camp lay ahead. Bladder pushed ahead, nosing between the bushes and tiptoeing forward. He waved Sam to follow him, and Sam peeked at the tongues of golden fire licking upward and hiding the stars. They could make out a deformed shape hunched at the campfire and framed in living red and gold. When it moved, they both jumped.

"Ogre?" Bladder hissed. He scuttled back to the rocks.

Sam crept back too. The giant's twin humps shifted until its covering fell away: a blanket. Then enormous white wings stretched wide against the flames, a coo rang out, and the dark figure turned.

Sam ran forward. "Daniel? Bladder, it's all right. It's Daniel!"

"Yeah, brilliant news," Bladder called back, but Sam could tell it made him happy.

The angel smiled. His face glowed; his wings were golden in the firelight. Yonah fluttered onto Sam's shoulder. A pair of shadows peered out from under the angel's wings.

"Imp!" Wheedle screamed. "Oh, my stars! Bladder! You're alive!"

Spigot shrieked, and the pair rushed forward, jumping on the stone cat like puppies. When they had pounded him enough to make sparks fly off his stone skin, the pair came over to Sam.

Spigot shoved his beak into Sam's hand, and Wheedle licked his face. "I missed you, Imp." "You put His Miserableness back together."

Sam laughed. "I did. But how'd you find us?"

Daniel pointed up. "A few lost souls told us all about a baby and an imp called Sam."

"Daniel made us show him where we'd thought you might come up. Nothing but hundreds of pixies and brownies flooding the streets," Wheedle added. "When you didn't come out the usual places, we knew exactly where to try."

Spigot squawked.

"No, not Stonehenge," Wheedle said. "Here. Mên-an-Tol. It's always been a place for bringing babies."

"It's my fault the imps are all over the place. There might be some ogres and trolls on the loose too," Sam said.

Daniel smiled. "They told us. They also told us you destroyed the Vorpal Sword and freed them from their slavery."

"But what will control the monsters now?"

Daniel gathered Sam into his arms and put his warming hands on Sam's back. "That is a problem for another night and maybe another hero. You've done enough good for a little while. Let it be someone else's responsibility for now. It's time to rest." The angel untied Beatrice and pulled out a bottle of milk from under a wing. Beatrice clamped dirty hands on it and guzzled. Daniel flourished a wing at the fire. "Help yourself, Samuel."

A meal of stew and hot chocolate had been laid out, but Sam didn't bother with it until he'd found a bottle of water and tipped the contents into his dry throat.

"You were thirsty," Daniel said.

"Thirsty? Is that the word?"

"Yes it is!" Bladder cheered, and sank up to the eyes in a bowl of hot chocolate.

"Now, what don't we know?" Daniel asked. "Tell us everything."

Wheedle and Spigot shuffled closer to the fire and stared at Sam. Bladder gargled hot chocolate.

"I have a soul," Sam said.

"That explains a lot. Your glow tonight was visible from the distance. A little bit of joy can do that."

"I'm glowing? Why can't I see it?" He looked at his hands and all he saw was dirt, but he felt cheered and his story spilled from him, nodding at extra comments Bladder threw in, as well as the unnecessary insults. When he finished, he felt emptied—his muscles weak, his bones like stone.

"It's interesting, isn't it?" Daniel said.

"What?"

"If Maggie had managed to grab you at your Hatching. If Thunderguts had taken you straight to the sword . . . what do you think you might have done?"

Sam remembered how nice it had been to be held by Maggie, even being told he would be a prince. If he hadn't had anything else—no gargoyles, no Kavanaghs . . .

"I would have taken the sword up for them, I guess. I would have done what they asked." He hung his head.

Bladder stormed toward the angel. "Give it a rest, wing-flapper!"

"It just seems that . . ."

"No, no, no! You are not going to start with 'there's a reason it all happened' and 'this is all part of a plan.' Blahdy blah! Can't you see, this boy's tired and miserable and can do without your trash. He don't need you to tell him why he had to go through all that muck. Me neither. He's been brilliant! Can't you leave him without trying to say there was some sense in it?"

Daniel glanced at Sam's weary face. "You're right, Bladder."

Bladder stopped. He opened his mouth a few times. When no words came out, he took seat.

"Wheedle and Spigot might have something to discuss with you, Bladder."

"What? What?" Bladder thumped his forepaw into the dirt.

Wheedle nosed a box forward.

"Chocolates?" Bladder asked.

"No, it's pamphlets we been reading," Wheedle said. "We've been given some options. Just looking for two, of course, but now we're back to three, thought we might look at a new cathedral. Maybe a museum."

Spigot squawked around a photo in his mouth of a TV with a bed in the background.

"Is that a hotel room?" Bladder asked.

"We been doin' a lot of house hunting," Wheedle said. "We have options."

"Does it have a bar fridge? With chocolate?"

"Think so."

"Where's this one?"

Daniel stood. "Brighton. The hotel already has some gargoyles, chimeras actually. On the staircase. Now, you'll be all right here. Sam needs my help to return him to the Kavanaghs. It's time to take Beatrice home."

Sam hung his head.

"Don't you want to go home, Samuel?" Daniel asked.

"It's . . . it's not my home. Can't we stay here for a night? Just one? We can go in the morning."

Daniel brushed the hair from Sam's forehead. "Don't you want to see the Kavanaghs? Don't you think they've waited long enough to see you? Humans have hearts, and theirs have broken at this loss."

Sam hunched. "They won't want to see me. You should take Beatrice back. By yourself. I know she should be with her mom and dad . . . I want them to be happy, to be their best. I love them."

Sam looked up at the angel. How could he explain? He did want to see the Kavanaghs, but it would be the last time. "It's because of me that Beatrice was taken. They aren't going to want me around."

Daniel sighed. "Well, we aren't out of options, but we do need to take this baby home."

Bladder's tongue didn't finish licking the hot chocolate under his eye. He plunked himself next to Sam. "This is probably the stupidest thing I've ever said, 'cause normally I hate humans, but I think you might really be one. And I've seen your face when you look at that baby. You light up like . . ." He sneered at Daniel. "Like some glowy angel. Better. Like sunshine. I think you should try. We'll have you back in a shot, if it don't work. You will always belong to our pack, and it'll just prove to me how ridiculous they are if they don't want you."

Sam hugged the gargoyle. "I love you too, Bladder."

"That's not what I said."

Wheedle snorted.

Daniel laughed. "It sounded like it."

Bladder's cheeks puffed, and his mouth opened and closed. He stared at Spigot and Wheedle, who were capering about him. "You're a complete bunch of . . ."

Daniel bowed to Bladder. "Would you like to find a new home or not?"

Bladder shut his mouth. Yonah and Spigot sat on the ground next to the gargoyle, giggling.

Daniel pulled Sam and Beatrice under his arms and took off.

Bladder's voice followed them as they flew away. "Stupid overstuffed turkey, obviously don't know anything about gargoyles. He's got dirt between his . . . and what are you two laughing about?" Then Sam couldn't hear them.

Daniel rushed up and up into the star-flecked inkiness of night. Sam held tightly to Beatrice and kept her from falling.

"It's astonishing how much it sounds like he loves you, Samuel," Daniel said. "What is it about gargoyles that they can do that?"

"Gargoyles have hearts." Sam pressed his lips closed. He realized he wasn't supposed to tell.

Daniel's wings stopped flapping. The air quietened as they glided on a night current. The angel chuckled. "Well, that makes sense. Absolutely." He muttered something to himself before saying, "What are their hearts like?"

Sam smiled, remembering. "Bladder's is beautiful, white like a star, and it glows like a soul. But it broke very easily. I bet Wheedle and Spigot's are the same. You won't tell them I told you?"

Daniel closed his eyes. Sam could not read the expression. "It'll be our secret," the angel said.

The sky was magnificent, but as soon as Sam saw the Kavanaghs' house, he decided that nothing was as magnificent as the slumping little house with its decaying brickwork and flower-filled yard.

"Over there." Sam pointed to where the trees grew thickest. They set down in the middle of the pixie circle.

The house felt dark, like a stew of black gathered about it.

Daniel stepped back into the yard, behind a hedge of purple flowers, and pointed Sam to the front entrance.

"I'm just going to leave her at the door, she'll cry soon enough," Sam said.

"Take your time."

Sam waited a few minutes before he took slow, short steps to the door. He stared at it: on the other side Michelle, Richard, and Nick slept. He supposed they were sleeping, maybe they were awake staring at the ceiling. He couldn't hear snoring, just shallow breathing.

"There you are."

Sam jumped and, startled, he bit the inside of his mouth. Beyond the end of the porch, in a canvas chair among a bank of wilted flowers and greenery, Great-Aunt Colleen sat. She stared at him with one eye open, as if he'd just woken her.

"I dreamed you'd come back. I dreamed you were watching us. Were you watching us, imp child?"

Sam shook his head. "Not on purpose. I didn't mean to."

"Well, you came to them for a reason, it's true. They already lost one baby, twelve years ago. The worst thing for a family, you know that, my boy?"

Sam nodded. His heart had broken the moment Beatrice was taken.

"Then here you were, the very day their new baby was taken. The very day."

Sam felt his heart beat. He did have a heart, and a soul, but it was questionable how human he was. He'd wanted to leave before he had to find out how badly they all thought of him.

"You were brought here to watch over us, I'm thinking. So I've been telling them not to worry. 'Samuel will bring her back,' I said. I told them. 'Raised by angels, he was, so whatever he is he knows how to guard a body. He's gone to fetch her back for us; don't worry about it.' I don't want to offend you, Samuel, but there may have been some swearing involved on both sides."

Sam stared at her. "I thought everyone would think it was my fault. So I ran. When I met you, you asked me if I meant you harm."

"And so I did, but you said 'no,' Samuel. And you have my brother's face. That's not the face of a liar. Mischief he was, and a danger to hisself certainly, like you're wont to be, but never a liar, my Samuel, and I believe the same about you." Great-Aunt Colleen nodded at the shifting lump in Samuel's arms. "I'm not wrong, am I?"

"No, Great-Aunt Colleen."

"Look at you, you're in need of a bath and some shut-eye, aren't you?"

Sam knew about baths, and he hoped shut-eye wasn't painful.

"I'm in need of some shut-eye meself," Great-Aunt Colleen continued. "Couldn't sleep, a voice kept telling me I needed to be up an' watchin'. It's a good voice, that'un, an' has always guided me right. Have you enough strength in your spare arm to help an old lady out of a chair?"

Sam shot over and offered his free hand.

"I'm not sure I've seen a grubbier fella than you. What you must have gone through to get our Beatrice back. Tell them what they need to hear. I think they'll listen." She winked at him. "Then you can tell me the whole truth later."

She groaned as she stood upright, and grabbed the walking stick leaning against the chair. "Let's see then."

Sam looked at the front door. He didn't know if he could walk through it again.

Then it opened. Nick stood on the other side, yawning and stretching. "Did the postman arrive?"

Great-Aunt Colleen laughed. "It's two in the morning, you great donkey."

Nick looked at the dark sky and blinked a few times. "Oh, yeah. I thought I heard someone say there's been a delivery. I must have been dreaming."

"Well, there has been a delivery, so I think it may have been more than a dream."

Nick stared blearily around at the world outside. He rubbed his neck and shivered. Then he stared at Sam and the baby. He frowned. "Who's that?"

Sam knew he looked like a filthy animal, with his

dirt-painted face and torn clothing. He smelled too. "It's Sam. Samuel."

"Sam?" Nick opened his mouth, the sleepiness dropping away like a stone. He was awake and dashing toward him. "Sam! Sam!" Nick yelled, then screamed. "Mom! Dad! Sam! Sam!"

The young man grabbed Sam's arms, shaking him. The ache in Sam's shoulder woke with a groan. If he'd been a normal human, he would have bruised. Nick stared at him with wild eyes, and then he spotted Beatrice's filthy, funny face staring back. Nick's yells startled her and she joined in the bawling. "Beatrice! Mom! Dad! For crying out loud, get down here! Beatrice!"

The movement upstairs started sluggish and slow like flat-falling troll-tread. As Nick's yells continued, their pace quickened, then raced. Sam heard Richard slip on the stairs and travel the last three steps on his butt.

"Nick? Are you all right?" Michelle's high, anxious voice called.

Nick yelled: "Beatrice! Sam!" as if he'd lost all other words.

Michelle's pale face appeared in the doorway, Richard just over her shoulder. They were both wearing ratty pajamas, looking sallow and thin. Michelle took three steps toward him. Her gaze took in Beatrice's face. Sam handed her over, and Michelle took her with greedy hands.

She looked back up, and stared at him, her eyes filled with tears.

Sam held his breath.

CHAPTER 23

Daniel was hunched over the chocolate-shop table. He watched May walking behind the counter.

"You are right, she is powerful."

Sam nodded. "She's the only adult I've seen that glows."

"You'll meet quite a few of them. All the ones you've been around until now have been at funerals and worrying about work. Admittedly, she is on constant high beam."

Sam kept his voice low, watching Mrs. Dancy, the lady from Children's Services. She was pretending to study chocolates.

May smiled at him. "Something else, Rumpel?"

"I'm fine, May, thank you."

Daniel called out. "So, do you intend to keep working in a chocolate shop, May?"

"Actually, Rumpel, I don't. I've applied to get into social work. I think I want to work with the homeless."

"She can hear you?" Sam said.

"The real glowers always can," Daniel replied. He grinned at Sam. "So, did you see everyone?"

"Mrs. Dancy let me pop into the church." Sam grinned, remembering the okay hand signs he'd exchanged with Beth and Ben behind Mrs. Dancy's back.

Daniel rummaged under his wing and yanked a few times until a newspaper came out. "Read this."

Daniel turned to page fifteen, and Sam found a small article with a fine black-and-white photo. "Yesterday, local residents found three gargoyles in a Sussex playground. East Sussex Police believe it is an impressive prank but do not know who placed the statues. Each one weighs half a ton. One had been positioned at the top of the slide.

"Mrs. Elizabeth Lane, who lives opposite the playground, said, 'My children came home screaming about monsters chasing them around. Such lively imaginations they have.'

"A crane hire company has been called out to move the pieces, although some locals thought it an interesting art installment and are petitioning the council to leave it in place."

Daniel complained. "They've gone crazy since they moved into that hotel."

May looked up. "Who are you talking to, Rumpel?"

"Reading to myself."

"Where did you get the paper . . ." The sudden baby squawk at the door interrupted her. "Ah, here they are."

Sam felt his stomach lift as the Kavanaghs rushed toward him. He stroked the creases out of the front of his shirt.

Richard and Nick crowded around him. Michelle sat Beatrice on Sam's knee. Sparkles unwound and twisted themselves around Michelle, even as Beatrice's head rested on Sam's shoulder. The writhing light encircled him, then stretched beyond him toward Nick, wrapping the young man in a scarf of blue stars before wriggling onto Richard, copying his fingers in glowing pink.

Michelle reached to touch Sam's face, her other hand rubbing Beatrice's back. "Don't waste time with small talk—tell him the good news."

"The paperwork's been approved: just one more hearing and you'll be part of the family," Nick said.

Michelle wrapped him and Beatrice in her arms. He heard her steady heart racing. "We can take you home with us, Sam. Where you belong."

Beatrice laughed.

ACKNOWLEDGMENTS

I'd like to say thank you first to my family. To Tess, for telling me I should try to get my books published, and Rick who told me he agreed, that I had to take the risk or I would regret it. To Sue, for telling me I could write. To Mum, Nell, Julie, Jen, Jenny, and all the nieces and nephews who said they'd buy a copy. I have used your names throughout my books, maybe not this one, but you'll see them in print.

I also need to thank my fabulous agent, Catherine Pellegrino, who has been a powerhouse, and it amazes me what she can do. I fell on my feet when I found her. Also, Hannah Sandford, my editor, for her encouragement and advice and helping me turn my words into a story. To Jessica Bellman, my desk editor, for making everything perfect.

And to God, for all the Samuels, Daniels, Beatrices, and gargoyles.

Thank you to you all.